TH

OF WIGHT

MURDERS

A gripping crime thriller full of twists

PAULINE ROWSON

The Solent Murder Mysteries Book 5

Originally published as *Blood on the Sand*

CW01645661

JOFFE BOOKS

Revised edition 2022
Joffe Books, London
www.joffebooks.com

First published by Fathom in Great Britain in 2011
as *Blood on the Sand*

© Pauline Rowson 2011, 2022

This book is a work of fiction. Names, characters, businesses, organizations, places and events are either the product of the author's imagination or are used fictitiously. Any resemblance to actual persons, living or dead, events or locales is entirely coincidental. The spelling used is British English except where fidelity to the author's rendering of accent or dialect supersedes this. The right of Pauline Rowson to be identified as author of this work has been asserted in accordance with the Copyright, Designs and Patents Act 1988.

Cover art by Dee Dee Book Covers

ISBN: 978-1-80405-155-9

To Eileen and Bernard Haley who gave me the joy of reading

CHAPTER ONE

Wednesday

Eight o'clock in the morning, a grey light in the January sky. The sea the colour of frosted glass. Everything was perfect, Andy Horton thought as he stepped off his yacht and struck out along the pontoon of Bembridge Marina on the Isle of Wight. For the last seven days he'd hardly thought about work, let alone dreamt of chasing villains and arresting scum on his CID patch in Portsmouth just six miles across the Solent — though it could have been a million miles away as far as the landscape, population and crime statistics were concerned. The Isle of Wight was a haven of tranquillity and a desert of crime in comparison to the rainforest of the inner city where he'd grown up and worked.

As he headed for the small marina shop, he wondered how Sergeant Cantelli was faring in his absence. Fine, was the answer, he thought with a smile. Barney Cantelli was one of the best sergeants an inspector could have, and he was also a very close friend; the only person who had stood by him during his suspension last year over those ridiculous rape accusations, which had proven unfounded but had cost him his marriage.

His daughter, Emma, flitted into his mind and with her came the usual gut-churning anguish. She was eight years old and he should be with her. He didn't understand why Catherine was so determined to keep him away. She had no right. Hopefully his solicitor would sort out the access problem soon and then he and Emma could go sailing together, and do all the things a father should with a daughter. The thought of what he was missing filled him with bitterness and anger and it was with an effort that he pushed such negative emotions aside. A good long walk by the coast, lunch somewhere, and then another walk back would help. Tomorrow he'd sail around to Cowes and maybe after that across the Solent to Lymington. He had a whole week left to enjoy before being swallowed up again in crime and station politics.

His thoughts had taken him to the marina shop, which was closed.

It didn't matter; there was nothing he needed from it. He'd grab a coffee on route somewhere.

He struck out across the soft sandy soil and grass of the Duver, recalling that it had once been a golf course. The steadily increasing number of walkers suing for being hit by flying golf balls, however, had finally been too much for the club and they'd given the land up for a nature reserve. It was, he thought, a much better use of the beauty spot. Perhaps the seagulls agreed. Glancing up, he watched as they swooped low and then glided up on the keen morning air. God, they were noisy and big buggers too. Wouldn't like to make enemies of them; they'd peck your eyes out as soon as look at you — which reminded him of his boss, DCI Lorraine Bliss. Still, she was safely on secondment at HQ, thank God, and would be until the end of March. They were welcome to the ice-maiden.

Something seemed to be getting those gulls going. A dead fox probably, he thought, pushing his way through the thick and overgrown wind-sculpted gorse. The gulls were directly overhead now. Maybe he should turn back and leave them to their carrion. But he'd come too far; a few more paces and he'd be out of this gorse and onto the shore, breathing the fresh, salty sea air and feeling great.

He rounded the bend and drew up sharply. Kneeling in front of him he was surprised to see a woman crouching beside what looked like one of the derelict sandy bunkers. A polite smile formed on his lips, he made to speak when she spun round, and the words froze in his throat as swiftly he took in her terrified pale blue eyes, ashen face, wet blonde hair and dirty, sodden clothes. But it was what she was holding that sent his heart into overdrive. He was staring at the barrel of a gun aimed at a part of his body that he hoped he'd still have some use for despite his marital break-up.

'It's OK. I won't hurt you. I'm a police officer,' he said as steadily as he could, and he hoped reassuringly, not sure whether stating his occupation would calm her or incite her to violence. He held up the palms of his hands, willing her not to shoot either intentionally or accidentally. The magazine could still be loaded with cartridges, which could go off with the slightest pressure on the trigger. And she didn't look as though she was in control of her emotions, let alone her movements.

She did nothing. Her eyes were blank with horror — or was that terror? He didn't have time to analyse as his brain suddenly registered the smell of rotting flesh, forcing his stomach to contract at the thought of what might lie beyond the woman in the bunker. If she had killed once, she could easily do so again.

Keeping his gaze fixed firmly on her stricken face and his palms in the air he cautiously stepped forward, saying gently, 'Why don't you give me the gun?' He lowered one hand, stretching it towards her, holding his breath. The moisture was pricking his forehead and a cold sweat was trickling down his back, but these were the least of his problems. 'The gun,' he urged more firmly this time. He saw her start before her eyes flicked down to the weapon, then surprise gave way to disgust and she thrust it at him.

He took it with a silent sigh of relief then deftly removed the magazine, noting what he had already surmised by the smell emanating from the bunker: the SIG P220 semi-automatic pistol had been discharged. Removing a tissue from the pocket of his sailing jacket he wrapped the magazine and gun in it, then seeing that the woman wasn't about to go anywhere, he stepped past her and peered into the bunker.

The body was worse than he'd expected. The maggots were feeding off the soft dead flesh, animal life had made inroads into other parts of the corpse and the birds had pecked at the eyes. His stomach somersaulted and bile filled his mouth, and though he wanted to look away, he knew he couldn't. First impressions were vital.

The man was on his back, clothed in stout walking boots, heavy dark-green corduroy trousers and a navy-blue waterproof jacket smeared with mud. As Horton's eyes once again travelled to what was left of the face, he saw that he'd been very fair, like the woman hugging herself on the edge of the bunker, and was, he reckoned, aged somewhere between thirty-five and forty-five though it was difficult to tell. Finally, Horton registered what he thought was a gunshot wound on the left temple. She'd killed him.

Then his brain kicked into gear. This poor soul had been dead some days. Was he therefore looking at a suicide and this unfortunate woman had inadvertently or instinctively picked up the gun? Time to find out.

'I'm Detective Inspector Horton,' he announced firmly. He didn't bother with his warrant card; he doubted she'd see a billboard if he stuck it in front of her. She was younger than he'd first thought, about late twenties, and still on her knees. 'What's your name?' he asked gently, recognizing that she was in a deep state of shock. Who wouldn't be?

She made several attempts before any sound emerged. 'Thea Carlsson.'

She began to shiver. Horton whipped off his sailing jacket and draped it around her shoulders, noting how thin she was. Pulling her up, he led her trembling body a short distance away. She made no protest.

Reaching for his mobile he said, 'Where do you live, Thea?' He had to ask her twice before she answered.

'Cowes.'

That was to the west of the island, about fifteen miles away.

'I came to find . . . I came to see . . .' Her eyes dashed towards the bunker.

So this wasn't a chance discovery. She knew the victim. How? Had she arranged to meet him here and arrived some time ago to find him dead, and had then been unable to move for shock? It was possible. It would account for her appearance.

'We'll get you to a hospital.' He began to punch in the emergency number but she stopped him.

'No. Please. Not that. I'll be all right. I need . . .' Again her eyes travelled in the direction of the bunker before she screwed them shut as if she could blot out what she'd seen. She obviously couldn't though, because she quickly threw them open again.

'Sit down,' Horton commanded. She obeyed without question, sinking on to the grassy hummock. It was soaked from the heavy rain of the night, but getting her jeans wet was the least of the poor girl's concerns.

'I'll call the police. This won't be my case,' he explained, studying her harrowed expression and feeling there was something vaguely familiar about her. Stepping a short distance away, he swiftly searched his memory for his past cases but nothing registered with him.

He was tempted to call Superintendent Uckfield, head of the Major Crime Team in Portsmouth, but there was no indication yet that this was murder. It could still be suicide. So he rang the head of the island's CID, Detective Chief Inspector Birch.

'What do you want? I'm busy,' came a voice like a dry twig snapping underfoot. Birch by name and Birch by nature, thought Horton, recalling the thin-lipped, gaunt man with whom he'd had a run-in when he had been a sergeant and

Birch a DI on the mainland. What had stuck in Birch's gullet was the fact that Horton had been right about a case. He'd insisted that the man Birch had arrested for murdering a pensioner was innocent. But Birch had wanted a result and hadn't much cared how he'd got it. Birch had coolly and verbally bludgeoned the vulnerable, simple soul they'd arrested until he'd confessed. Two days later, in police custody, Brian Gooding had hanged himself and Horton had found the real killer, an evil bastard called Fred Hemmings. But Birch had got his promotion to DCI, and Horton was still a DI, which just went to show there was shit justice in the world.

Crisply Horton said, 'Possible murder, the Duver, St Helens. I'm with the woman who discovered the body, male Caucasian.'

'The victim's name?'

'Haven't got that far.' Horton relayed the location, knowing it wasn't far from the car park.

'Stay there,' Birch commanded.

'I wasn't thinking of leaving. No sirens.'

The line went dead. Birch probably didn't like being told that but Horton didn't want the world and his wife coming to take a look, though he didn't think they'd draw a crowd on a cold January morning.

Relieved to see that the dog-walking brigade hadn't yet woken up, he sat down beside Thea Carlsson, feeling the wet grass soak through his cargos. He wished those seagulls would go away. After a moment he said gently, 'Who was he, Thea?'

Her head swivelled round. She appeared shocked to find him there. 'I never thought . . . I didn't expect Owen to do that,' she stammered.

'Owen?'

'He's my brother.'

Horton hadn't expected that. Her shock seemed genuine enough, but being a police officer, he knew there could still be a reason why she had wanted her brother dead. This could be an act. If it were though, it was worthy of an Oscar.

'You think he took his own life?'

Her head came up and she eyed him with suspicion. 'What other explanation is there? You saw him.'

He had indeed. But there were certainly more isolated spots on the island to commit suicide, so why come here? And why hadn't anyone found him before now when clearly he'd been dead for days?

'Did he own a gun?'

'No.'

Where had it come from then? He didn't believe her. 'Where does your brother live?'

'Cowes.'

'With you?'

'Yes. If the police had listened to me in the first place then Owen might still be alive,' she added with a flash of anger. 'I reported him missing on Sunday, but they said he'd probably just taken off for a few days. They thought I was being neurotic. But I knew Owen wouldn't go away without telling me. I knew something was wrong.' Her voice faltered.

She stared into the distance, but not in the direction of her dead brother. Wherever she looked though, Horton guessed she was seeing the rotting corpse. He studied her angry, hurt and bewildered expression, knowing all too well how it felt to live with the pain and emptiness of someone 'missing'. Her mystery had been resolved, albeit tragically, within three days. He'd been living with the mystery of his missing mother for nearly thirty years. What had happened to her after she'd left their council flat that November day, he still didn't know. She'd mixed with some dubious characters, admittedly, one of whom he'd come across recently while working on a case, but that trail had gone cold.

Had she ended up like Owen Carlsson, he wondered, staring across the Duver. He didn't want to think so but knew it was possible. Suddenly and unexpectedly a distant memory nagged at a dark corner of his mind. There was something here that had prompted it, but no matter how hard he tried, whatever it was it refused to step into the light.

The sound of vehicles approaching brought him back to the present. Birch had got here quicker than he'd expected.

'When was the last time you saw Owen?' he asked, bringing his mind fully back to the case, only it wasn't his case.

It took her a while to answer. 'Saturday morning. Owen went out walking. When he didn't return by late afternoon I called him, but got no answer. I tried most of Saturday night and Sunday. Then I went to the police. I tried again all day on Monday and Tuesday but got nothing.' She shivered violently. Her eyes darted to the bunker.

'Did your brother have any financial worries?' Horton could hear people making tracks through the gorse and the low rumble of voices. Of course it might not be Birch.

'No.'

'Had he been unwell?'

'You mean depressed? A bit. You see his . . .' Her words trailed off. Horton looked up to see two uniformed officers heading towards them. Behind them was a lean man in his late forties wearing a long raincoat and a sour expression on his grim, unyielding face. He was accompanied by a short, corpulent balding man in a shabby jacket that didn't quite meet across his stomach.

Horton rose, and leaving Thea in the care of the woman police officer, crossed to Birch. He'd lost more of his hair since Horton had last seen him and what he still had was now grey, but his eyes were exactly as Horton recalled, hard and full of cynicism.

Birch curtly introduced the short, balding man as Detective Sergeant Norris. There was no smile of greeting. Working with Birch had obviously inoculated him against using those particular facial muscles.

'What are you doing on the island?' Birch demanded, as if Horton should have applied for a visa.

'Sailing. I'm on leave.'

Birch regarded him disbelievingly. That was his problem, thought Horton, as he led them to the corpse. The young uniformed officer retched at the sight of the rotting body before scuttling away. Horton didn't blame him, but Birch's expression never altered. If he blinked Horton must have missed it. He gave no sign of being moved by what he saw, and neither did Norris. Given that a violent death such as this happened on the Isle of Wight about as frequently as a total eclipse of the moon, this pair were remarkably indifferent. Too indifferent for Horton's taste.

Horton held out the gun. 'I took this off the woman; she's the dead man's sister. She claims it's not her brother's.'

'We'll check,' Norris said, taking it.

Horton quickly briefed them on what he'd learnt so far. Birch showed no recognition of the name, but Horton knew a missing person's enquiry, especially one that had only been reported three days ago, wouldn't have involved a DCI unless, of course, it had been a child.

When he finished, Birch said, 'She could have killed him earlier, then dumped his body here this morning. When she heard you crashing through the undergrowth, she picked up the gun to cover her fingerprints and to make you think it was suicide.'

'So how did she get the body here?' asked Horton stubbornly. 'She doesn't look strong enough to have carried it from the car park.'

'She had an accomplice.'

Unfortunately, Birch could be right. How else would she have known where to find her dead brother?

Crisply, Birch said, 'We'll deal with this now. You can make your statement later.' He turned away to give instructions to Norris.

Feeling irritated at the abrupt dismissal but determined not to show it, Horton returned to Thea Carlsson. He studied her forlorn, bedraggled figure still sitting hunched on the grass, with his sailing jacket swamping her; he simply couldn't see her as a killer though he knew he should keep an open mind. He'd been in the job long enough to know that even the most innocent-looking people were capable of mass cruelty and murder.

He said, 'Is there anyone I can contact for you? Any friends or relatives?'

'No. There's no one.' She stared at him for a moment then added, 'But there is something you can do for me. Would you feed my cat, Bengal?'

Horton swiftly hid his surprise at the unusual request. Not of the fact that she had a cat but that she trusted him to enter her house and feed it.

She took a key from the pocket of her jeans and stretched it out for him. As his fingers brushed hers, Horton felt a strange sense of connection. She held his gaze and he got the distinct impression she was speaking to him, though what she was saying he couldn't fathom.

Reluctant to relinquish her touch, but with the beady-eyed female police officer breathing down on them, Horton pocketed the key. The policewoman took Thea's arm and gently eased her up.

Now was probably his last chance to ask the question that was bugging him. 'How did you know where to look for Owen?'

'He told me where to come.'

Horton eyed her curiously. How was that possible when he was dead? And, despite her appearance, he simply couldn't believe she'd been keeping vigil over her dead brother's body for days. Someone would have found her. Had Owen Carlsson posted her a note on the Saturday of his disappearance which she'd only received this morning? But that would make her postal delivery incredibly early, which, Horton thought, was highly unlikely.

'It's difficult to explain,' she added, with a quick glance at the exasperated-looking police officer who was obviously keen to get Thea Carlsson to the station. 'It's why I knew Owen was in trouble.' Again the nervous glance at the policewoman. 'I sensed danger. I knew that something had happened to Owen. I didn't know the exact spot. I've been walking around for hours.'

Now Horton was really puzzled. She wasn't making any sense. But before he could comment, she drew a deep breath and said, 'You see, I'm psychic.'

Horton gave a silent groan. She was clearly unhinged. Enough to have killed her brother? Probably. The policewoman obviously thought so, judging by her expression. And if Thea Carlsson was going to stick to that as the reason for being here then he didn't hold out much hope of her convincing Birch she was innocent.

Eyeing him regretfully but unapologetically she said, 'I can see that you don't believe me. It doesn't matter.'

Then why did he feel a stab of guilt? It was as though he'd been tested and found wanting, he thought as he watched her climb into the police car.

He took the key from his pocket, recalling the sensation as their fingers had touched; something had passed between them. There had been some kind of silent pleading in her eyes. What had she been trying to tell him? What did she want him to do? He stared down at the key.

'She wants you to feed the bloody cat,' he said aloud, slipping the key back into the pocket of his cargos. And that was exactly what he was going to do.

CHAPTER TWO

Horton studied Thea Carlsson's house. It was detached, double fronted with sturdy stone bays up and down, and built most probably in the early part of the twentieth century. It stood in a road of similar properties in a quiet residential area above the town of West Cowes and the River Medina. Horton was relieved to see no sign of Birch nor any police presence but he knew it was only a matter of time before they showed up. And maybe that would be sooner rather than later if Birch discovered that Thea had given him a key.

Where once the front garden had been there was now hard-standing for two cars, but only one was parked, a small Citroen. Thea's or her brother's? He peered inside. Nothing lying about on the seats. And no blood stains or maggots, he thought wryly, though the boot might reveal something. He tried it. It was locked. But if it had been used to transport Owen's body, and if Owen had been killed inside this house, then surely Thea Carlsson wouldn't have given him a key. And, another thing, if this was Thea's car then why hadn't she driven it to the Duver? Perhaps she didn't drive, he thought, reaching for his mobile phone. He called Cantelli.

'Missing us already?' Cantelli joked.

'I need you to check a car registration number.'

'Andy, you're on holiday.'

Horton heard the exasperation in the sergeant's voice. 'Humour me.' He gave Cantelli the number and said, 'Call me back.' He could have checked it himself by using his laptop computer on the boat and logging on to the police computer with his password, but he couldn't wait that long.

He glanced around the deserted street before striding up the path to the house, and letting himself in. For several seconds he stood in the spacious hall testing the silence. It was total. He was alone. He hadn't expected anyone to be here, except a cat, and that didn't make an appearance.

The cord-carpeted stairs to the first floor were directly in front of him with closed doors to both his right and left. The old wooden floor boards in the hall had been stripped and primed to perfection. They led down a narrowish hall to a door at the back of the house but it was the one on his right that he pushed open. As he stepped into a spacious sitting room he wondered what Thea and her brother did for a living. Perhaps he'd find some indication here.

The room had been expanded by knocking the front and back rooms into one, giving it a light and airy feel. Beyond this he could see a conservatory and then the garden. It was tastefully and comfortably furnished with pale blue drapes at the windows and cream painted walls. There was a scattering of rugs on the stripped-wood floor and the paintings were modern seascapes.

He caught the faint smell of paint. He wasn't sure that was a good sign. That, and the fresh looking cream sofas, confirmed to him the room had recently been decorated and refurnished. It was also spotlessly clean with nothing out of place. He didn't yet know how long Owen Carlsson had been dead, but if he had been killed in here then Thea and her accomplice might have had time to clean and redecorate. And if Birch believed her to be the killer, then the crime scene officers would take this place apart to find evidence to prove it.

He crossed to the cabinet of books to the left of the chimney breast and tilted his head to read the spines. There were books on walking, birds, nature and the environment. His phone rang.

'The Citroen belongs to an Owen Carlsson,' Cantelli announced. 'He lives at 18 Grafton Street, Cowes.'

Where Horton was standing. 'Does he own the house?'

'I expect the mortgage company *own* it but he's listed as the owner-occupier, not a tenant. I've checked him out. There's no previous on him.'

Horton might have known that Cantelli would go one step further than he'd asked him to. So Thea simply lived here with her brother. She didn't have a financial share in the ownership of the house.

'Anything wrong?' Cantelli asked, when Horton didn't instantly reply.

Horton told him what had happened, excluding the bit about Thea being psychic.

'Blimey, can't take you anywhere. Do you want me to see what I can find on them?'

Horton did but he said, 'Haven't you got anything else to do?'

'It's been fairly quiet lately.'

'Not saying I'm jinxed, are you?'

'Well, you do have a habit of running into trouble.'

Horton sniffed. Unfortunately Cantelli seemed to be right. 'Maybe this isn't trouble and is suicide.'

'You don't sound too sure. I'll check them out.'

Horton found Bengal's food trays in a modern kitchen which opened up into the conservatory. Again, it was spotlessly clean and he found everything in its place as he opened cupboards and drawers. He dished out some food for the cat before returning to the hall, where he pushed open the door opposite the lounge and drew up surprised at the contrast with what he'd already seen. Books and box files were everywhere: on the floor, on shelves straddling a black iron Victorian fireplace, and piled on the ancient desk in the bay window. Horton made for the shelves where he found books on the depleting rainforests, weather systems, climatic change and the balance of the ecosystems. Whose office was this, Owen's or Thea's, he wondered? And was this interest in the environment a hobby or profession?

Then his eyes spanned the handwritten notes on the box files noting the names of projects: *Estuarine, marine and coastal ecotoxicology in the south-west Solent*; *The determination of seabed reference conditions for potential offshore windfarm sites off the Isle of Wight and Hayling Bay*; *Sea temperatures and global warming* and, judging by the name on the reports, this was clearly Owen Carlsson's profession and his office.

Horton picked out the file on *Estuarine, marine and coastal ecotoxicology in the south-west Solent* and glanced through the covering notes unable to make much sense of them. Stuffing the papers back, he extracted notes from a second folder. It was a study on the impact of onshore and offshore wind farms on and round the Isle of Wight. An environmental pressure group called REMAF, which stood, Horton saw, for Renewable Energy Means A Future, had commissioned it. A shrill-piercing tone shattered the silence, making him start. Scrabbling under some papers on the desk, Horton located the phone. The light was flashing on the answer machine, showing that three messages had already been left. He let the phone ring and listened as the answer machine clicked on, shuddering slightly as he heard the dead man's voice.

'Hi, this is Owen Carlsson. I'm out trying to save the planet. Leave a message and I'll get back to you when I've completed my mission. If I don't return your call you'll know I've failed, but you and no one else will be around to care very much by then anyway.'

Horton smiled. Clearly, Owen had had a sense of humour and had been passionate about his work. Then Horton remembered that rotting body and the smile died on his lips.

A male voice bellowed, 'Where the devil are you, Owen? I had to cancel the meeting with Laura. Call me — and I don't mean next week. I mean now.'

The last word was shouted before the phone was slammed down. Horton punched in 1471 and jotted down the telephone number of the caller. It was a mobile number. He pressed the play button and found that the same man had left the other three messages since Monday, growing increasingly cross with each one, and not leaving his name. It was obviously someone well known to Owen. Who was this Laura he kept referring to? From the messages the meeting had been arranged for today, Wednesday.

He shoved the papers on wind farms back into the box file, wondering why Thea hadn't answered the telephone in her brother's absence, explaining that her brother was missing. Perhaps she'd been too upset, he thought, pulling open the desk drawers and rummaging around inside, thinking that maybe he should have put on his latex gloves. She must have heard the phone. Even if she had been out of the house on each occasion why hadn't she come in here and played the messages? Had Owen banned her from doing so? But why would he do that, unless she was one of those women who couldn't resist tidying up, like Catherine who was obsessed with maintaining his former marital home like a show home. Perhaps what he'd seen of this immaculately kept and tastefully decorated house was down to Thea, and her brother had drawn the line at any make-over in here.

There was nothing of interest in the desk. He wondered where Owen Carlsson kept his more personal documents: birth certificates, passport, examination and school certificates, old photographs. There was also no sign of a gun licence and neither was there anything that resembled a gun cabinet. Sergeant Norris would have checked out the ownership of the gun by now, but Horton found himself once again calling Cantelli.

He asked Cantelli to check the National Firearms Licensing Management System, and the police computer to see if either Owen or Thea Carlsson owned a gun.

Then he told Cantelli about the telephone message left on Owen Carlsson's machine and gave him the mobile number. 'Find out who is on the end of it and whatever else you can get on him, but don't tell him about Owen Carlsson. I don't want him alerted.'

'OK.'

Horton called to the cat as he climbed the stairs, remembering what he was meant to be there for, but Bengal didn't show. He checked out the bedrooms at the front of the house, finding that one of them was Owen Carlsson's while the other was a plainly decorated spare room. There was nothing in either of them to tell him why Owen Carlsson had been killed. And if he'd been hoping for love letters, pornography or even guns he was disappointed.

Staring around Owen Carlsson's immaculately tidy bedroom he was intrigued by the contrast here with the man's chaotic office below. It made him wonder who the real Owen Carlsson was — the tidy one or the more carefree one indicated by his office and that answer phone message. Was there an inner conflict in Owen Carlsson, a split personality perhaps that had somehow resulted in his death?

God, he was beginning to sound like a psychologist, a breed he didn't have much time for after his experiences of them as a child. It didn't take a degree or professional training to know why he had been so unruly. A police officer and his wife, who had been his last foster parents, had managed to interpret his moods and needs and channel his energy into making his life more constructive, not any trick cyclist.

His attention was caught by the sound of a car pulling up, and hurrying to the window he saw a smartly dressed woman in her fifties enter the house to his right. It could be worth having a word with her. He checked the bathroom — nothing out of the ordinary unless there were blood stains invisible to the naked eye — before pushing open the door of the last room along the landing. Here he found the cat curled up on a dark blue duvet.

The huge tabby opened one eye and contemplated him warily as he moved around the bedroom. Judging by the female clothes and smattering of toiletries in the adjoining shower room this was clearly Thea Carlsson's bedroom, but he was struck by the fact that she had few possessions and even fewer clothes. There was also no laptop computer, no mobile phone and no personal letters. On the mantelpiece though were two framed photographs and Horton crossed to these. He found himself looking at what must surely be Owen Carlsson. Here were the same thin face, white-blond hair, pale blue eyes and wide mouth as his sister. They could almost have been twins except that — judging by this photograph — Owen had been some years older than Thea, who was standing next to him in a cap and gown. Horton wondered what her subject had been; she could hardly have graduated in psychic mediumship. Where did she work? What did she do? He hoped Cantelli would enlighten him because there was nothing here to tell him.

He replaced the photograph and picked up the other one. It was of a man and woman, in their mid to late twenties, standing beside a motorbike, which Horton recognized instantly as a Triumph. He also knew immediately who the couple were. There was no mistaking the parents of Owen and Thea Carlsson, and judging by their clothes, it looked as though the picture had been taken in the early 1970s. Where were they now, he wondered? Why hadn't Thea mentioned them? They would need to be told about their son's death. But then he recalled that Thea had said there was no one. They must be dead, he thought, replacing the picture, unable to stop himself thinking of his own parents.

He'd never known his father, and as far as he could remember his mother hadn't spoken of him. Was he alive, and if so, was he even aware of Horton's existence? He doubted it. And there was no way of knowing or finding out, unless he located his mother. And that seemed highly unlikely. The past was better left where it was. If only it would stay there, he thought bitterly, turning his attention to the books in the low bookcase.

He found several on spiritual healing and psychic phenomena, which were obviously Thea's given her earlier declaration. He thought of Birch and Norris's reactions to her claims of being in touch with the dead and winced. Was she sticking to her story? He hoped not but what was the alternative? That she was a killer? There was a vulnerability about her that bothered him. And he didn't much like the vision of Birch's cynicism and derision as he questioned her.

Had she asked for a solicitor? He told himself that Birch's officers would have explained her rights, but he was concerned that her shock might make her say something which Birch would misinterpret or seize upon as evidence of her guilt — like that damn psychic thing. And if she hadn't been charged . . .

Telling himself he was an idiot, he rang the solicitor who was handling his divorce. Frances Greywell came on the line almost instantly. She didn't give him the chance to speak.

'I've heard nothing more from Catherine's solicitor about you seeing Emma. I'll chase them up.'

'I'm not calling about that. Do you know any good lawyers on the island who specialize in criminal law?'

'Why?' she asked, surprised. 'Are you—?'

'It's not for me,' he hastily interjected and quickly gave her an edited version of his discovery that morning, and details of Thea Carlsson.

'There's Michael Braxton. He's well thought of.'

'Call him and ask him to contact DCI Birch or Sergeant Norris at Newport station. If Thea hasn't got a solicitor, ask Braxton if he'd represent her. I want someone with her as soon as possible despite anything she says to the contrary.'

'Of course. I'll do it now,' she said crisply.

'Give him my mobile number and ask him to call me as soon as he's spoken to her and to DCI Birch.'

She rang off. Horton knew that she would have liked their relationship to be more than a professional one, but he didn't want to get involved with his solicitor, no matter how attractive she was. He had half an idea that it would backfire on him and that somehow Catherine would use the information to be even more difficult and obstructive than she was already being.

He picked up the book beside Thea's bed. *The Lost Ghosts of the Isle of Wight.* Poor buggers, he thought, opening it and reading the handwritten dedication: 'To darling Thea who has the gift, Helen.' What gift? Being physic? Who was Helen?

His phone rang, making him jump. He wasn't usually so edgy. The cat started too, shifted a paw and cast him an angry glance before deciding that he and his phone were no threat.

It was Cantelli again. 'Know much about ghosts?' Horton asked, putting the book back where he had found it.

'Why? You seen one?'

'Not yet. But give it time. Thea Carlsson claims to be psychic,' he found himself confiding.

'Well, she's not employed as a medium. In fact, she's not employed anywhere in the UK according to Her Majesty's Revenue and Customs. Or if she is then she's not paying tax and never has.'

Maybe she relied on Owen for money, thought Horton, and lived here as his dependant. But if so, why so few clothes and limited personal possessions? Unless Owen had kept her short. Was he some kind of control freak and she'd finally flipped?

'What about Owen Carlsson?' Horton gazed down at the sloping roof of the conservatory and beyond that into a good-sized garden, which backed onto the gardens of another street. At the bottom of Owen's garden was a group of bare-branched trees and shrubs, and a small summerhouse.

Cantelli said, 'He's a self-employed environmental consultant, and, according to the Internet, has written tons of articles on the environment. He's had some pretty impressive national media coverage on global warming. And there's no record of either of them owning a gun. Want me to carry on digging?'

'With a spade.' Horton ignored the small voice inside him that told him to leave well alone and get on with his holiday. He could be wasting precious police time by getting Cantelli to do work that DCI Birch must surely be doing. But then perhaps Birch thought he was staring at Owen Carlsson's killer sitting opposite him in the interview room. And maybe he was.

'What do your psychic powers tell you about Owen Carlsson's death, Barney?'

'They say get the hell out of there and finish your holiday.'

Horton thought it good advice.

'But knowing you, you won't,' Cantelli continued, with a smile in his voice. 'You might like to know that Taylor and his scene of crime team are on their way over and Dr Clayton's doing the autopsy later today. She can't get over to the island until six.'

So Birch was treating it as suspicious and not suicide. Horton didn't see that he had any choice. 'What about Uckfield and the major crime team? Are they coming?'

'Not as far as I know,' Cantelli answered.

Which meant Birch was pretty confident he had the killer. Horton didn't much like the sound of that. He'd found nothing in this house to show why a sister had killed her brother, but then maybe Thea had motives that weren't on display. Who knew what past secrets lay between brother and sister, he thought, seeing again that maggot-infested body in the dunes.

He said, 'Tell Taylor I'll see him when he's finished at the scene.' Sergeant Elkins of the marine unit would bring the police launch bearing the SOCO into Bembridge. Horton knew it was nothing to do with him, but he felt he couldn't simply walk away.

He locked up and knocked next door. Introducing himself as a friend of Owen Carlsson he broke the sad news of Owen's death to the neighbour he'd seen earlier climb from her car, but he made no mention of how Owen had been killed or where.

She showed him into a small over-furnished room and waved him into a seat before perching her slender backside on the chair opposite.

'How awful for Owen's sister,' she said, after the usual expressions of horror and shock and introducing herself as Evelyn Mackie. 'Not that I really know her. She only arrived a week ago, Monday before last. Owen introduced Thea when they were in the garden that Friday. I was hanging out the washing when I saw them talking in what Owen called his natural garden. It's right at the bottom, bordering on to the houses over the back of us in William Street. My husband calls it a wilderness, but Owen said it was full of wild flowers and grasses and helped to encourage bees and insects. Since then I've not spoken to her. Shy, I suppose.'

Horton got the impression that Evelyn Mackie either didn't like Thea or disapproved of her. She'd given him some new information though, and putting that with what Cantelli had said about no record of Thea paying taxes in the UK, Horton guessed that Thea must normally be resident abroad, or perhaps travelling. Certainly not living under her brother's tyrannical rule as he had hypothesized.

Evelyn Mackie continued. 'Owen said his sister would be staying with him for a while. I've only heard her calling the cat since then. He arrived about the same time.'

Clearly she didn't approve of the cat either.

As if to confirm this she said disparagingly, 'He's a stray. Thea must have encouraged him, because Owen wasn't a great cat lover. Oh, not that he hated them or would harm them, but he told me once he didn't much care for the way they tormented their prey.'

Bengal had found a comfortable billet then. 'Didn't Thea ask you about Owen's disappearance?' Horton asked, curious.

'Had he disappeared? I didn't know.' She scowled, as though annoyed at missing out on a piece of gossip. But why hadn't Thea checked with Owen's neighbours for sightings of her brother? Perhaps Owen had told Thea that he didn't like his neighbour. Or perhaps, as Evelyn Mackie had said, Thea was shy. Did that also explain why she hadn't answered her brother's telephone calls and taken messages? Or maybe Owen didn't like her meddling. Perhaps then he was a bully and Thea had been terrified of him. He'd ordered her to come home and she didn't have the courage to refuse. Then once here, she'd cracked up and killed him. Or, maybe, she'd come home with a lover specifically to kill her brother. He didn't want to believe that either, but he knew that if these thoughts were running through his mind, then they would be galloping through Birch's.

Evelyn Mackie's cultured tone broke through his thoughts. 'Owen was a lovely man, so polite and friendly.'

That didn't mean he was kind to his sister and animals though. Bullies often put on a false facade to the outer world whilst tormenting their victims. But the man on that answer machine message hadn't sounded like a bully.

Heaving a sad sigh Evelyn Mackie added, 'I can't believe he's dead. I only saw him on Saturday on the chain ferry crossing to East Cowes. He seemed fine then.'

Horton's ears pricked up at that. Thea claimed to have last seen her brother leaving the house on Saturday morning. 'What time was this?'

'It must have been just after ten. I was in my car heading for Fishbourne to collect a friend from the ten twenty-five car ferry from Portsmouth.'

'Was Owen in his car?'

'No, on foot. He was dressed for walking; boots, stick and a rucksack. I asked if he wanted a lift anywhere, but he said no. He didn't say where he was going.'

Pity. Horton recalled that Owen had been wearing boots when he'd seen the body, but where were the rucksack and the walking stick?

'Can you remember what he was wearing?'

She thought for a moment. 'Dark-green corduroy trousers and a navy-blue waterproof jacket. Why?'

'Just curious,' he said dismissively, but seeing that his comment didn't convince her, he expanded, 'Thea told me Owen had disappeared on Saturday so I was just checking if it had been when he went for that walk. It sounds like it to me.' Horton rose. 'Maybe I should tell Owen's neighbours on the other side.'

'It's a second home,' she said scathingly. 'They only come over in August for Cowes Week and at Christmas.'

Horton could tell she didn't like that either. And it did seem a waste of a house going empty for much of the year. He would like to have asked her more about Thea but that might have made her curious about him, and besides, if Thea had only just arrived then Mrs Mackie probably wouldn't know much anyway.

Horton took his leave and headed for the chain ferry. But the ferryman couldn't remember seeing Owen Carlsson. 'All these walkers look alike to me, mate,' he said. Horton doubted the man would have remembered even if he'd shown him the photograph from Thea's mantelpiece.

It had started to drizzle. There wasn't much more Horton could do. It would take resources and a media appeal to discover where Owen Carlsson had gone, and that was down to Birch, he thought gloomily.

By the time he'd reached the marina the drizzle had turned to a cold penetrating rain, and a chill wind was barrelling off the sea. What had started as such a beautiful day had turned into a grim one in more ways than meteorologically. He was tempted to revisit the scene to see what Taylor and his team had discovered, but curbed his impatience. Taylor would be with him soon enough, and besides he was wet and cold.

There was no sign of Sergeant Elkins or PC Ripley on the police launch moored five boats along from his yacht. Probably inside having a cuppa. Horton didn't blame them. It was Elkins' friend who had loaned him this yacht until April, after Horton's little yacht, which had been his home since Catherine had ejected him, had been set alight. Soon he would have to start looking for a boat of his own. He couldn't contemplate living in a dingy flat even though he'd been told by Frances Greywell that it would be viewed more favourably than a boat by the children's court judge.

He reached for his key and froze. The hatch was open. Surely to God he'd locked it before leaving. OK, so he'd been in a hurry to get to Thea Carlsson's house before DCI Birch, but not that much of a rush to forget to lock up.

His eyes narrowed. The padlock had been forced. Someone had broken in. In Bembridge this sort of crime, or in fact any type of crime, was highly unusual.

In the space of six hours he'd managed to unearth two. Maybe Cantelli was right and he was jinxed.

Stealthily he stepped on board, his ears straining for the slightest noise. The intruder could be below. But only the sounds of the water slapping against the hull, the rain drumming on the decks and the wind moaning through the halyards greeted him.

He eased back the hatch. Nothing. Silently he crept down the steps into the cabin, then stiffened with fury as he registered the devastation around him. Every cupboard had been opened and the contents strewn over the floor and seats. But no maniac rushed out to assault him. He was alone. Whoever had done this was long gone.

Swiftly he made his way to his cabin where his clothes were tossed on the bed, his holdall upended. Since the fire on board *Nutmeg*, he had learned not to keep anything of value on the boat. His passport and a copy of his birth certificate, along with the missing person's file on his mother, were now safely held at Framptons Solicitors. He carried with him credit and debit cards, a photograph of Emma and his warrant card. All his post he'd had redirected to the station. The only thing of any real value on the boat was his laptop computer, and that was still here, intact and in its bag, and as far as he could see the zip hadn't been tampered with.

Why hadn't the intruder stolen it? It would have been valuable in its own right, and if someone had cracked his password allowing access to his emails and the police computers it would have been worth a fortune. Did this suggest someone unfamiliar with technology? Or the opposite — someone who knew enough about computers to know that hacking in and finding the password would take time, expertise and blind guesswork and, by that time, Horton would have changed it anyway, so had left it behind.

Whatever, this clearly wasn't the work of an opportunist thief, or someone high on drugs or drink looking for something to sell for a quick fix. This intruder, Horton figured, had been searching for some clue as to his identity. And he wouldn't have found it.

He climbed back on deck and stared around in the slanting rain. The pontoon was hardly on the criminal's usual route, so why here, why now and why his boat? And why hadn't he stolen anything? There was only one answer: Owen Carlsson's murder.

CHAPTER THREE

'There are no prints, except yours,' Taylor mumbled nasally two hours later.

Horton wasn't surprised. Even the most stupid of thieves watched enough television to know they should wear gloves. But that didn't always guarantee they couldn't be identified.

'Can you get anything from the glove prints?'

Taylor sniffed and shrugged an answer. It didn't inspire Horton with much hope. If the intruder had worn gloves, then it meant he'd either had a pair on him to save his fingers from the cold — which didn't sound like your average toe-rag criminal — or he'd come equipped for breaking and entering. If he had, surely he would have stolen the laptop computer. No, Taylor's findings confirmed Horton's initial thoughts: this intruder had come equipped with gloves because he had already dumped Owen Carlsson's body in that bunker earlier that morning after killing him, and had then hung around to see Carlsson's sister turn up to discover it. Which meant he either must have told Thea where to find it and all that stuff about her being psychic had been a lie, or he was Thea's accomplice in crime and her horror-stricken act had been staged for his or some other passer-by's benefit exactly as DCI Birch had suggested. The thought depressed Horton.

'We might get something from these hairs,' Taylor said, holding up a tiny plastic bag, 'Unless they're yours?'

'Mine aren't that long.' Horton ran a hand over his cropped hair. And unless they belonged to the owner of this boat, or a friend of his, then they must belong to the intruder, because Horton certainly hadn't been entertaining on board this yacht. It was something, but it was useless if they didn't already have this person on the DNA database to match it against. And then, he thought, he could have brought the hair in himself on his clothing picked up from the bus or Evelyn Mackie's house . . .

Taylor said, 'I've taken scrapings from various items that the intruder must have touched. That might give us something.'

And, Horton thought hopefully, it might match with evidence found on Carlsson's body, which made him once again think of Thea Carlsson. Angry with himself for letting her get under his skin, he flicked on the kettle and said tersely, 'What did you find at the scene of crime? The other crime,' he added.

'It's too early to say.'

Horton had expected that. 'Coffee?'

'Allergic.'

Horton had yet to find something that Taylor wasn't allergic to. Work, he supposed. The man was mournful, nasal and mostly monosyllabic but he was efficient, dedicated, thorough and hard-working. What more could a police officer ask?

'There was stuff that could have been there for days, weeks even,' Taylor added. 'Cigar and cigarette butts, couple of condoms, used.'

'Not much good if they haven't been,' muttered Horton. 'You didn't find the bullet then?'

'No.'

So it would be down to Dr Clayton to excavate it from Owen Carlsson's body.

'Anything strike you as unusual?' Horton asked, making himself a coffee. Taylor had over twelve years' experience, a sharp eye and a good brain. Not much got past him.

'There are no obvious signs that the body was transported there: no broken or trampled gorse bushes, no footprints, and no vehicle could get to that spot. But there was a lot of rain last night, and wind, so the sand has shifted and some of the gorse bushes have been uprooted; it's difficult to tell if that was because of the weather.'

'But you don't think he was killed there?' Horton pressed.

'We've got photographic images; we'll enhance them and they might give us a clearer picture.' Taylor slid out of his seat. 'I'll get everything examined and relay our findings to DCI Birch.'

It was a gentle reminder to Horton that he wasn't in charge of this investigation. Feeling irritable and restless, he watched Taylor go, knowing he was right; this case had nothing to do with him. Tomorrow he'd make his statement at Newport police station, and return home to Southsea Marina on the next high tide. He'd forget all about Thea Carlsson and her dead brother.

The trilling of his mobile sliced through his thoughts.

'For Christ's sake, Andy, can't you go anywhere without causing trouble?' Superintendent Uckfield bellowed.

'I didn't shoot him.'

'Just don't ask me to go on holiday with you!'

Perish the thought.

'Well?' commanded Uckfield.

'Well what?' How come Uckfield was suddenly interested? 'You'll have to talk to Detective Chief Inspector Birch.'

'He reckons he's got the tart who did it.'

'She's not a tart,' Horton said stiffly, and too quickly. He took a breath, not wanting Uckfield to read too much into his reaction, but it was too late.

'Oh, like that, is it?'

Hearing the sneer in Uckfield's voice, Horton cursed himself for over-reacting. But his response to Uckfield had told him he could no more walk away from this than streak naked through Portsmouth's busiest thoroughfare in the middle of market day. Forcing his voice to sound more casual, he said, 'Has Birch charged her?' He heard the deep throb of the police launch as it headed out of the marina.

'Says it's only a matter of time.'

'Motive?'

'Claims brother and sister could have fallen out.'

'Over what?'

'He'll find out.'

Or fabricate it, thought Horton uneasily. He didn't trust the emaciated Birch one inch. 'She was very distressed to find her brother's body.'

'Could be guilt.'

Horton gave him that, but he still wasn't convinced, despite his earlier thoughts. She hadn't looked guilt-ridden. But there was more to it than that. He told himself he wasn't attracted to her, and yet there was something that he couldn't explain, even to himself — a feeling, a bond? He didn't know exactly and was irritated at not being able to pinpoint it.

Uckfield said, 'How come she found him?'

Horton hesitated; he certainly wasn't going to tell Uckfield the psychic bit. The big man would laugh from here to John O'Groats and back again and then think the same as everyone else: that Thea was off her trolley or guilty as hell. So Birch hadn't told Uckfield about that. He wondered why. He must know by now; the woman police officer would have relayed that nugget of information even if Thea hadn't repeated her claim in the interview room. To distract Uckfield, Horton said, 'Owen Carlsson was seen on Saturday on the Cowes chain ferry.'

'How the hell do you know that?'

'I've talked to his neighbour.'

'Thought you were on holiday. Does Birch know?'

'No idea.' Horton waited for the reprimand and was surprised when it didn't come. Instead Uckfield almost chuckled.

'Tell me what you've got.'

So Uckfield was another one who wasn't a member of Birch's fan club. Horton wondered who was; Sergeant

Norris probably. He quickly briefed Uckfield about his visit to Owen Carlsson's house, but still said nothing about Thea and her psychic warning, or about the break-in on his yacht.

'We're coming over,' Uckfield abruptly announced when Horton had finished.

'The major crime team's been called in?' asked Horton with a mixture of surprise and relief. It meant that Birch must have doubts about Thea being the killer. Or more likely he couldn't prove it. That solicitor, Michael Braxton, must be doing a good job.

Uckfield said, 'Strange as it might seem, murder, or suspected murder, counts as a major crime.'

But Horton knew that wasn't the real reason. He could hear it in Uckfield's voice. And if Birch hadn't asked for assistance, who had?

Uckfield said, 'We'll be there just before eight.'

'Who's we?'

'Marsden and Somerfield—'

'DI Dennings?' Horton asked sharply. He didn't want the man who had taken his job in the major crime team plodding all over the place. Since appointing Dennings, Uckfield had realized his mistake and had been trying to ease him out, but unfortunately Dennings was sticking to Uckfield like treacle to a spoon, much to Uckfield's chagrin.

Uckfield said, 'He's sick.'

'Can't be with stress,' Horton quipped. 'He'd need to be overworked for that.'

'Flu,' Uckfield replied curtly.

'And the Port Special Branch post you're trying to persuade him to take?'

'Still trying. There's that vacancy on my team, remember?'

Not yet there isn't, thought Horton, *if Dennings refuses to go*. 'I'm on holiday,' he said, hoping Uckfield would ignore that. But he didn't.

'Cantelli's coming with me.'

Poor Cantelli. He got seasick just looking at water. And he didn't think Charlotte would be very pleased at having her husband dragged away from the bosom of his large family. He said, 'Then you'd better ask him what he's already got on Owen Carlsson.'

'Jesus! Has everyone been investigating this case except me, who should be?'

Horton said nothing, forcing Uckfield to continue. 'Trueman will co-ordinate the incident room at Newport station. Can't trust these islanders to do that properly.'

Birch and Norris were going to love this, Horton thought gleefully.

'And Somerfield might be able to get close to Thea Carlsson. You know, woman to woman kind of thing. Birch has had to release her. Seems she's got a pretty good lawyer and Birch had no real evidence to hold her, though he could have applied to do so, if he'd thought about it a bit longer. But thinking is not Birch's strong point.'

Why the hell hadn't Uckfield told him this immediately? And why hadn't that damn solicitor told him when Horton had left clear instructions that he should do so? Had Thea told him not to? Maybe Frances Greywell hadn't relayed the message.

Uckfield rang off. Horton thought about calling Cantelli then changed his mind. The sergeant was probably packing his bag and taking his sea sickness pills. Instead Horton called Braxton, after getting his number from Frances Greywell's office, only to be told that Mr Braxton was unavailable.

'I bet he is,' Horton murmured, throwing his mobile phone down in disgust. He paced the cabin feeling uneasy. He flicked on the light hoping it would dispel his concerns about Thea, but it didn't. The image of her terrified expression haunted him. She simply couldn't be guilty. A chilling suspicion began to form in his mind. Was she being threatened? Had her brother been killed as a warning and she'd been told where to find his body? Was she in that house alone? She had to be unless Evelyn Mackie had seen her return and had called on her. Would Thea have let her in though? Given Thea's past record of keeping to herself he didn't think so.

God, he wished he'd taken down Owen Carlsson's home telephone number; he could have called her. But again, he doubted if she would have answered it. Why would she have told the solicitor not to notify him that she'd been released? There was only one answer he could think of: because she didn't trust the solicitor. Correction, she didn't trust anybody. But she'd asked him to feed her cat! She'd given him a key. Why? He didn't know, only that he was certain that her life was in danger. He could feel it — and bollocks to Uckfield or anyone else who would laugh at him because of it.

Before he knew it he was locking the boat and hurrying towards the marina shop in the rain-soaked night, wishing he had his Harley-Davidson.

Scouring the window he spotted a faded, dog-eared card advertising a local taxi company and without much hope rang the number. He was relieved and pleased when it was answered promptly by a cheerful voice which announced it would be with him in five minutes. That usually meant ten and on this island that would no doubt stretch into fifteen. By the time the headlights swept into the marina seventeen minutes later Horton was ready to throttle the man, but he held his tongue and his temper long enough to give clipped instructions for Cowes.

While he had waited for the taxi to arrive, he'd considered calling Birch and asking him to send a car to Thea's house. But he didn't. Why, he couldn't say, except that it had something to do with Thea not trusting anyone, which meant he couldn't either.

He cut off the taxi driver's friendly chatter with a mixture of monosyllabic replies and stony silence. He soon got the message. Although the rush-hour traffic on the island was nowhere near as heavy as that on the mainland, tonight it seemed exceptionally busy. Horton cursed silently every time they stopped, which seemed like every five minutes. If he'd had the Harley he'd have been there by now.

Finally they were heading into Cowes. But even then it wasn't plain sailing. It would have been easier to get out and run! At last they turned the corner and pulled up outside Thea's house. It was in darkness. Had he rushed here like an idiot and Thea was with friends or relatives? But she'd said there was no one. He rang the bell. No answer. He called through the letter box. Still no reply, and yet he felt sure she was inside. Could she have done something stupid like take her own life? He shuddered at the thought and, quickly extracting the key, opened the door.

Now his sense of danger was stronger than ever. Everything was silent. Too silent. Perhaps she was next door. But he didn't feel it. This psychic stuff was rubbing off on him. Yet he couldn't bring himself to call her name. Some sixth sense was telling him there was someone here. He could feel a presence, and he didn't think it was a spook.

Silently and swiftly he covered the rooms on the ground floor. There was no one and no sign of Thea, though she had been here: a cup was on the drainer that hadn't been there this morning. A noise suddenly alerted him. His senses strained to place it and its location. It was the cat, Bengal. He was meowing and the sound was coming from upstairs.

Taking the stairs two at a time with his heart pounding like a piston engine, he paused on the landing and listened. Silence. Then Bengal mewed again. He was in Thea's bedroom.

Holding his breath, Horton thrust open the door hoping to slam anyone lurking behind it, but it only bounced back on him. The brief glimpse inside made his blood freeze. Swiftly he crossed the room where Thea was lying face down on the bed and pressed his fingers on her neck. There was a pulse, thank the Lord. But he barely had time to register this when a movement caught the corner of his eye. He dodged to his right at the same time as trying to turn, but he was too late. A violent blow caught him on the side of his head. He heard the crack before he felt the pain. Then the bed raced up to meet him. He sensed someone hovering, but the lights were fading fast. Muffled footsteps. Then nothing, only blackness.

CHAPTER FOUR

Something was licking his face and screaming in his ears. He opened his eyes with a groan, which turned into a throat-clenching choke. A sharp pain stabbed his head so it took him a few seconds to connect his choking with the acrid smell of smoke. Bloody hell, the house was on fire!

He pushed Bengal away and staggered up, trying to stop the room from spinning, and desperately struggling to remember what had happened. He didn't know how long he'd been unconscious but it could only have been seconds, maybe a couple of minutes at the most. It was long enough to feel the heat through the floorboards. Time to get out. His mind was rapidly calculating that using the stairs wasn't going to be an option — a view that was confirmed as he slammed the bedroom door shut, noting its thickness with a small glimmer of hope. A quick glance at Thea told him she was still unconscious or even dead by now. Then she groaned. Thank God! The heat was scorching and Bengal was on the window ledge, screaming like mad.

Horton dashed into the en-suite shower room, which he realized, too late, was where Thea's assailant had been hiding, and tossed the towels under the shower, quickly soaking them. He rushed back to the bedroom door and stuffed one along the bottom of it, but he could do nothing about the fireplace and smoke was already beginning to drift in through it.

With the other wet towels he crossed to Thea and shook her. The heat was growing more intense through the soles of his feet and he could hear the wood of the floors and stairs crackling. Bengal had jumped off the window ledge and had scurried under the bed.

Horton shook Thea again and gently slapped her face, trying to shake her into full consciousness.

'Wake up. We've got to get out of here,' he urged.

'My head . . .' She coughed as the smoke began to permeate every narrow crack in the room. He handed her a soaking towel.

'Wrap this around your mouth and nose. Come on, get up.' Roughly he hauled her up, holding the other wet towel to his face.

She slouched against him, but her eyes were open and he could see her quickly taking in the situation.

'Bengal,' her muffled voice cried through the towel.

'He's under the bed. There's no time. We have to get out. Now!' The fire was already on the landing. Soon it would be licking at their door. But Thea was on her stomach, reaching under the bed.

Seeing there was nothing for it, Horton groaned and said, 'Help me shift the bed over,' otherwise they'd never get the ruddy cat and they'd all be fried alive. 'Get ready to grab him.'

The cat started violently as the bed was shoved against the wall. Horton grabbed him by the collar as he tried to scamper out, obviously scared out of his wits. He wasn't the only one.

He thrust Bengal at Thea, who swiftly wrapped the towel around him. She was coughing like mad. Horton picked up a chair and smashed the window, praising God it hadn't been double-glazed. He could hear the siren of the fire engines, but he couldn't wait. It would be too late. Looking down, he saw that the fire had reached the kitchen, and had spread into the conservatory directly below them. He turned back and saw the flame coming through the door. The room was filling with thick black smoke and he could hardly breathe. Thea looked as though she was going to pass out and there was no sound or movement from the cat. They had no choice.

'Out,' he commanded, quickly clearing the jagged glass from the window with the towel wrapped around his hands. 'Slide down the roof as quick as you can and jump on to the grass.'

'I can't—'

He scooped her up, momentarily stunned at just how thin she was, plonked her on the window ledge, grabbed Bengal and pushed Thea out. She coughed, then screamed. Out of control, she slid down the roof and seemed to fall or somersault over the edge. He had no idea how she had fallen, or if she was alive or injured. Any moment now the smoke would get him.

He climbed onto the window ledge just as the roof below him collapsed inward with a great crash and billowing of smoke cutting off his escape route. The sirens were louder now; the firefighters must be outside, but he couldn't hang around to find out. With the lifeless Bengal under his arm, he saw the drainpipe to his right. It was wet and therefore probably slippery but that was the least of his problems. He'd need two hands to climb down it. Bengal was probably dead. He should leave him behind. But he couldn't. He knew Thea would never forgive him.

With Bengal under his right arm, and sitting on the window ledge facing the garden, he reached across his body with his left hand for the drainpipe, grabbed it, praying that it would hold, and then eased the rest of his body over the sill whilst somehow managing to slide Bengal between his chest and the wall and wrap his other hand around the drainpipe. Scrambling, sliding, stumbling, he fell down the drainpipe until Bengal slipped from his body and Horton rolled onto the ground.

He looked up to see three firefighters wearing breathing apparatus crash through the back gate. One, quickly seeing Horton, rushed towards him as the flames from the kitchen seemed to want to reach out and consume them. Horton grabbed Bengal and staggered up, marvelling that no bones were broken as the firefighter helped them both to safety.

'There's no one in there,' Horton managed to cough and splutter. The firefighter nodded his grateful thanks, and rushed away to give instructions to his colleagues. Horton gazed wildly round for Thea. Then, with overwhelming relief, he found her squatting on the grass, staring blankly at the blazing spectacle of her brother's home.

'Are you all right?' he asked. It was a stupid question — how could she be? But she was alive and so was he, which, looking at the blaze and feeling the intense heat of the fire, was a miracle.

She nodded, dazed. No bones broken either. She'd had a lucky escape and so too had he. He wasn't sure about Bengal. Unwrapping the towel, he stared down at the comatose tabby cat.

'Bengal!' she croaked, her voice turning to a sob. 'Now I've got nothing.' Her words, and the anguish in them, wrenched at Horton's heart. Swiftly he crossed to one of the firefighters.

'Have you got any compressed air to give the cat? He might still be alive. She's lost everything else. Her brother died this morning.'

The firefighter hurried back to Thea with Horton. He put a mask over the cat's face and shot the compressed air into its nose and mouth. They waited. Was it too late? It seemed as if it had been an age since Bengal had lost consciousness and they'd climbed out of the window, but in reality, Horton knew it was only a couple of minutes at the most. Then Bengal stirred.

'Thank you. Oh, thank you!' Thea whispered, stroking the cat, her tearful eyes radiating out of her smoke-blackened face.

Horton's heart skipped several beats. He had to fight off the urge to take her in his arms and hold her, to soothe away her pain.

'That's one of his nine lives used up,' he said, nodding his thanks to the firefighter, thinking he was using up his own at a fast rate of knots. His throat and chest hurt from smoke inhalation but not as badly as he'd once suffered. And this time, unlike his past brushes with fire, it hadn't been primarily aimed at him, but at Thea. Thank God he had responded to that sense of urgency, that gut feeling that something was wrong. He shuddered to think of the outcome if he hadn't. Anger surged through him. Holiday or not, he had to catch the bastard who had done this to her.

Forcing himself to speak gently, despite the searing rage inside him, he said, 'Who attacked you, Thea?'

'I don't know,' she answered after a moment's hesitation.

She was lying. He could see it in her eyes, and the way she hastily glanced away. He decided not to press her, there would be time enough later. Bengal struggled free from her grasp and skittered down the garden path. An ambulance man appeared with a thermal blanket.

'Bengal!' she cried, twisting round to watch the cat's vanishing tail.

'He'll be OK,' Horton quickly reassured her. Tom cats could look after themselves, and, according to Mrs Mackie next door, Bengal had been doing just that for some time. Seeing Thea's obvious distress though, he added, 'I'll ask Mrs Mackie to feed him.' She wasn't a cat lover, but surely she couldn't refuse putting out a bowl of food in the circumstances?

Thea's grateful smile turned into a cough as the ambulance man escorted her through the narrow side entrance into the street. Following them, Horton crossed to Evelyn Mackie who was hovering nearby, along with most of the neighbours, huddled under umbrellas. He managed to divert her from her verbal sympathetic onslaught on Thea and persuaded her to take pity on Bengal. To her credit Mrs Mackie agreed quickly. She also offered Thea a bed but Horton declined. If the killer was still watching Thea then it would put Mrs Mackie in danger. Not that he told her that. If his boat hadn't been broken into, he might have suggested Thea stay with him. At least he could have protected her then. But this killer had already seen he was close to Thea, and Horton couldn't take that chance.

Anxiously he watched as she was wheeled into a curtained cubicle in A & E at St Mary's Hospital in Newport. Then, far from reassured she'd be all right, he walked to another cubicle where, with remarkable speed, a doctor who looked as tired as Horton felt checked him over and told him he was suffering from mild smoke inhalation and a blow to the head. Horton already knew this, and was advised that if he were to experience any effects of delayed concussion, he was to return immediately. Discharged, and in the privacy of the relatives' room, just off the private room where Thea had been taken for the night on Horton's insistence, he called Uckfield.

'What is it with you and fires?' Uckfield demanded with exasperation, after Horton had quickly explained what had happened.

Horton winced as Uckfield's remark hit home — his ability to attract danger wasn't necessarily going to commend him to Catherine, or her lawyers, in respect of his demands for regular contact with his daughter.

'They're keeping Thea Carlsson in for the night,' Horton said. 'Someone's tried to kill her once. They'll try again when they learn they've been unsuccessful.' He went cold at the thought of how close she and he had come to death. 'She needs a safe house until we find this lunatic.'

'We?' Uckfield said pointedly.

Horton tensed. He had to be on this case, even if it meant Uckfield would go running back to Catherine to confirm that it was as she thought — he was incapable of keeping his promises to Emma because of his job.

'I can postpone my holiday,' he said anxiously.

'No. You're still on holiday,' Uckfield insisted, then before Horton could protest, added, 'That is as far as DCI Birch and his team are concerned. You're undercover.' Horton heaved a silent sigh of relief as Uckfield continued. 'Start asking questions, sniffing around, stirring things up. Whoever is doing this will think you're either a nosy parker or a friend of Thea Carlsson, which means they might try and get at you.'

Uckfield was right. It could be dangerous, but it could also be a short cut to finding their killer.

Uckfield went on. 'Anyone know you're a copper?'

'No. There was nothing on my boat to say I was.' Horton realized what he had said too late. It had slipped out before he could stop himself. He ran a hand over his face, suddenly exhausted. The adrenaline rush of facing danger had subsided, leaving him feeling that every bone in his body was about to crumble into osteoarthritis, and every muscle was aching beyond even the most arduous of workouts he could possibly imagine. Besides that, his head was thumping and his throat was sore.

'Your boat?' Uckfield picked up sharply.

'It was broken into.'

'Thanks for telling me. When?'

It didn't matter now; all that did was he was on the case. He quickly told Uckfield about the break-in and his theory that the killer must have seen him with Thea Carlsson and wondered who he was.

'Is there anything else you've forgotten to tell me?' Uckfield asked scathingly.

Only the bit about Thea being psychic, but Horton wasn't about to divulge that to the biggest sceptic this side of the equator.

'So who knows you're a cop?' Uckfield repeated.

Horton pulled himself up even though he felt like collapsing in a heap and sleeping for a few months. But Uckfield's words made him recall the feeling he'd experienced earlier when he had decided not to reveal to Mrs Mackie that he was a police officer. Maybe there was something in this psychic stuff, after all. His mind raced to recall who knew he was a policeman and came up with the doctor attending Thea. He told Uckfield and added, 'I'll tell him to keep it quiet.'

'Good. We're on the ferry. Cantelli's looking green and keeps running to the bog, so he'll be about as much use as a rubber spanner when we arrive. Maitland, the fire investigation officer, will be over first thing tomorrow to examine the house.'

It was arson, that much was obvious, but Horton hoped that Maitland might be able to tell them exactly how the fire had started, which could give some clue as to the background of the offender, though he doubted this one would have been stupid or careless enough to leave any traces behind.

'What about Taylor and SOCO?'

'Elkins will ferry them into Cowes in the morning. Any more incidents like this and it'll be easier and cheaper to put the buggers up in a hotel. I've scheduled a full briefing at Newport station for eight a.m. Either I or Cantelli will liaise with you after that, if he's stopped throwing up by then. And I'll get Birch to set up a twenty-four-hour watch on Thea Carlsson until we can get her moved. Then she'll be under continuous protection in the safe house.'

Horton felt relieved. Glancing through the window of the relatives' room, he said, 'DCI Birch's just arrived with Sergeant Norris.' They were talking to a nurse. He'd expected them to show up sooner.

'I'll call him. Now make like you're a distressed friend, which doesn't sound like a problem, and get the hell out of there.'

The line went dead. A few seconds later Horton saw Birch reach for his phone. It had to be Uckfield calling him because Birch looked as though he'd swallowed a lemon with the pips still in it. He gestured at Norris to stop him heading for Thea's room. There was obviously some kind of disagreement between Uckfield and Birch judging by Birch's pinched expression before he rang off and consulted with Norris. As Horton stepped out of the relatives' room, Norris reached for his mobile with a glare at Horton that could have frozen the Solent.

'Just what were you doing at that house, Inspector?' Birch demanded icily.

'Visiting someone I was concerned about.'

Birch narrowed his eyes, clearly not believing him, and stepped so close that they were almost touching noses. With an expression of such loathing that it made Horton shiver inside, though he took pains not to show it, Birch hissed, 'If you so much as put a toe out of line on my patch, I'll make you wish you'd never joined the police force.' Then swiftly turning, he marched towards Norris.

'Nice to feel appreciated,' muttered Horton, heading back to A & E reception unperturbed by Birch's threats. The man was vindictive and spiteful but Horton could handle that. He'd met his type several times both in the criminal world and as colleagues, and had decided long ago that retaliation might be sweet but it wasn't worth the effort. It was better to bang the bastards up if they were criminals, or avoid them as much as possible if they were colleagues. That way you saved wasting a lot of energy. Avoiding Birch would be one of life's pleasures.

Finding the doctor he'd spoken to earlier, Horton quickly explained the situation and asked him to say nothing to anyone about him being a policeman. The doctor nodded wearily. Horton might just as well have saved his breath. He appeared to have forgotten anyway.

He stepped into a cold night with rain like stair rods and climbed into a taxi that had just dropped off a fare outside the hospital. Giving the driver instructions to return to his boat he once again wished he had the Harley. He toyed with the idea of sailing back to Southsea Marina tomorrow to collect it and then return to the Isle of Wight by car ferry, but that would lose him a day's investigation and he couldn't afford that. Besides, he had to stick around to see if Owen Carlsson's killer got curious about him again. Glancing at his watch he was surprised to see it was only eight o'clock. It felt a hell of a lot later. Suddenly he knew what he had to do.

'Take me to Ryde Pier and the FastCat to Portsmouth.'

'But you said—'

'The FastCat, and as quick as you can.' With luck and a following wind he'd make the twenty fifteen crossing. From Portsmouth he could get a taxi to Southsea Marina, collect the Harley and return on the car ferry to the Isle of Wight. He could have hired a car on the island, but he much preferred the Harley. On that he could think.

It was ten minutes before midnight when he finally returned to Bembridge Marina. He'd grabbed a pizza in a restaurant in Oyster Quays while waiting for the ferry to the island, and had snatched half an hour's sleep on the crossing, but that had only served to make him feel more exhausted than when he'd set out. He'd ridden through the quiet streets of the Isle of Wight carefully, grateful for the sheeting rain and cold night to help keep him alert.

His yacht was as he had left it, chaotic, but there were no further signs of an intruder. Tidying up would have to wait. He gulped down a tumbler of water hoping it would ease the rawness in his throat, then showered and lay down in the darkness listening to the soothing sound of the water slapping against the hull, and the rain drumming on the coach roof.

His mind sped back over the day's events, trying to make some kind of sense of the information he'd gleaned, but there were too many gaps. Perhaps Uckfield would be able to fill some of them in tomorrow — or rather today, he thought, glancing at the luminous digital clock beside him. And at least he'd get the chance to talk to Thea and find out who had told her where to look for her brother's body, and who had tried to kill her.

Had the killer lured her to the Duver with the intention of making it look as though she'd killed her brother, and had then intended to shoot her and make her death look like suicide? Horton's arrival on the scene had scuppered that plan so the killer had tried again by knocking Thea out and setting fire to the house. It was possible. And he reckoned she knew who that person was. But why not say? Why protect him? Could it be a boyfriend?

His phone rang. He was surprised to hear Sergeant Trueman's voice.

'What's up? Can't you sleep?'

'Not unless the boss tells me to. Actually I'm just on my way to our hotel. Hope I didn't wake you.'

'You didn't.'

'Thought not. Owen Carlsson—'

'Yes?' Horton sat up, all thoughts of sleep obliterated with those two words.

'He was involved in an incident nineteen days ago. A woman he was with was killed in a hit-and-run at Seaview. Carlsson was paying the bill at the Seaview Hotel, where he'd been dining with Arina Sutton, his companion. She said she wanted a breath of fresh air. It was eleven fifteen. When Carlsson stepped out of the hotel he saw a car speeding towards her. He called out, but it was too late; she was knocked flying. Died instantly. No witnesses, apart from Carlsson.'

What a waste. Was this woman's death enough for Owen to have killed himself? But it hadn't been suicide. Tonight's events had proved that.

'Did we get the driver?'

'I'm not sure what the Isle of Wight police have done to trace him.'

Horton heard the underlying criticism in Trueman's voice. Why hadn't Birch or Norris mentioned this to him, Horton wondered? They should have recognized the victim's name when he'd given it to them at the scene of the crime, especially when putting it together with the fact that Thea had reported her brother missing. Was Birch holding out? That was highly probable given the man's dislike of him. But perhaps Birch considered the fact that the death of this woman and now her partner was pure coincidence. But Horton didn't trust coincidences one tiny little bit.

'Did Carlsson get a registration number?'

'According to the report he said it all happened too quickly and he was hardly thinking about that.'

No, only police officers were trained that way.

Trueman said, 'All Carlsson could say was that it was a dark-coloured saloon car.'

Which were two a penny. Then a thought struck Horton. Had Owen recognized the driver and been killed because of it? Or perhaps Owen was mixed up in something dangerous; he'd known the accident was intended for him — a warning for him to tow the line. Over what though? And how did that affect Thea? Were Thea and Owen both involved in something dangerous? Had Owen ignored this warning and so had to be eliminated? Perhaps the killer thought that Owen had confided in his sister, which was why she had to be killed. Or was he just reading too much into this? Probably.

Rubbing his eyes, Horton said, 'Where did Arina Sutton live?'

'Scanaford House, Arreton.'

Horton knew the village. It was strung out along a busy road between the island's capital at Newport and the coastal resorts of Sandown and Shanklin.

'There's something else,' Trueman added.

Horton could hear by Trueman's tone it was significant.

'Helen and Lars Carlsson, the parents of Owen and Thea, were killed in a road traffic incident in 1990.'

The couple in the photograph with the Triumph motorcycle. Thea had told him there was no one. She hadn't lied. 'So?'

'They died in almost exactly the same spot as Arina Sutton.'

Horton felt a prickling sensation crawl up his spine.

'What happened?' he asked quietly.

'Their car went out of control, careered over the sea wall on to the stones below and caught fire.'

And a child and teenager were orphaned. 'Who was driving?'

'Lars Carlsson. He hadn't been drinking.'

'Suspicious?'

'No.'

Or rather it hadn't been. Not until now.

CHAPTER FIVE

Thursday, 8.35 a.m.

The narrow street in Seaview which led down to the sea was deserted. That wasn't surprising, thought Horton, given the time of day, the season and the fact that most of the houses were second homes owned primarily by the London set and frequented only in August.

Horton drew the Harley to a halt by the low sea wall and gazed across a grey choppy Solent into a cloud-shrouded horizon. The shores of Portsmouth and Hayling Island were invisible. It was as though they were marooned here from the rest of the world. Throughout the night his thoughts had been haunted by Thea and the new mystery that Trueman had tossed into his lap — the deaths of Helen and Lars Carlsson in 1990. Did that have anything to do with the incident here nineteen days ago? Had the killer mistaken Arina Sutton for Thea Carlsson and been determined to murder the Carlsson children in exactly the same spot as where their parents had died, only it had gone wrong? But why the hell should he want to do that?

He swivelled round to peer up the road where Arina Sutton had been killed. The first thing that struck him was the driver would need to have been very skilful, or lucky, to have sped down the road and slammed into poor Arina Sutton before taking the sharp bend to the left, without careering over the low sea wall and crashing onto the stones and rocks below, as the Carlssons had done. And another thing: how could the driver have got up so much speed in such a short distance to create an impact powerful enough to kill? OK, so the road was on an incline and pedestrians did die even if hit at low speed, but it was less likely.

Leaving his Harley, Horton made his way up the centre of the quiet road until he was standing at the crossroads and staring back down it towards the sea. Then he turned and climbed the steep incline up the approaching road. It curved slightly to the right. Stopping after a few yards, he turned. Yes, he had a good view of anyone leaving the hotel, especially if Arina had stood in the middle of the road, perhaps taking the night air and waiting for Owen. With his engine already running, the killer had raced down the road, shot across the crossroads, taking a gamble that nothing would be coming — although Horton knew there wasn't much chance of that — and had slammed into her, maybe as she had turned on hearing the roar of the car. Perhaps she had tried to run, or dive, out of the way, but the driver had swerved into her. But if the engine had already been running to allow the driver to get up speed quickly, how had he known when to strike?

Horton's mind grappled with the possible answers to that question. It could mean there had been two of them: one driving the car, and the other watching the hotel — perhaps from the shadows of the narrow street almost opposite it, ready to relay to the driver when Arina Sutton stepped outside. Alternatively, the driver himself could have been inside the hotel watching Owen Carlsson and Arina Sutton. When he'd seen them finish their meal, he'd made his way to his car parked here, switched on the engine and waited until he saw her step outside. And if that was so then he wouldn't have confused Arina Sutton for Thea Carlsson.

Horton began walking back to the Harley, mulling this over. It meant that either Arina was the target, probably killed as a warning to Owen Carlsson, or the killer thought he'd get Owen Carlsson and didn't much care if Arina also got killed in the process. By some quirk of fate Owen had been late joining Arina but the driver — once embarked on his mission — couldn't, or didn't want to stop. Yes, that was possible, and it fitted. And the killer had missed Carlsson once, so he had tried again and this time he had succeeded.

Of course, that didn't account for how Thea had known where to find her brother's body, discounting the psychic bit. Horton reached for his mobile and called Cantelli. The briefing would be over by now and Horton was keen to get an update.

'How's the stomach?' he asked when Cantelli came on the line.

'Still in my throat. And I'm not sure it's going to stay there either.'

'I can't persuade you to join me for a bacon buttie then?'

Cantelli groaned.

'Coffee?'

'Yeah, I reckon I'll just about keep that down. Where are you?'

Horton told him and added, 'But I'll be in the café in the Quay Arts Centre in Newport in thirty minutes.' He couldn't risk going to the police station in case someone was watching him. He didn't think they were, but it was best to be on the safe side. And he figured that Thea's attacker wouldn't know that Cantelli was a copper. 'Did you manage to track down Owen Carlsson's caller?'

'Yes. Terry Knowles. I spun him the yarn that we believed his car had been stolen. He told me rather rudely that seeing as he didn't own a car he thought it highly unlikely. He lives in Winchester and runs an environmental consultancy based in Southampton. He's clean.'

So, Owen could have been working with Knowles on an environmental project. Now they had to find out who this

Laura was that Knowles had mentioned in his message. Horton doubted if Thea knew, but it might be worth asking her later. And if she didn't know they could go back to Knowles in an official capacity, and with the real reason for contacting him.

Horton said, 'Has Dr Clayton reported back on the autopsy?'

'She's just finished briefing Uckfield. He's in with DCI Birch.'

'See if you can get her to join us in the café. I'd like to hear what she's discovered. Is Maitland at the scene of the fire?'

'Yes, and Taylor.'

'How's Thea?'

'No permanent physical damage, but as for mental scars . . .'

And Horton knew they would never heal.

Cantelli said, 'Trueman's digging out background information on her and her brother. Uckfield said we'd leave interviewing her until she's in the safe house and then Somerfield can talk to her. She's with Thea at the hospital. The safe house is being organized now.'

And Horton would feel much happier when she was there. 'See you in half an hour.' He rang off.

As it was, he made it in twenty minutes and didn't have long to wait before he saw the red-headed, diminutive figure of Gaye Clayton, in jeans and a sailing jacket, enter the café. Behind her was Cantelli, looking rough. His dark eyes quickly scanned the café before alighting on Horton. There was a nod of recognition and a brief smile. No one followed them in and Horton knew that no one had come in after him. There were only a handful of people in the café, none of whom seemed the slightest bit interested in them.

'It was murder,' Gaye said, after settling herself in the chair opposite Horton. There were dark shadows under her soft green eyes, and the faint, pleasant smell of soap about her, which was a darn sight better than her usual perfume — formaldehyde.

Horton hadn't really doubted the verdict. Cantelli pulled up a seat next to him and yawned into his coffee.

Looking over the rim of her espresso, Gaye continued. 'There are some highly unusual circumstances surrounding the victim's death, which I am sure you will find extremely interesting. Superintendent Uckfield did, though he wasn't quite sure what to make of them, but to someone with your intellect, Inspector, it will be child's play.'

'Flattery will get you nowhere,' he said, smiling.

'Pity.' Her return smile turned into a yawn, which she gallantly stifled.

Horton leaned forward eagerly, wondering what was coming next. He already knew that this case was exceptional. From the moment he'd first seen Thea he'd had the impression or instinct, call it what you will, that there was something out of the ordinary about her and the murder of her brother. He couldn't explain it but he had the uncomfortable feeling that something had led him to this. It was stupid and irrational, and he knew that Uckfield and others, with the exception of Cantelli, would think he'd cracked up. Maybe he had and Thea's psychic claim had tipped him over the edge into paranoia or insanity. He'd been under considerable pressure since his return to duty in August, and what with the impending divorce and access to Emma . . . With irritation he pulled himself together; only facts would help solve this murder and bring this evil killer to justice, not airy-fairy feelings.

'Fire away,' he said brusquely.

She winced at his pun. 'When a weapon is held against the skin the bullet usually produces a round hole. Not so in our victim. This time it's irregular in shape, more like a letter D, which means that instead of travelling in a tight spiral the bullet wobbled as it struck the victim's skin. The cause of that could be a gun that has malfunctioned or the ammunition is defective—'

'Ballistics are examining that and checking that the fragments Dr Clayton found in the body match the weapon you took from Thea Carlsson,' Cantelli interjected.

'And it was a hell of a job picking them out, I can tell you,' she added with feeling, running a hand through her spiky auburn hair.

Horton tried not to imagine those small, slender fingers probing the soft tissue of Carlsson's brains. He swallowed his coffee as she continued.

'But that isn't the only reason for an atypical shaped wound. If I put that with the fact that there were no soot or powder deposits either, then it is my opinion that the gun was fired from some distance, certainly over two or maybe three feet, which rules out suicide.'

Horton said, 'Was he killed where the body was found?'

'No. He'd been moved.'

'Taylor couldn't find any evidence of it.'

'He'd been moved,' Dr Clayton repeated firmly.

Horton believed her. 'The killer covered his tracks very carefully.'

'And left the weather to do the rest,' she finished.

Horton thought back to Evelyn Mackie's evidence. 'As far as we know Owen Carlsson was last seen on Saturday morning on the chain ferry between West and East Cowes—'

'The super's giving a press conference.' Cantelli glanced at his watch. 'About now. He's appealing for anyone who saw Owen. And we've got a description of Carlsson's rucksack and walking stick from DCI Birch's interview with Thea. Uckfield's got duplicates. He's showing them on TV.'

And I bet DCI Birch is pissed off about that, thought Horton with some relish.

'There's more, if you want to hear it,' Gaye said.

Horton put her tetchiness down to fatigue. He suspected she'd had less sleep than him and that was precious little. 'Go on. Please.' He tried a smile but didn't get one in return this time.

'The fact that the shape of the entrance wound is atypical combined with the absence of soot and powder, not to mention the fragmenting of the bullet inside the body and the impact on the internal injuries, suggests to me that the gun was fired through a window, or a sheet of glass, which made it ricochet.'

Horton stared at her tired elfin features. This he hadn't expected.

'Are you sure?'

She eyed him disdainfully. He shouldn't have asked. It was what Uckfield must have said. He'd obviously gone down in Dr Clayton's estimation, which wasn't a very pleasant thought.

His mind went back to the scene. Was there anywhere near where Owen's body had been found that could have harboured a killer who had shot him as he walked past? There was a café — closed this time of year, a handful of very large houses — mostly divided up into holiday flats, some holiday caravans and beach huts, all facing the sea, again some distance away, and mostly empty. There was also the marina shop. If Owen had been killed as he'd walked past any of these, his body would then need to have been dragged over the nature reserve to the bunker where he'd been found. It was possible, he supposed, but that didn't answer the question why nobody had discovered him before yesterday, *if* he'd been killed on Saturday, and he didn't know that for sure. He was about to ask Gaye Clayton when she started talking again.

'I've sent his clothes to the forensic lab and I also took radiographs; they might reveal tiny fragments of glass, although at the distance from which he was shot I'm not hopeful.' She swallowed the remainder of her coffee and pulled a face as though not liking the taste. 'I've been living off this stuff all night. Doctor's curse. Takes me back to the old days on A & E. I'll probably have a thumping head tomorrow.'

Horton had difficulty seeing Gaye Clayton with living patients after having watched her cut into the flesh of dead people. 'How long had Carlsson been dead?' he asked.

'Ah, an intelligent question! You're redeemed, Inspector. There was a great deal of rigour in the body and lividity was extensive and permanent. The flies had laid their eggs in the soft tissue and they'd hatched. Sorry, Sergeant, is this making you queasy?'

Cantelli took a deep breath and said, 'After-effects of sea sickness.'

Horton smiled grimly and tried not to see the carcass of Owen Carlsson, or think about that smell.

'The eggs will usually hatch within eight to fourteen hours depending on the body temperature and the conditions outside. The maggots had gone through their first stage, which means that your victim had been dead two to three days, maybe four, but they hadn't reached the second stage so he certainly hadn't been dead as long as seven days.'

Cantelli swallowed hard.

Horton said, 'Which fits with his sister seeing him on Saturday morning and Mrs Mackie seeing him on the chain ferry later the same morning.'

'He was probably killed either late Saturday or sometime during Sunday. Early Monday morning, at the latest, and that's the best I can do,' said Dr Clayton, almost apologetically.

Thea had said that she'd got no answer from her brother's mobile phone on Saturday evening, which suggested that Owen Carlsson was already dead. So where had he gone when he'd left the chain ferry in Cowes?

'Did you find anything in Owen's pockets?'

Gaye shook her head. 'Not even a handkerchief.'

Cantelli said, 'His wallet must have been in the rucksack. Could robbery have been the motive?'

'Has anyone used his debit or credit cards?'

'Not yet. But he could have had cash on him.'

'Villains don't usually go round shooting people on the Isle of Wight for cash,' Horton ventured. 'This is hardly an inner city.'

'No, but it is possible,' Cantelli insisted. 'They could have been high on drugs, or drunk, saw Owen out walking, alone, and thought him an easy target.'

Horton thought it unlikely. He reckoned this killer had known exactly where Owen Carlsson was every minute, probably every second of the day. And again he thought of Thea. What did she know that she wasn't saying?

Cantelli continued. 'Let's say they shot him through a car window, saw him fall, screeched to a halt, jumped out and stole his money. Then they tossed his rucksack in a ditch or hedge and bundled the body into the boot of the car.'

'I can tell you're feeling better; your creative juices are working well.'

'Must be this coffee.'

'Any views on that, Dr Clayton?' asked Horton.

'If he was kept in a car, he wasn't there for long. I didn't find any traces of oil on his clothes or skin, but there were fibres that looked as though he'd been covered with something: a rug, blanket, or similar. His clothes were wet, and there are salt residues, but given that he was found so close to the sea that's hardly surprising. The lab will give you a more accurate analysis.'

Cantelli resumed. 'The villains could have driven to the car park at the Duver, bundled Owen Carlsson out of the car late Tuesday night, carried him to the sand dune and then left him with the gun, which they wiped free of their prints, before pressing it into Carlsson's hand to make it look as though he'd shot himself.'

Gaye interjected. 'His prints were on the gun, but there was no gun residue on his hands.'

Horton looked thoughtful. 'I just can't see your average yobbo going to so much trouble. They'd have left the body where they shot him. And they certainly wouldn't have left their gun behind.'

'OK, not yobbos and not drunks,' Cantelli conceded, evidently reluctant to give up on his theory. 'But someone who set out to kill Owen Carlsson and make it look like suicide.'

But Dr Clayton was shaking her head. 'They failed.'

'Perhaps they're not very bright.' Cantelli added. 'After all, they got the wrong person first time round when they ran into Arina Sutton.'

'Ah, but that would mean Owen's death was planned and not a random attack. And was Arina the wrong person?' posed Horton.

Gaye looked up, more alert than previously. 'Sutton?'

'You know her?' Horton asked, curious, hearing a note of recognition in her voice.

'I know a Professor Sir Christopher Sutton.' She gave a tired smile and half a shrug. 'But it's a common enough surname.'

'Who is he?'

'A neuropsychiatric consultant.'

'A what?' asked Cantelli.

Gaye smiled wearily. 'Neuropsychiatry is the study of mental disorders attributable to the nervous system. Sutton is a clever man and a very entertaining speaker, egocentric like a lot of consultants, but brilliant. He must be retired by now. I heard him talk years ago, at a seminar, when I was studying personality, profiling and criminology. He was about sixty then and a legend in his field.'

Horton doubted if there was a connection, but he'd ask Trueman to check just to be sure. Not that it had any bearing on this case. Still, any information was better than none. Addressing Cantelli, Horton said, 'Did Thea Carlsson mention anything to Birch about Arina Sutton being killed in the same spot as her parents in 1990?'

'If she did he didn't bring it up at the briefing this morning. He claims she said practically nothing before the solicitor showed up and afterwards just sat there looking forlorn. All she did say was that she went to the Duver because she had a feeling that was where she'd find her brother. Of course Birch doesn't believe her.'

And neither does anyone else, thought Horton, studying Cantelli to see what he thought. Cantelli simply raised his dark eyebrows, as though to say 'who knows?'

Gaye scraped back her chair with a yawn. 'Sounds like you've got quite a case on your hands, Inspector.'

'I'm on holiday,' Horton replied, rising.

'Looks like it,' she rejoined sarcastically. 'Well, I'm going home to catch up on my beauty sleep.'

He should have answered, 'you don't need it', but he'd never been one for smooth talking. Not that Gaye Clayton expected it, but she was eyeing him slightly curiously.

'I'll give you a lift to the hovercraft,' volunteered Cantelli as they headed out of the café.

Outside Horton paused and peered through the heavy stinging rain. There was no one loitering suspiciously. In this weather there wasn't anyone about at all.

Turning to Cantelli he said, 'How did Thea get to Bembridge? She didn't use her brother's car.'

'She phoned for a taxi to take her to St Helens and walked down to the Duver from there. The taxi driver has confirmed it.'

'Is she still at the hospital?'

'She was when I left the station.'

'I'll pay her a visit. If someone's watching her it'll reinforce the belief that I'm a friend.'

Cantelli's phone rang. Sheltering in the doorway of the café, he answered it as Horton escorted Dr Clayton towards Cantelli's car parked opposite the Harley.

'I hear you had a close call last night,' Gaye said, ramming her hands in the pockets of her sailing jacket and seemingly impervious to the rain lashing into her face.

'Could have been worse.' His chest was still raw, but it would get better.

She halted and stared up at him with an expression of concern. 'Be careful, Andy.'

'Why the warning?' he asked with false lightness as alarm pricked his spine.

'Perhaps I'm just tired, but I don't like this case. There's the smell of evil around it.'

Horton grew even more concerned though he tried not to show it. She'd echoed his sentiments exactly. 'I didn't think scientists had premonitions,' he teased.

'Well, this one does and she's just had it. I haven't met Thea Carlsson, only her dead brother, but this is a clever killing by a clever killer. And, despite Cantelli's theories, it is not yobbos. Your killer never for a moment thought it would be construed as suicide, but he's done his best to make it difficult for us to ascertain time and place of death. Anyway, I've said my piece. I just don't want you ending up on my dissecting table — no matter how much I'd like to see you without your clothes.' She smiled to lessen the impact of her words but Horton shuddered at the thought of being laid out on the mortuary slab.

'That was Somerfield,' Cantelli said, hurrying towards them. Horton saw instantly that something was wrong. 'Thea's gone.'

'How? When?' Horton rapped.

'About half an hour ago. She said she wanted a shower before she left the hospital for the safe house. The WVRS volunteer had brought her some clothes. Well, she could hardly walk out in a hospital gown and Somerfield couldn't go in the shower with her,' Cantelli said defensively.

'Why not? She's a woman too,' Horton snapped. This was the last thing he'd expected.

'She's not gone back to the burnt-out house,' Cantelli said, the rain pouring off his face, his dark eyes anxious. 'I suppose she could have returned to where she found her brother's body.'

Horton cursed. 'Check the hospital staff for any sightings of her, Barney. I'll head for the Duver.'

'Andy,' Gaye called out after him. 'Remember what I said.' He would, but it wouldn't make any difference.

CHAPTER SIX

He reached the car park at the Duver in record time, and miraculously, without getting a speeding ticket or killing himself. There wasn't a car in sight. The rain was sheeting down. The biting wind cut into his flesh and shook the gorse with the fury of an outraged god. From beyond the beach huts came the thunderous pounding of waves crashing onto the shore. Not a day to be at sea, he thought, hurrying to the place where he'd discovered Thea leaning over her brother's body, without any real hope of finding her there. She wasn't. Only the flapping blue and white police tape greeted him.

So where was she? Had she voluntarily left the hospital or had she been abducted? Christ, he didn't even want to consider the latter, but he had to. Her abductor could be the arsonist and his intruder and the person who had been watching him and Thea here yesterday.

His eyes searched through the slicing rain for a hideout where this person could have watched the sorrowful scene being played out. There were plenty of places to hide: the numerous bushes, the caravan park to the north on the hill and the large houses on the gentle hill slopes to the west, which rose to the village of St Helens. Anyone with a pair of binoculars could have seen them.

Frustrated and concerned, he returned to the boat and punched in Cantelli's number.

'There's no sign of her,' Cantelli greeted him mournfully. 'We've put out an all-ports alert but we're keeping it from the media in case it puts her life in danger.'

'I'll skin Somerfield alive,' snarled Horton.

'It's not her fault, Andy,' Cantelli said gently, then added, 'But if it makes you feel any better Uckfield's already done that.'

Horton took a breath and mentally got a grip on his emotions. For someone whose personal motto was 'control at all times and never show what you're feeling', he was failing miserably.

Cantelli continued, 'There is one bit of news though; a nurse on A & E says she saw Thea climb into a car. She's definite about that because she was on duty when Thea Carlsson was brought in so she recognized her.'

'What car? Description of the driver?' asked Horton eagerly.

'She didn't get the registration or make, she was in a hurry and she didn't think much of it, but it was a dark-coloured saloon, a newish model. No description of the driver. Doesn't help us much, but the nurse says that Thea went willingly. No one was forcing her inside.'

Horton wasn't sure he liked the sound of that, especially the bit about a dark-coloured saloon. But if it wasn't Arina Sutton's killer, was it a friend? Had she lied about not knowing anyone? Had she telephoned this person from the hospital and asked him to collect her? Did that mean she could be involved in the murder of her brother after all? No. He didn't want to believe it.

Cantelli said, 'Uckfield's on his way to see you, Andy. Says he'll meet you at the nature reserve opposite Port St Helens. Do you know where he means?'

Horton did. Uckfield could have picked a drier location, but there was logic in his choice. No one would be on the footpath that skirted Brading Marshes in this weather. And it was screened from the road by trees, shrubs and the lagoons.

Locking the boat, Horton hurried across the harbour causeway to find Uckfield's silver BMW already parked in the small yard opposite the entrance to the reserve. He hadn't gone far into it before he spotted a short, square-set man wearing a long green waxed coat with a cap pushed low over his head, peering through binoculars across the salt marshes. Horton smiled to himself. Despite the clothes and binoculars, this was not Uckfield's natural habitat. The big man stood out like a hooker at a high-class wedding. Uckfield had never been any good at covert operations.

'Seen anything interesting?' Horton asked as he drew level.

'Not a dickie bird. Anyone follow you?' Uckfield lowered the binoculars.

'No.'

'Can't say I blame them in this shit-awful weather.'

Uckfield was right. There was no hiding place from the relentless rain, which had already seeped through Horton's trousers to his skin. He refrained from sounding off about Somerfield's incompetence — it would achieve nothing — and instead asked what Trueman had dug up on Thea Carlsson. He was curious to know more about the girl who had got under his skin so much.

Uckfield said, 'She's twenty-eight, has dual nationality, British and Swedish, like her brother, and works as a translator for the European Union. Or that is she did until eleven days ago when she sent an email to her boss saying she was going on unscheduled leave and wasn't sure when she'd be back.'

Horton rapidly calculated the day as having been Sunday, which tied in with what Evelyn Mackie had told him — Thea had arrived at her brother's house on the following Monday.

Uckfield said, 'She gave no reason and no one's heard from her since.'

What had prompted her to take such drastic action? Horton wondered. Had Owen told her he was in danger?

Uckfield continued. 'She lives in Luxembourg and speaks Danish, German and Swedish.'

A clever girl. But there was more, Horton could see it in Uckfield's scowling expression. 'And?'

Uckfield sniffed noisily. 'Owen Carlsson was working on a high-profile European environmental project. It's believed his death and his sister's sudden departure could have something to do with it.'

Ah, so that was it. He thought of those files in Owen's study. Could that be why the house had been set alight, to destroy one of them in particular? Perhaps the intruder couldn't find the file he wanted, or maybe Horton had disturbed him before he'd had a chance to properly search. Setting fire to the house with Thea in it would wipe out two problems with one match: the file and the chance that Owen might have confided in his sister. Or had Thea been involved in translating something Owen had been working on?

He said as much to Uckfield, adding, 'That could be why Thea looked so terrified when I found her. She could have known this person intended to kill her too, and now she's been abducted. The driver of the car she was seen getting into could have had a gun pointing at her.'

'In that case she's already dead.'

With a sinking feeling Horton knew it could be true, but he said, 'Who called you in?' It couldn't have been DCI Birch.'

'Reg.'

The Chief Constable and Uckfield's father-in-law. Given what Uckfield had just said about Owen's European environmental project, Horton had wondered if it might have been Europol.

Uckfield said, 'He had a telephone call from a woman called Laura Rose—'

'Laura!' Horton exclaimed. 'She's the woman Knowles mentioned on Owen Carlsson's answer machine. Owen had a meeting arranged with her for yesterday.'

'Yeah. She's an adviser to the European Commission Environment Directorate, and she was getting increasingly worried when this Knowles bloke said he had been trying to get hold of Owen Carlsson since Monday morning without any joy. When Carlsson still didn't reply by Wednesday morning, Laura Rosewood called the local station to be told that Owen had been posted as missing by his sister. She then called Reg. They're old friends. Reg called DCI Birch to be told that Thea Carlsson was being questioned and DI Horton had found Carlsson's body in a bunker. I've got an appointment with her tomorrow morning at eleven.'

'Not sooner?' Horton asked, annoyed.

'She's in London but she lives here on the island and doesn't get back until late tonight, and before you ask, I don't know what Owen was working on. Ms Rosewood told Reg it was too complex to explain over the telephone, and that it could be controversial. The chief asked me to keep it quiet for now.'

Horton stared at Uckfield disbelievingly. 'So in the meantime we twiddle our thumbs awaiting Ms Rosewood's pleasure. This could be vital information.'

'Twenty-four hours won't make much difference.'

Horton could hardly believe what he was hearing. 'It could to Thea's life,' he cried.

'It's probably got nothing to do with the case,' Uckfield said defensively.

'Well, I hope to God you're right because I wouldn't like it on my conscience.'

'She's really got to you, hasn't she?'

Horton didn't answer. He didn't like Uckfield's sneering tone but he knew better than to rise to his bait. After a moment, controlling his impatience and his anger, he said, 'What about this man Knowles? He must know what the project's about.'

'He's in the Shetland Islands.'

'Says who?' scoffed Horton.

'Ms Rosewood. Apparently he's examining how the Shetland Islanders use wind power. They get plenty of it up there. We're checking it out. Isn't this ruddy rain ever going to stop?' Uckfield glared at it as though he could frighten it into submission before turning and heading back to his car. Horton fell into step beside him feeling far from happy with the turn of events.

'Meanwhile we explore other avenues,' Uckfield continued. 'Maitland's confirmed that the fire at Owen Carlsson's house was started by igniting petrol which was poured all over the hall.'

Petrol meant car. Had the arsonist come with the intention of setting light to the house then? Had he known that the police had released Thea or had he been hoping to search alone and finding Thea there had to change his plans? Whoever it was who had attacked him, and set fire to the house, must have travelled there by car. Horton tried to recall the vehicles he'd seen parked in the road. In his anxiety for Thea he hadn't been paying much attention. There had been a white van, no lettering on it; a Volkswagen campervan behind it, a Golf GTI, a blue Ford Mondeo and a silver Audi. There were no motorbikes and he couldn't remember any registration numbers. He mentioned this to Uckfield.

'The fat sergeant is handling that,' Uckfield replied. 'He's knocking on doors.'

Horton guessed Uckfield meant Sergeant Norris, who was big, but not as overweight as Uckfield. They crossed the road.

'Marsden is checking out the gun clubs,' Uckfield added. 'And Somerfield is helping with calls after my appeal for sightings of Owen Carlsson.'

So no one was asking around Seaview for witnesses to Arina Sutton's death. Horton said as much and got the tart reply that it wasn't a priority. Horton understood that, but he couldn't help thinking it might be significant.

Uckfield zapped open the car. As Horton's wet trousers squelched on Uckfield's leather seats, Uckfield said, 'Birch believes Thea Carlsson is involved in her brother's death. She got someone to kill him who then attempted to silence her.'

'Why the devil would she do that?'

'People do kill their relatives.'

Horton could see that Uckfield agreed with Birch, which was probably why he was in no hurry to interview Ms Rosewood. Horton thought back to the fire. He had let himself into the house using the key Thea had given him, which meant she must have had a second key, or perhaps Owen kept a spare hidden somewhere. The front door had been shut when he had arrived. So the intruder must have been known to Thea, and she'd refused to say who it was. He blamed himself for not pressing her on it. He'd let his personal feelings get in the way of his job.

Uckfield started up the car and switched the heater on full blast.

Despite not wanting to admit it, Horton said, 'Thea must have gone willingly with whoever she let into the house up to her bedroom.'

'A lover?'

Horton wondered why he didn't much care for that thought either.

'Perhaps it was a friend of her brother's or someone claiming to be a friend.' Terry Knowles flashed into his mind again — but he was apparently in the Shetland Islands.

'Then why not tell us who it is?' Uckfield growled. 'If she's innocent.'

'She could be scared.'

Uckfield grunted but seemed disinclined to believe it.

Horton said, 'If we discount the environment theory, and Thea's involvement in her brother's death, Owen's murder could have something to do with the death of his parents in 1990.'

'How the blazes do you work that one out?'

'Isn't it an odd coincidence that Arina Sutton, the woman Owen Carlsson was with that night, was killed in the same place as his parents all those years ago?' Uckfield was eyeing him as if he were mad.

Horton suddenly felt weary. The full pelt of the heater was making him incredibly tired. His throat hurt and his head ached with going around in the same old circles. With an effort he roused himself to explain.

'Let's say Owen Carlsson is the hit-and-run driver's intended victim but because he leaves the restaurant late the driver kills Arina Sutton instead. Owen calls Thea on Sunday morning to tell her his girlfriend's been killed in exactly the same spot as their parents in 1990.'

'You don't know she was his girlfriend.'

'Why else would he take her out for a meal?'

'She could have taken him out. It could have been business.'

'Whatever,' Horton dismissed impatiently. 'The accident brings back terrible memories for Thea and she rushes home upset—'

'A week after the incident is hardly what I call rushing home.'

Uckfield had a point.

'There is another possibility.'

'Go on, amaze me.'

'Only if you turn that damn heater off.'

Uckfield silenced the engine.

Horton continued. 'Owen's death could have nothing to do with his work, and nothing to do with his parents dying in the same place as his girlfriend. Arina Sutton's death could have been caused by a drunk driver, and one whom Owen recognized. Maybe not at first but after the shock wore off. Or perhaps he saw the car some time later, and when he realized who the driver was, he couldn't believe it. He kept silent because he knew this person well; he went to confront them with it on Saturday, to tell them to own up, and got himself killed as a result.'

'Then he was an idiot.'

'But it's possible.'

Uckfield grunted an acknowledgment that it was.

'And it's possible that the killer thought Owen had confided this to Thea, hence the attack on her.' Uckfield opened his mouth to speak but Horton pressed on, 'And seeing as you don't get to talk to the elusive Laura Rosewood until tomorrow, I'd like to check out the Arina Sutton angle, talk to her relatives, posing as a friend of Owen Carlsson, of course,' he hastily added, seeing Uckfield was about to protest. 'Owen might have said something to a relative, like "I think I know who killed her." There's also the possibility that Arina's death might not have been an accident. Arina Sutton could have been the target and Owen knew why, which was why he was killed.'

Uckfield exhaled. 'My God, you've got more theories than my wife's got shoes. All right. Let me know what you come up with.'

'And you let me know the moment you get anything on Thea Carlsson.'

Uckfield promised he would.

On that note, Horton returned to his boat, changed into his leathers, and set out for Arina Sutton's home: Scanaford House.

CHAPTER SEVEN

Thursday, midday

It was old. Georgian, Horton reckoned, drawing to a halt in front of the brick and stone house that resembled a minor stately home. The tree lined driveway must have been almost a mile long. Whatever Arina Sutton's background it was certainly one of wealth. The house had to be worth a million pounds plus, and it was a million miles away from the cramped flat in a council tower block that had once been his childhood home. He told himself he wasn't resentful, but who the hell was he kidding?

Climbing off the Harley, Horton removed his helmet, glad the rain had finally ceased, though the darkening sky threatened more. He pushed his finger on the brass bell beside a solid oak door and ran a critical eye over the facade. The place had a shut-up, forlorn feel to it and, judging by the flaky paintwork and grass growing out of the drainpipes, was in need of some tender loving care. He wondered who he was going to upset by calling here and asking questions about Arina's death. A grieving mother or father? A sister or brother? Whoever they were, clearly they weren't at home.

There was no letter box for him to peer through, only a black-painted post box fixed to the outside wall. He flicked it open. Empty.

Disappointed, he made his way around the left-hand side of the house where the lawn gave way to a lake about the size of the one on Southsea seafront, on which they hired out paddle boats. Beyond this was a small copse of elms and some other trees whose species he didn't know. The sweeping lawns and the lake made him feel like a bit-part actor in *Brideshead Revisited*. Perhaps Arina Sutton had married well before meeting Owen Carlsson and had got a whacking great divorce settlement, which was more than Catherine was going to get. Her position as marketing director of her father's international marine manufacturing company paid well, and 'daddy' would always see she was all right. Horton figured that although he'd have to give her the house or his pension, he was damned if he was going to give her both.

The gardens were deserted except for the odd crow and magpie. Irritated that his journey had been a waste of time, he continued to the back of the house, but got the same story — closed for business. The bereaved had obviously departed to seek comfort elsewhere. His attention was arrested by the sound of a car pulling up. Great. Now he might get some answers.

He hurried back to the front where, with a slight quickening of pulse, he saw a dark-coloured saloon car. His eyes swivelled to the lean, grey-haired man wearing cowboy boots, a ponytail and leather flying jacket who was peering at Horton's Harley with suspicion rather than admiration. At the sound of Horton's footsteps, he looked up with hostile eyes and a scowling countenance.

'Who are you?' he demanded aggressively.

Horton would like to have asked him the same question, but he said, 'I'm looking for a relative of Arina Sutton.'

Horton wondered if he was Arina's brother, or husband. At a push he supposed he could possibly be her father if he'd had her young, say at eighteen. Arina had been forty when she'd died and this man was somewhere in his late fifties. He didn't look the type to own this pile but then he could be a former rock star, or even a drug dealer for all Horton knew.

'There aren't any relatives,' the man said warily.

Clearly not related then. *Maybe he thinks I'm a burglar, or worse, an estate agent.* Horton didn't trust the skittering eyes and narrow mouth. And he wasn't sure he believed the bit about there being no relatives.

'Were you a friend of Arina's?' Horton probed, eyeing him steadily.

The man's eyes refused to meet Horton's. 'I knew her father, Sir Christopher Sutton. He died just before Christmas. Cancer.'

So no suspicious circumstances there, though a ponytail always oozed suspicion. Horton recalled what Dr Clayton had said. It had to be the same Sir Christopher. Time for introductions.

With a smile he stretched out his hand. 'Andy Horton.'

Ponytail eyed it as though it contained a grenade before sniffing and taking it briefly and damply. 'Roy Danesbrook.'

Resisting the urge to wipe his palm down the side of his trousers, Horton said, 'Isn't there anyone I can speak to about Arina?'

'Depends what you want to know.'

What you're doing here for a start, thought Horton, getting fed up with Danesbrook's evasiveness and recognizing the same defensive tone he'd heard many times in an interview room. Although he'd never met Sir Christopher, he couldn't believe that such an eminent man could have been friends with so shifty a bastard. He wished he was here in his official capacity as a police officer, then he could have been as blunt as he wanted. But maybe he could be.

'I want to know why Owen Carlsson is dead,' he said briskly.

Danesbrook's eyes widened. His lips twitched nervously.

'I take it you knew Owen,' Horton pressed.

'Not really. I saw him at Arina's funeral. Did he kill himself?'

'Why should he do that?'

'I just thought . . .' Danesbrook shifted and fiddled with his ponytail.

'When was her funeral?' Horton asked, sharper this time.

'Tuesday before last. She's buried alongside her father. They're in the churchyard.' He jerked his head to his right. 'The last plot before the graveyard opens out into the new section. Sir Christopher is with his late wife and Arina next to them. Look, I've got to go.'

But you've only just got here. As if reading his mind Danesbrook said, 'I only came up to the house because I saw your bike from the road and wondered who you were.'

Oh yeah? Horton didn't believe that for a second. 'Did Owen say anything to you about Arina's death?'

'No, nothing. I'm late. Sorry, I can't help you.'

He watched Danesbrook slither into the car, jerk it round and skid away, but not before he noticed a dent in the front passenger door. He reached for his phone and relayed Danesbrook's registration number to Cantelli, adding, 'Find out all you can about him, and who formally identified Arina's body. Ask Trueman to get some background information on Arina Sutton and her father, Sir Christopher, and find out who their solicitor is. Any news on Thea?'

'No. Sorry.'

Horton had hoped but not expected. He crossed to the church. Now that he was here he might as well take a look at the graves. He doubted they'd reveal anything, but no harm in hoping. He wondered why his news about Owen Carlsson's death had so rattled Danesbrook.

He pushed open the wrought-iron gate and eyed the church. Saxon, he reckoned. Not that he was an expert but he'd once had a girlfriend who was and she'd dragged him around the churches of southern England in the hope that she'd educate him. *He'd* gone in the hope that he'd get his wicked way with her, which he hadn't. The romance — though he could hardly call it that — had fizzled out somewhere in Dorset.

He found the graves without too much trouble. On Arina's there was a mound of earth and decaying flowers, and on her father's a wooden cross with his and his wife's name etched on it. Horton surmised that the headstone had been removed to accommodate the death notices of husband and wife. He bent to read the inscriptions on the cards on Arina's grave, but the weather had made the writing illegible.

Hearing footsteps, Horton turned to see a tall, athletically built man with fair shoulder-length hair approaching him. His weather-worn face and the name on his green sweatshirt told Horton he was a landscape gardener, either called Jonathan Anmore, or he worked for Jonathan Anmore. The former was confirmed after a brief introduction.

'I look after the gardens at Scanaford House,' Anmore explained. 'Sir Christopher was a real gent and his daughter, Arina, was a lovely lady. Sad to think they're both gone now. She came here in July to look after the professor when he got ill. Are you a friend of Arina's or the Prof's? I don't remember seeing you at their funerals?'

'I didn't know either of them. I was a friend of Owen Carlsson's.'

Anmore's expression deepened into one of concern. 'I heard about his death on the radio.'

Which was more than Danesbrook had. Horton said, 'I had hoped Arina's relatives might tell me something that would help me find out why Owen died, but I met a man called Danesbrook at the house who said there aren't any relatives.'

Anmore ran a hand through his hair and nodded. 'That's right.'

'So who inherits?'

'No idea.' After a short pause Anmore added, 'Do the police know how Owen died?'

'Probably, but they're not saying much to me. Could be suicide, could be murder?'

'But who would want to murder him?'

Horton shrugged. 'How did Owen seem at Arina's funeral?'

'Upset, like we all were.'

'And was that the last time you saw him, Tuesday week?' Horton tried not to sound like a policeman.

'Yes. What about his sister? Can't she help?'

So he knew about Thea. 'I don't want to upset her any more than she already is.'

'No. I guess not.'

'Did you meet her at Arina's funeral?'

'No. I heard Owen tell Bella Westbury that she was staying with him for a few days.'

And who else had heard this, Horton wondered? He asked who Bella Westbury was.

'The professor's housekeeper. She lives in the village.' Anmore glanced back towards Scanaford House. 'It's that house, you know. It's cursed. Everyone who comes into contact with it ends up dead. Except me and Bella. It's haunted, you know. No, it's true, all documented fact. A father killed his daughter there in 1865 and threw her body in the lake. She's said to walk the house before a death.'

Anmore's words had pricked Horton's memory. He recalled the book by Thea's bedside, *The Lost Ghosts of the Isle of Wight*, and the inscription inside it, 'To Thea who has the gift — Helen.' It must have been given to her by her mother and now that book, like all the others in the house, and Owen's environmental papers, were ashes.

'Did Arina see this ghost before her father's death?' he asked, not particularly seriously.

'She never said.' Then Anmore grinned. 'I don't believe in ghosts either, but the murder bit's true.'

And that was one murder that Horton didn't have to solve.

Anmore's mobile phone rang. There was nothing more to be gained by hanging around here. Maybe this Bella Westbury could provide him with more information.

Horton headed for the village, but not before he paused at the top of the driveway and looked back at Scanaford House. The driveway curved to the left and was screened from the road by evergreen trees. It was as he had thought. Whatever Danesbrook had come here for, it hadn't been to check out Horton's Harley — because unless the man had X-ray eyes there was simply no way he could have seen it.

CHAPTER EIGHT

'Tea?' asked Bella Westbury crisply.

Horton accepted with alacrity, even though he would have preferred a cold drink for his still sore throat. But if it meant he'd learn something that could help them with the investigation then he'd swallow castor oil and like it.

He stepped into the narrow terraced cottage a few yards along from the village shop where the sales assistant had given him Bella Westbury's address. He hadn't expected her to be in or so friendly, a decided bonus after Danesbrook's evasiveness. He'd introduced himself as a friend of Arina's, saying that he had lost touch with her over the years and had only just learnt of her death. She accepted it readily.

'Sling your jacket down anywhere and come through to the kitchen. It's warmer.'

The room felt warm enough to Horton with a wood-burning stove belting out heat but he wasn't going to argue. Bella Westbury was not the type of woman to mess with.

Horton did as instructed and followed her short, sturdy figure through a small living room crowded with an assortment of old and worn furniture, which appeared to have been thrown together without any regard to design, space or colour. It reminded him of his childhood days spent in rented accommodation before the council flat had become his and his mother's home.

'Arina's death was tragic,' she tossed at him over her shoulder. 'Such a bloody waste of a life.'

Horton ducked his head to avoid the wind chimes in the kitchen doorway and didn't quite succeed. Their musical tingling was accompanied by a feline chorus. Horton counted five cats crawling over the small kitchen, which was five too many for his liking. Bella Westbury lifted one from the table where it had been licking at a plate of Ginger Nuts.

She said, 'Arina was cultured, educated, gentle, kind and intelligent. But of course, you'd know that, being an old friend.'

Shrewd green eyes examined him out of a weathered face of about fifty-five years. Horton gave what he considered to be a sad smile of acknowledgement, which she seemed to accept as genuine. Quickly, to forestall her asking any questions about his relationship with Arina, he said, 'I was talking to Jonathan Anmore in the churchyard. He spoke very fondly of Arina.'

'He would. No one had a bad word to say about her. Why should they when she was one of the best? Jonathan always fancied his chances there. But then Jonathan fancies his chances with any female under forty. Arina would joke with him, but that's as far as it went. Biscuit?'

Horton politely declined. Maybe she saw his distaste because she said, 'I'll just let the cats out.'

The wind rushed in as she threw open the door, setting off the wind chimes. Horton let his eyes roam the cramped, untidy kitchen. They came to rest on the wall beside him that displayed several framed newspaper cuttings.

'Is that you?' he asked, trying to keep the surprise from his voice as he stared at a young woman with long auburn hair and fire in her eyes.

'Greenham Common, September 1981,' she answered crisply and proudly, throwing a tea bag into two mugs. 'Twenty-five and full of ideals. Still am, thank the Lord. Not like the namby-pamby kids these days. They're too intent on climbing the greasy pole to the top of a corporation that is as corrupt as they are.'

Horton thought that a bit harsh but didn't say so. She filled the mugs with hot water and plonked them on the table. Gesturing him into a seat she said, 'I met Ewan there.' Her brow puckered.

Horton hoped he wasn't about to hear the gory details of a troublesome relationship. But then it was his own fault for raising the subject.

'He was a miner from South Wales,' Bella continued, sitting down opposite Horton. 'His mother was one of the first women who marched for ten days to set up the Greenham Common Peace Camp. I heard about it on the news and went there like a shot. I was there until 1983 when I married Ewan and went to live in South Wales and we all know what happened after that. I will never forgive Margaret Thatcher and the Tories for their treachery and the police for their brutality.'

Her voice became harsher and Horton's eyes flicked to the framed newspaper cuttings of a crowd of miners being beaten back by the police. He was glad he hadn't come here as a police officer. He certainly wouldn't have been offered tea and biscuits. Although only a teenager at the time and more interested in playing football, he'd seen films of the miners' strike of 1984 and 1985 during his police training. The conflict had produced clashes between the state and the miners in epic proportions, eleven miners had died, tens of thousands had been arrested, and scores of police had been injured. The mines the colliers had been fighting to keep open were all eventually closed down. The miners lost, big time.

'I fought beside Ewan,' she said, proudly. 'We were a real community then, not like now where no one knows a single bugger in his street, although it's not so bad here on the island, the last bastion of Olde England. It's so important — community — despite what that mad woman said. We're still suffering the consequences of her reign now.'

Horton took it that she meant Margaret Thatcher. He could well imagine Bella Westbury on the picket line. So where was Ewan Westbury now? He'd seen no evidence of a man living here. Dead or divorced, he wondered? He needed to get her back to talking about Arina Sutton and then hopefully Owen Carlsson, but before he could speak, she was off on her reminiscences.

'We all stuck together. The railway workers, seamen, printers, they all came out in support of the miners, and we had international help. It was 1926 all over again with the women running soup kitchens. We staffed food centres and collected cash, but it was all a waste of time in the end. And now look at the mess we're in: oil shortages, petrol prices sky high, power rationing, dependent on overseas countries for coal when we've got a rich resource right under our feet.'

'But coal isn't environmentally friendly,' chanced Horton. Despite his intentions to get her back on his track he recognized she'd given him a lead into discussing environmental matters, which could take him to Owen Carlsson.

'Of course it is,' she declared, slamming her mug down with such force that he was amazed it didn't break. 'There's new technology that makes it cleaner and there could be more and even better technology to help get it out of the ground without scarring the countryside and killing men, or having to go cap in hand to other nations. If the so-called brains and techno kids put their minds to it we could benefit big time. Christ! If they can invent mobile technology, nuclear weapons and God alone knows what, surely they can find a way of processing our rich natural resources into clean and efficient energy?'

Horton wondered what Sir Christopher and Arina Sutton had thought of Bella's views. Somehow he couldn't see her keeping them to herself while dusting the furniture or cooking the dinner.

'Instead, they talk about wind farms,' she snorted. 'They wouldn't keep this kitchen in energy let alone the rest of the village or the island. You'd need thousands of the ugly monsters blighting the landscape and I for one don't want them ruining the beauty of the countryside. Besides it's all bollocks you know, this eco-friendly crap, designed to make the government look as though they're doing something to save the planet, when it's already too late.'

'Isn't that a somewhat pessimistic view?'

'Not if you read the global warming reports and hear Owen Carlsson talking. He was Arina's boyfriend. He'll tell you. He's studied the oceans. He knows just how bad things are, but people simply don't want to hear what he's saying.'

And was that why he was killed, Horton wondered, thinking back to his earlier discussion with Uckfield at the nature reserve, and Uckfield's meeting tomorrow with Laura Rosewood. Had Owen been saying too much? Was the controversial environmental project he'd been working on something to do with global warming? The reports Horton had glimpsed in Owen's study again sprang to mind. He wished he'd had time to read them.

Then he registered that Bella Westbury had talked about Owen in the present tense. So, another one who hadn't heard the local news. He'd tell her soon, but he wanted to fish a little longer.

'I read something about there being a local opposition group to the wind farms.'

'You bet there is! WAWF, Wight Against Wind Farms, both the onshore and offshore variety. Like I said, they won't make a blind bit of difference. Not while they keep aeroplanes in the sky. Did you know that after 9/11 when the USA grounded all flights for three days the temperature in America actually fell? If that isn't proof of the harm they do I don't know what is. And this pathetic, stupid government tell us to stop buying carrier bags and use energy-efficient light bulbs. I mean what the hell difference is that going to make?'

Horton smiled. 'Not much, I guess. But isn't there another group called REMAF?' he recollected from Owen's office.

She eyed him curiously.

'I read about it in the local newspaper,' he quickly explained.

She seemed to accept this. 'Renewable Energy Means A Future. Owen had to conduct a report for them on the viability of the wind farms. I tried to get Owen to tell us the results at a meeting in October, but he wasn't having any of it. That's how he met Arina. It was love at first sight. Then to be killed by some idiot bastard with no brains between his ears who didn't even bother to stop. And just when she'd found happiness. If it hadn't been for me they'd have never met. I arranged for Owen to give a talk on the environment, and I cajoled Arina into coming with me.'

'I understand you were her housekeeper,' Horton asked casually, sipping his tea and trying not to pull a face. Not a great lover of the brew, this tasted like cats' piss.

'Sir Christopher's really. Arina was an interior designer but she shot home from London to help nurse her father when he became too ill to manage alone. Sir Christopher died on the thirteenth of December. Twenty-one days later Arina is killed by a lunatic driver. She didn't want to stay on at Scanaford House after her father's death. She never really liked the place.'

'Not because it's supposed to be haunted!'

She gave a laugh that reminded Horton of the laughing sailor in the glass booth on Clarence Pier in Southsea. 'Jonathan Anmore tells everyone that old tale.'

'It's not true?'

'Who knows? There was a murder there yonks ago, but if you give Jonathan half an ear, he'll embellish it with so many ghosts you'd think they were holding a convention there.'

'Who inherits now Arina's dead?'

'No idea,' she answered sharply. She probably thought he'd come with the intention of making a claim on her estate. 'You'll have to ask Gerald Newland, the solicitor. He's in Newport.'

And Horton, or someone in the major crime team, would. He reckoned that neither Bella Westbury nor the gardener, Jonathan Anmore, had been named in the wills otherwise one of them would probably have said. Or perhaps Bella Westbury did know and wasn't about to confide in a stranger.

'How long have you worked there?' He could see by the slight narrowing of her eyes it was one question too far. She was getting suspicious about his purpose, but she answered him, albeit curtly.

'About a year.'

Horton was surprised. The way she'd been talking he'd assumed she was the old faithful family retainer. Who had Bella replaced? Was it relevant? He didn't really think so, and the way she was eyeing him he guessed he would be pushing his luck asking. It was time he broke the bad news.

He tried a bit of disarming honesty. 'I'm sorry if I'm being too nosy, but I'm trying to understand not only why Arina was killed, but why her boyfriend, Owen Carlsson, is also dead. But I guess you might have explained that already, with him and Arina being—'

'What do you mean dead?' she interrupted sharply. Her green eyes, as hard as emeralds now, peered at him with such intensity that he felt like a suspect in one of the interview rooms at the station.

'You've not seen the news or heard it on the radio?' he asked, curious.

'I don't listen to that rubbish.'

He found that slightly puzzling for a woman who was keen on political fighting, and one who had obviously *been in* the news as well as *making* it over the years.

He said, 'His body was found at St Helens Duver yesterday morning. He was shot.'

'Good God! He killed himself?'

Which was what Danesbrook had concluded. Horton supposed that was only a natural reaction. He shrugged. 'All I know is that he went missing on Saturday. You didn't see him by any chance?'

'No.' She sipped her tea, but she seemed preoccupied rather than upset.

'Did he say anything to you after Arina's death?'

'Like what?' Her head came up and she eyed him warily.

'Like who might have killed her?'

'Are you saying that he might have known who ran Arina down and was shot because of that?'

'It's just an idea.'

'And not a very realistic one. This is the Isle of Wight not Washington DC.' She rose and poured what was left of her tea down the sink before turning and brusquely saying, 'There's not much more I can tell you about Arina.'

Horton didn't agree but he could see that pressing her would only arouse her suspicions, which, judging by her frosty stare, were already at sub-zero temperatures. He thanked her for her time and the tea and made his way thoughtfully back to the Harley. She, like Danesbrook, had seemed very keen to get shot of him after he'd mentioned Owen Carlsson's death.

He had hoped for one small piece of information that could help him find Thea Carlsson. He hadn't got it. But he did know one thing. Scanaford House was worth a great deal of money, and money was a powerful motive for murder.

CHAPTER NINE

Thursday, 6 p.m.

'Arina Sutton must have left a considerable fortune,' Horton said some hours later in a pub not far from the station. Over his Diet Coke, he'd brought Uckfield, Cantelli and Trueman up to speed on his encounters with Danesbrook, Anmore and Bella Westbury. He added, 'We need to talk to the Suttons' solicitor: Newlands.'

'That's also Owen Carlsson's solicitor,' Cantelli said. 'He telephoned this afternoon after hearing about Carlsson's death on the local radio. Says Thea Carlsson hasn't been in touch with him but that Owen made a will. He saved me a call because he formally identified Arina Sutton's body along with Owen Carlsson. I've made an appointment to see him tomorrow.'

'Good. Ask him about both Sir Christopher's and Arina's wills.'

Cantelli nodded. 'I've checked out your man, Danesbrook; he's got form.'

Horton wasn't surprised. 'Drugs?'

'No. Affray and assault. He was arrested in 1996 during the Newbury by-pass campaign for assaulting a security officer.'

Horton recalled the by-pass protest vividly. The road contractors had suffered numerous delays and setbacks. Clearance had been hampered by well-organized activists employing highly effective disruption tactics. They'd built tunnels and tree houses and used themselves as human shields to prevent security men and diggers from moving in and ripping up the countryside. It became known as the 'Third Battle of Newbury' — the other two had occurred in the seventeenth-century English Civil War. There had been a number of arrests and the Thames Valley Police had to ask the government to help towards the enormous cost of policing the protest.

It was a year Horton would never forget for two reasons. Early in the New Year he'd confronted a youth robbing a sub-post office and got himself stabbed in the process, earning a commendation for bravery for managing to arrest the toe-rag. It was also the year he and Catherine had married. His memory conjured up the delicious moments when she used to call round to his flat after work . . . But that was the past and a treacherous place to be. Thankfully, Cantelli rescued him from it.

'Danesbrook was also arrested in 2000 during the fuel protests.'

'Bit of a rebel then. And violent.' Uckfield looked hopeful. He downed the remainder of his pint and started on a whisky.

Horton thought of Bella Westbury's rebellious past. 'What does he do now?' he asked.

'Draws the dole,' replied Cantelli. 'Or rather lives on benefits, like he seems to have done for most of his life.'

Horton raised his eyebrows. 'How come he drives a new car? Did they give it to him as a Christmas box for loyal service?'

Cantelli smiled. 'It's in his name and it's not stolen.'

Uckfield looked sceptical.

Cantelli said, 'He lives in Ryde, divorced, aged fifty-three.'

'He looks older.'

‘Probably the life he’s led.’ Cantelli took a sip of his tomato juice and pulled a face.

‘If you don’t like it, why do you drink it?’ asked Horton.

‘Charlotte says it’s good for me, though she might not think the same about the crisps.’

Horton said, ‘Glad to see you’ve got your appetite back after your sea voyage.’

‘Don’t remind me, the memory’s only just fading.’ Cantelli consulted his notebook. ‘Danesbrook served eighteen months in prison, from 1996 to 1998. He had some kind of mental breakdown after six months and was transferred to a secure hospital where he stayed until he was released.’

Uckfield beamed. ‘So a nutter too, this gets better.’

Cantelli continued. ‘He was convicted again in 2000 but got a community sentence for the fuel protest affray. Everyone wanted that hushed up.’

‘But he is violent,’ insisted Uckfield.

‘Was,’ corrected Horton, then added, ‘But his car is a dark saloon and it’s got a dent in the passenger door. It could be from the impact on Arina’s body.’

Cantelli looked puzzled. ‘Why would he want to kill her? I know I’ve not met him but I can’t see the likes of him inheriting Scanaford House.’

And neither could Horton. He only had Danesbrook’s word he had been a friend of Sir Christopher’s.

Trueman piped up. ‘He could have been paid to kill her.’

‘If her death is deliberate,’ Uckfield stressed. ‘Birch thinks not.’

‘All the more reason to think it was then,’ muttered Horton. He thought of that skilful drive down to the sea ending in striking Arina with enough force to kill her. It also made him think of Owen Carlsson’s parents’ death in the same place. Turning to Trueman he said, ‘Did you get anything on Helen and Lars Carlsson?’

Uckfield huffed but said nothing. Horton knew he didn’t think it had anything to do with their current case.

Trueman put down his lager and said, 'Lars Carlsson was in the UK attending a conference. He was an architect in Sweden. He and his wife decided to combine business with pleasure and take a holiday on the Isle of Wight.'

'Does that mean they lived in Sweden?' asked Horton.

'Yes. Stockholm. Lars was highly respected, a modernist and something of a pioneer in architecture in Sweden in the 1980s—'

'Which means concrete and crap buildings that no one wants to live in,' carped Uckfield.

'Go on,' said Horton to Trueman.

'They rented a house in Yarmouth. Thea Carlsson was in Sweden at school but Owen Carlsson was at Southampton University at the time of their death. Helen Carlsson was a professional photographer and an acclaimed one. She'd won awards for her photographs of Chernobyl and the fall of the Berlin Wall. I found an obituary on them both in *The Times*. Here.'

Horton was impressed. He took the copy of the newspaper cutting from Trueman and saw the same good-looking couple as in the photograph on the mantelpiece in Thea's bedroom, only this time they were in evening dress. The picture had obviously been taken at an awards ceremony and again he saw the striking resemblance between Thea and her mother. He made to pass it to Uckfield.

'I've read it. Doesn't tell us much.'

'I'll read it later.' Horton thrust it in his pocket. 'What about the accident?'

Trueman continued. 'It was a wet and windy night, in March. Visibility was poor. The autopsy on Lars Carlsson, who was driving, showed that he hadn't been drinking. The car skidded off the road and crashed over the wall onto the rocks and stones on the beach. The Carlssons were wearing seat belts but the impact was so severe that their charred remains were embedded in the wreckage. The engine was still running, petrol leaked from the fuel tank causing it to ignite. It was the early hours of the morning. There was no one around. They didn't stand a chance.'

'It was an accident then?'

'Looks like it.'

Horton considered this for a moment before saying, 'So did Arina Sutton's killer know about the Carlssons being killed there?'

Uckfield scratched his neck. 'If he did then we're back to finding a motive for Owen Carlsson's death and Arina Sutton was killed accidentally.'

'But we still have to consider that she could have been murdered for her father's money.'

Cantelli interjected. 'We don't know yet that she did inherit it.'

'OK, but let's assume she did.' Horton addressed Uckfield. 'We should get a team into Seaview and ask around for possible witnesses to her death. And we should conduct a house-to-house to see if we can get a better description of the car and interview the staff in the hotel.'

'Not asking much, are you?' Uckfield sniped. He drained his glass. 'It was nineteen days ago! Most buggers can't remember what they were doing yesterday.'

'A photograph of Arina and Owen might jog some memories and I mean a picture of them alive not on the mortuary slab,' he added, quickly pre-empting Uckfield.

Cantelli said, 'I'll see if the solicitor can let me have a photograph of Arina and I'll check if the newspaper archives have one of Owen Carlsson.'

Horton said, 'There must be one in Thea's apartment. What are we doing about that?'

Trueman answered. 'Luxembourg are waiting for a search warrant.'

And it seemed a long time coming, thought Horton. 'Why can't we just go in?'

'They want to do everything by the book.'

'Bloody book,' muttered Horton before his mobile rang. Glancing at the display he recognized his old home number and tensed. What did Catherine want now? Whatever it was he wasn't expecting good news. He thought about letting it ring then changed his mind.

'Yes?' he snarled.

'Daddy?'

Christ! His heart skipped several beats. The world froze for a second as the picture of his dark-haired daughter sprang before him, causing a lump in his throat and a tightness in his chest. Quickly he rose and headed for the exit. Uckfield was the last person he wanted to be privy to this conversation.

'How are you, poppet?' he said, trying desperately to inject his voice with a lightness he didn't feel. This was the first time Emma had called him since he'd been forced to leave his home. Had something happened to Catherine? He was damned sure that Catherine wouldn't let Emma within a planet's distance of a phone to call him and she'd never have given her his mobile number.

'Mummy says I've got to go away.'

Horton gripped the phone. Catherine couldn't be moving abroad. She couldn't be taking Emma from him.

He heard the tremor in his daughter's voice and as evenly as possible said, 'Where does Mummy say you're going?' Silently he prayed it wasn't true. He hurried towards the Harley, not wanting the others to come out and disturb him.

'I don't want to go away to school.' She began to cry. It ripped at Horton's guts. He would have given the world not to be here now, on an island. He silently cursed. Uckfield could solve his own damn cases. Then the image of Thea's smoke-blackened, fearful face flashed before him. He felt torn, and angry that he felt that way.

'Don't cry, darling. It's all right. You don't have to go.'

'But Mummy says I do and that I'll like it. I won't. I'll hate it,' she sobbed.

Horton felt sick with anguish and tried to steel himself but his mind was full of visions of Emma abandoned. A child of eight. God, how the memories fled down the years and there he was, a boy of ten, standing alone in a barren, cold room, rejected, abandoned, confused and hurt. Cruel taunts ringing in his ears. 'Your mother doesn't love you.' The pain of the memory gripped him, making him feel sick. He'd see Catherine in hell before she subjected his daughter to the same terrible fate.

It took every ounce of control for him to make sure he sounded normal when he said, 'Where's Mummy, Emma?'

'With Uncle Edward. Angie's looking after me, but she's on the computer.'

Uncle fucking Edward! So Catherine was still seeing that fat git. He'd like to punch him from here to kingdom come and back again. Taking a breath and forcing a smile into his voice he said, 'Don't worry, Emma. I'll talk to Mummy. I'll see that you don't have to go away to school.'

'Promise?'

'Of course. Now tell me what you've been doing all day.'

Horton listened to her chatter, which became steadily more joyful as it went on, whilst he became more depressed at the realization of what he was missing. This was a life that Catherine had denied him — his daughter's. It was like being shown all the toys in a shop as a child knowing you could never have access to any of them. And that was the story of his life. He'd always been on the outside, except at work. There he was on the inside. And that, he thought, with growing despair, was all he had left.

Finally his conversation with his daughter came to an abrupt close with, 'Angie's calling me. I'd better go. Bye, Daddy.' And she was gone.

Horton quickly selected Catherine's mobile phone number. She'd know it was him. She'd recognize his number. Would she answer? He doubted it, but miraculously she did.

'What is it, Andy? I'm busy,' she snapped.

Before he could stop himself he was saying icily, 'Shagging Edward Shawford I expect.' Then realizing that she could just hang up on him he quickly added, 'Is that why you want to send Emma away to school?'

'How do you know that? Who told you?'

'It's true then. You know I won't allow it.'

'It's got nothing to do with you.'

'She's my bloody daughter,' Horton roared, stung by her callous words, fighting desperately to hold on to the control that was his usual master, but which now seemed in severe danger of deserting him. A young couple brushed by, eyeing him strangely. He stepped further back into the shadows of a shop doorway.

'Don't swear at me!' Catherine hissed down the line.

He took a breath and silently chanted his mantra. *Don't let the buggers see you're hurting. Don't let them see you care.* It didn't work, because he cared too deeply. All he could see was Emma, alone and frightened. And all he could feel were the bitter memories of a little boy, terrified and hurt, standing in that empty prison of a room.

'Emma is not going to be abandoned,' he reiterated slowly and deliberately, as if each word weighed a ton and cost a million pounds. His hands were clenched, his insides contorted in a tight knot.

'No one's abandoning her,' Catherine said scornfully.

'So being shut up in a draughty old boarding school, deprived of her mother and her father, isn't abandoning your child?' he snapped.

'You're living in the wrong century. Northover is not something out of a Dickens novel. It's an excellent school where all the best people's children go—'

'So that's all she is to you, a status symbol!'

'I'm not going to have this conversation with you, Andy, and especially now. Emma is in my care and I'll decide what's best for her.'

In a flash Horton saw what game Catherine was playing. Coldly he said, 'You're doing this so that I can't see her, aren't you?'

'Don't be ridiculous.'

But he knew he was right by her false tone of indignation.

'I'm her mother and I'll—'

Horton punched his mobile off. He didn't want to hear any more. And he couldn't face returning to the pub to discuss the case. With a heavy heart he climbed onto the Harley and with no idea where he was going, letting his mood take him, he rode through the quiet streets of the island, occasionally stopping to look at the sea in the rain-sodden night.

Eventually he found himself back at Bembridge Marina, amazed to see that it was over four hours since he'd left the pub. He felt mentally exhausted. He'd considered every possible alternative to how he could prevent Emma from being sent away to school, from abducting her — foolish — to finding something against the school, a criminal activity — possible. He'd have all the staff checked, double-checked and triple-checked. Finally he'd turned his mind to how he could gain permanent custody of Emma, which included resigning, showing Catherine up to be a terrible mother, bribing the judge and coaching his daughter to say she wanted to live with him. His brain ached with it all.

Angry and emotionally exhausted, he stripped off and stood under the hot shower long enough for his skin to wrinkle. Every nerve within him cried out for the chance to sink into drink-induced oblivion, something he hadn't done since April. He knew it wouldn't help matters and that drunk or sober he wouldn't sleep.

He made a coffee and sought distraction from his mental turmoil in thinking about the case. It was then he remembered the obituary on the Carlssons. Fishing it out of the pocket of his trousers, he sat down with his coffee and read it through twice. The first time quickly, the second slowly, taking in every word and linking it in his mind with Thea and Owen Carlsson, looking for anything that might help him connect the cases, but he didn't find it.

What he did learn, however, was that Helen had been the daughter of a Dorset butcher. Secondary school educated, she'd come up through her profession the hard way, forcing herself into what was then a male dominated world — the business of being a newspaper photographer — putting herself into extreme and dangerous positions until her talent, and hard work, had finally been recognized.

Lars, by contrast, had come from a wealthy Swedish family. He'd been educated privately and gained his degree in art and history from Cambridge before returning to Sweden and architecture as his chosen profession. The two had met in America in October 1967 when Helen had been photographing the massive protest in Oakland, California, against the Vietnam War. Lars had been staying there with friends who had enlisted him in their protests.

Horton sat back thinking. What had happened to Helen Carlsson's photographs? Clearly they were worth a great deal of money. Had she made a will at the time of her death and bequeathed them to a close friend? Or had they been left to Owen or Thea? Perhaps they'd sold them. And what about Helen and Lars's personal papers: family photographs, mementos? Had they been in Owen's house and were now destroyed by the fire? Thea hadn't mentioned it. She hadn't even seemed upset that the book in which her mother had written a personal message had gone up in flames. She'd been more concerned about the cat.

A sound outside caught his attention. Someone was coming down the pontoon. It could be anyone, the harbour master perhaps. On the other hand, Horton realized, it could be his intruder returning and this time with a more sinister intent.

He rose. The footsteps grew nearer. They stopped. Holding his breath, Horton steeled himself for action. Then a voice hailed him — one he knew very well. Letting out a sigh of relief, he slid back the hatch and stepped into the cockpit to find a sopping wet and bedraggled Cantelli standing on the pontoon. Cantelli's grim expression killed Horton's smile in an instant.

'Thea. You've found her. She's dead.' An icy wind sucked the breath from him.

'No. Not Thea.'

Thank God. Relief washed over him. Then Cantelli's words registered. Someone was dead, and if not Thea, then who?

‘We’ve been trying to reach you,’ Cantelli said, looking worried.

‘Who is it, Barney? Who’s dead?’ His tired brain struggled to think who it could be.

‘Jonathan Anmore.’

It took Horton a moment to think who Cantelli was talking about before he recollected the athletic fair man he’d seen in the churchyard. ‘The landscape gardener! What the devil has he got to do with this case?’

‘That’s what Uckfield would like to know.’

And so would I, thought Horton. *So would I.*

CHAPTER TEN

'He's over there,' Uckfield announced, pointing to the far end of the barn.

From where Horton was standing he couldn't see the body, only a small wooden yacht on a trailer and, surrounding it, a couple of petrol-driven lawn mowers and other gardening implements.

On the six-mile journey across country to Dills Farm, Horton had trawled his memory recalling his brief conversation with Anmore in the churchyard, looking for some sign that the gardener would be their next victim, but only one thing stuck in his mind: Scanaford House. *Makes you wonder if it's cursed. Everyone who comes into contact with it ends up dead. Except me and Bella.* Perhaps he'd better put a watch on Bella Westbury, he thought, climbing into the scene suit. But ghosts didn't kill people, not unless Anmore had been frightened to death by one, and Horton thought that highly unlikely in the middle of a barn three miles from Scanaford House.

He said, 'How come DCI Birch called you in?' There was nothing to connect Anmore with Owen Carlsson's murder.

Uckfield pushed a toothpick in his mouth. 'He knew Anmore was the Suttons' gardener and because we're considering a possible link between Arina Sutton's death and Carlsson's he thought we should be here.'

Horton had a suspicion that wasn't entirely the truth and judging by Cantelli's expression he agreed. Birch probably knew they'd all been drinking in the pub and Horton wouldn't put it past him to tip off the press about this murder in the hope that they'd arrive to find the officer-in-charge stinking of booze. Uckfield smelt like a brewery. Horton wondered how long he'd stayed drinking in the pub in Newport after he'd left. He caught Cantelli's eye and an unspoken signal passed between them. They'd need to get Uckfield away before the media showed up, though thankfully with this being an island the national press wouldn't arrive until the morning, if at all. How to get him away without making him even more belligerent than usual was another matter.

Horton told Uckfield what Bella Westbury had said about Anmore's amorous tendencies, adding, 'He could have been killed by a jealous lover or husband.'

'Birch and Norris can follow that up. We'll examine any links between Carlsson and Anmore.'

That made sense, and three deaths around Scanaford House — four if you counted Sir Christopher — was four too many for Horton's taste. 'Did the doctor give any indication as to how long he's been dead?'

'Barely wanted to touch the poor sod, afraid he'd get that paint all over him.'

'What paint?'

'You'll see. Made me wish Doc Price was here; drunk or not he'd have done a better job than the streak of piss they sent along. But he was good enough to tell us he was dead.'

'Who found him?'

'Anmore's old man discovered him at about ten twelve p.m.'

Horton checked his watch, before slipping his arm into the white sleeve. It was just after midnight.

Uckfield said, 'Charlie Anmore says his son didn't return home for his tea at six. He tried his mobile and got no answer. He knew his son couldn't be gardening in the dark but he thought he might have got held up with a client, or gone to the pub, so he didn't bother too much about it. When it got to ten and Jonathan still hadn't appeared, Charlie rang round a few of his son's mates, tried the local pub, without success, and finally came here. His son hires the barn from the farmer.'

Uckfield's words had taken them to the body. Horton drew up with a start.

'You never said he'd been stabbed in the back with a ruddy great pitchfork.'

'Didn't want to spoil the surprise.'

'Thanks,' muttered Horton, ignoring his churning gut as best he could and focussing his gaze on Anmore. He was lying face down, with his arms outstretched and now Horton saw what Uckfield had meant about the paint. Anmore was covered in a russet-coloured liquid, which, if Horton wasn't mistaken, and judging by the discarded tin some two feet away, was antifouling paint for the boat's hull.

Uckfield belched loudly. 'Charlie Anmore eased the body over to check it was Jonathan, got himself covered in paint and then staggered out to summon help from the farmer, who thought Charlie was bleeding to death and nearly had a heart attack himself.'

'Where's Mr Anmore now?'

'PC Somerfield and one of Birch's officers took him home. Somerfield's still with him but the other officer has taken Anmore's clothes to the station for forensic examination tomorrow.'

'Shame the old boy touched him.'

'Yeah, but I doubt he killed his son, though you never can tell.'

Horton knew that was a sad fact of life. He studied the body, his revulsion replaced by curiosity. The pattern of death certainly didn't fit with Owen Carlsson's or Arina Sutton's. In fact, there seemed no pattern at all to any of the deaths except perhaps those of Helen and Lars Carlsson with that of Arina Sutton; both involved cars and both had been in the same location. But Anmore had been the Suttons' gardener.

'Why the paint?' he asked, intrigued.

Uckfield shrugged. 'Fit of temper after stabbing him? Or maybe Danesbrook did this. It looks like the work of a lunatic, though why he'd want to kill Anmore beats me unless he didn't like the azaleas he planted. Who knows what sets these people off?'

Was Roy Danesbrook involved, wondered Horton? He turned to Cantelli. 'Has anyone interviewed the farmer?'

'Sergeant Norris spoke to him earlier. He says he heard Anmore's van drive up the track at about six thirty. He was watching the weather forecast on the television, which is how he knows the time. He didn't see the van though and he can't see the barn from the house. He didn't hear any other car approaching the barn, but he did go out for a pint. Charlie Anmore came pounding on his door at about ten twenty. He called the police, left his wife to give Charlie a stiff drink and came up to the barn to see for himself. He says he touched nothing.'

'Did his wife hear or see anything?' asked Horton.

Cantelli shook his head. 'She was at a Women's Institute meeting in Newchurch until nine and there was no one else in the house. DCI Birch's officers will start a house-to-house tomorrow, but there are only three houses in the immediate area so it won't take them long and they're a mile away. This is a pretty isolated spot.'

Yes, and ideal for murder, thought Horton. The farmhouse was a mile up a muddy track, off a narrow country lane and surrounded by woods. Taylor might get something from the track, but Horton guessed too many police vehicles had trundled up and down it. There was something that had caught his attention, however. Dr Clayton had said that Owen Carlsson had been shot through glass and here, on his right, was a boarded-up window. Pointing to it he asked, 'When was that broken?'

Cantelli glanced at the window. 'The farmer might know. You thinking Owen could have been killed here?'

'It's possible, and then transported to the Duver in Anmore's van.'

Uckfield's phone rang and he hurried away, struggling to wriggle out of his scene suit as he went while reaching for his mobile phone.

Horton turned away from the body and with Cantelli followed Uckfield at a slower pace.

Cantelli said, 'There is another possibility, Andy.' He dashed an apologetic glance at Horton.

Horton knew what he was thinking. He said, 'You believe Thea Carlsson could have done this.'

'It's just an idea,' Cantelli shrugged. 'Perhaps it's like you said earlier. Owen recognized Anmore as the person who had killed Arina. Anmore could have been driving a car and not his van. Owen confronted him and Anmore killed him. But Owen had already told Thea about his suspicions and she came here to avenge her brother's death.'

Groaningly weary, Horton knew he had to consider it as a possibility. 'How did she know where to find Anmore?'

'Her brother could have told her before he died.'

'Then why didn't she tell us?' cried Horton.

'Maybe she wasn't sure until she let Anmore into the house and he tried to set fire to her.'

'That still doesn't explain why she wouldn't say anything to us,' Horton said stubbornly. 'And I don't see her having the strength to plunge a pitchfork into Anmore's back.'

'That might not be what killed him,' Cantelli persisted. 'She could have stuck it in him after he was already dead.'

Horton knew Cantelli could be right. Nevertheless, he had other ideas. 'Owen could have told Jonathan Anmore that he knew who had killed Arina and Jonathan thought he'd go in for a spot of blackmailing, especially after he heard that Owen Carlsson was dead. And the person he was blackmailing killed him.'

He thought back to his earlier brief conversation with Anmore. Anmore hadn't seemed worried or nervous when he'd told him Owen Carlsson was dead. He hadn't appeared smug either, just concerned. But both Roy Danesbrook and Bella Westbury had shown signs of unease.

Stepping out of his scene suit Horton's eyes swivelled to Anmore's van. Perhaps they'd get some forensic evidence from it, he thought hopefully, before his gaze travelled beyond it to where DCI Birch and Uckfield were head-to-head in conversation.

Following the direction of his gaze, Cantelli said, 'The Guv doesn't look very happy.'

And neither did Birch, thought Horton, as Uckfield turned on his heel and stormed towards them, leaving Birch to glower after him like a man who'd just had his tonsils removed without an anaesthetic.

'There's no point in you being under cover,' Uckfield growled. 'Every bugger here knows you're a cop. And the time for pussy-footing around is over. I want some answers on these murders and I want them quick.'

Horton wouldn't mind betting that the telephone call Uckfield had just received had been from the chief, and judging by Uckfield's mood, it hadn't been to utter words of praise and encouragement.

Horton said, 'I'll talk to Charlie Anmore.'

'Somerfield and Marsden can do that,' Uckfield said impatiently. 'I want you with me when I interview Laura Rosewood tomorrow. Be in at seven sharp.' Turning to Cantelli, Uckfield added, 'Let's leave this to the locals. DCI Birch can brief us tomorrow morning if his team find anything new. Meanwhile we need our beauty sleep. I want fresh eyes and brains. And I want results!' he boomed, storming off.

With raised eyebrows Cantelli followed Uckfield. Horton's eyes flicked to Birch who was eyeing Uckfield malevolently. Tomorrow morning Birch and Norris would be bleary-eyed and drunk with sleep deprivation and about as much use as an umbrella in a typhoon. That wouldn't stop Uckfield pushing them though; he'd push so hard that they wouldn't know what year it was, let alone what day. Birch had played the wrong card in snitching to the chief. A superintendent grassed up is a dangerous beast and they didn't come more beastly than Uckfield in a rage.

Horton swung the Harley round and headed back to the boat, thinking that Uckfield might have ordered beauty sleep, but obeying it would be another matter entirely.

CHAPTER ELEVEN

Friday, 10.15 a.m.

Horton slept fitfully, with dreams of Anmore's and Owen's rotting bodies, punctuated by images of Thea Carlsson as he'd rescued her from the blazing house. Even with a troubled sleep and judging by the look of them, he suspected he'd managed to grab more shut-eye than Birch and Norris who both remained resentful and sullen-looking throughout Uckfield's bad-tempered briefing.

On the journey to Laura Rosewood's home on the east coast of the island, Uckfield's mood, which was darker than a disused coal mine, didn't improve. He opened his mouth only to swear at any motorist or pedestrian who dared to get in his way, which seemed to be the island's entire population, and to comment that Ms Rosewood was bound to be a sandal-wearing, bead rattling Amazon with a moustache, or someone built like a shot-putter in the days of the Cold War and that this was all a ruddy waste of time. Horton was inclined to agree with the latter sentiment, but he envisaged a younger version of Bella Westbury, all slacks and common sense. He was relieved when they swung into a wide gravel driveway which culminated in a futuristic house of glass and steel, perched on the cliffs of Luccombe. It was, thought Horton, totally out of keeping with the grey-stoned and colour washed Victorian and Edwardian houses of the wooded area, and didn't look that environmentally friendly to him, which it should have been given the woman's position in the European Commission.

Laura Rosewood however was very friendly and not at all how either of them had imagined. As they followed her swaying hips clad in tight black trousers through a spacious hall Uckfield winked grotesquely at Horton. Clearly the attractive, slender, fortysomething woman with short blonde hair and immaculate make-up had lightened Uckfield's mood considerably. Perhaps, thought Horton, they should install her in the station.

'It's such terrible news about Owen,' Laura Rosewood said, gesturing them into comfortable armchairs in an airy and expensively furnished room. Horton's eyes were immediately drawn to the magnificent view of a tumultuous grey-green English Channel beyond wide glass doors, while Uckfield clearly had trouble taking his from Ms Rosewood's cleavage and the black bra beneath her dark-blue lacy top.

'We're hoping you can tell us what Owen was working on, Ms Rosewood,' Uckfield said solemnly.

'Of course. And it's Laura.' She flashed her perfect white teeth at him.

Uckfield's grin reminded Horton of a crocodile who'd just seen dinner in the form of a fisherman on the bank.

'When was the last time you saw Owen Carlsson, Laura?' Uckfield leered.

Horton tried not to wince. She was older than Uckfield's usual types but neither that nor the fact he was married would stop the big man from trying his hand.

'It was at Arina's funeral, a week ago Tuesday.'

'How did he seem?' asked Horton.

She swivelled her petrol-blue eyes to him. 'Upset, naturally. We all were. Are you any closer to finding out who killed Arina?'

Uckfield answered. 'Detective Inspector Birch is leading that investigation.'

This morning Horton had got his wish and Birch's officers were at Seaview conducting a house-to-house and trying to establish who had been in or around the hotel at the time of Arina's death. Another team were about to interview those in the houses near the barn where Anmore's body had been found. While Taylor's officers were going over the scene-of-crime with a comb so fine that not even a nit would get through. Cantelli had reported that the farmer couldn't confirm when the barn window had been broken. He said that Anmore must have boarded it up himself because he certainly hadn't done it. So not much joy there and neither had they found any witnesses to the fire.

'It's such a waste,' Laura Rosewood sighed. 'And now Owen's dead too. Is there any chance his death could have been suicide?'

'Would you have said he was capable of that?' asked Horton, knowing that it wasn't suicide, but eager to hear her thoughts and get an insight on Owen's personality.

'No, he was a very positive, cheerful sort of man. At least he was on the occasions I met him, barring Arina's funeral of course. He was recommended by Terry Knowles for a project I'm involved with for the European Commission, which is why you're here, of course.' Her eyes swung back to Uckfield. 'Can I offer you some refreshment? Coffee?'

'Thanks,' Uckfield replied before Horton could refuse. He would have preferred information to caffeine but he was outranked.

'I'll ask Julie to make us some. Excuse me.'

They both rose as she left the room. Uckfield's eyes followed her greedily. 'Wouldn't say no to a bit of that.' Horton didn't remind Uckfield that he was married. It would have been pointless. But it jogged Horton's memory that he hadn't yet called his solicitor regarding Emma being sent away to school. There had been the briefing and then the drive here. Once this was over, though, and he was alone, he'd call her.

'Nice place she's got; worth a few bob,' Uckfield added, prowling around the lounge and eyeing the exquisite glassware on specially designed shelves either side of an inset modern fireplace.

Horton agreed. There were also some expensive looking modern paintings on the pale cream walls and the widescreen plasma television and music system were both top of the range. Everything was neat, calming and spotless. The room barely looked lived in.

'Wonder what her old man does for a living,' Uckfield added, lifting and almost dropping a glass objet d'art which Horton thought had probably cost Laura Rosewood the equivalent of his annual salary.

'It could be her money.' He reckoned advisers to the European Commission were on a fair screw.

He crossed to the glass doors and stared at the great expanse of sea. In the sheeting rain he could just make out a container ship ploughing its steady way across the Channel. There was still no word on Thea. He had tried not to think that she could have killed Jonathan Anmore or that she might be already dead. It was useless to speculate. Uckfield said something to him but he had no idea what, and before he could ask him to repeat it footsteps sounded in the hall and the door swung open.

'Coffee won't be a moment,' Laura Rosewood announced, settling herself back in her seat. Uckfield resumed his. 'Now, you wanted to know what Owen was working on.' She fixed her eyes on Uckfield. 'Integrated Coastal Zone Management.'

'Come again?'

She smiled. 'It's complicated, but I'll try and make it as simple as possible.'

Horton took a seat to the right of Uckfield where he could see Laura Rosewood clearly. He removed his notebook from his pocket and began to make notes, something he rarely did, but knew he should. He had almost total recall but without Cantelli here, and with Uckfield bound to blame him if he missed anything which turned out to be vital, it was safer.

Laura said, 'Europe has a relatively long coastline in relation to its land area and there are a variety of different habitats, economic and social conditions surrounding it and impacting on it, but the greatest of these, and therefore the biggest threat to our coasts is us: humans. Many people have boats. Then there is fishing and other sea-based industries. As a consequence, our coastal areas and habitats continue to deteriorate. The European Commission Environment Directorate is extremely concerned about this, as are various governments and environmental bodies. So the Directorate set up a programme to monitor this.'

'The quality of coastal waters is a major cause for concern: oil slicks and algal blooms, buildings, urbanization, agricultural and industrial developments have considerably reduced the biological diversity and cultural distinctness of the landscapes in most parts of Europe. Recent research shows that climate change could involve a rise in sea level of several millimetres per year, and an increase in the frequency and intensity of coastal storms.'

There was one going on right now, thought Horton, as the rain hit the glass doors like a rapid round of machine-gun fire.

'Global warming,' he said, thinking about those files in Owen Carlsson's burnt-out study, and Bella Westbury had told him that Owen was an expert in oceans.

'Yes,' she replied, directing her gaze at him. 'And the pace of global warming is speeding up quicker than predicted.'

'We've all seen the film *The Day After Tomorrow*,' sneered Uckfield.

'You may be cynical, Superintendent, but the day after tomorrow is sooner than you think,' she clipped.

'Well, I'm more concerned with catching a murderer today rather than the day after tomorrow. So, what's Owen Carlsson got to do with all this?'

Before she could answer, the door opened and a slight, mousey-haired woman in her early forties entered carrying a tray. On it was a coffee pot, white porcelain cups and a plate of chocolate biscuits. She placed it on a glass-topped table in front of Laura Rosewood, who nodded her thanks. The woman smiled shyly at Horton and slipped away without a murmur or introduction. The silent and obliging Julie, no doubt.

'Depending on where these storms occur,' Laura continued, pouring the coffee with slender, well-manicured fingers, 'the combined effects of these two phenomena will have serious repercussions, such as major floods, which are already happening in our own country. Milk, Superintendent?'

'And three sugars.'

'Not for me.' Horton watched as she handed Uckfield his coffee, their fingers touching briefly.

'Where does Owen Carlsson fit into this?' Horton repeated, not bothering to disguise his impatience. He didn't have time to sit around listening to a geography and meteorological lesson.

She swivelled to face him. 'Expected growth — in tourism in particular — will increase human pressure on the natural, rural and urban environments. Look at the pressure to develop along our own Solent coastline, and here on the Isle of Wight. And I have to hold my hands up and admit that I am partly to blame.' She smiled somewhat ruefully. 'I ran a property development company, with my late husband, Jack, for fifteen years.'

That explained this house, thought Horton cynically. Only a property developer would have got planning permission for it.

She said, 'I was fortunate enough to sell the company three years ago at the height of the property boom.'

'Lucky you,' muttered Uckfield with his mouth full of biscuit.

Horton could almost see him thinking 'no husband to complicate things — ideal'.

'Or perhaps I was shrewd enough to see the bubble was about to burst. I've been in property a long time. I started as a surveyor a million years ago,' she smiled.

'I can't believe that,' Uckfield grinned back. Horton just about stopped himself from rolling his eyes at Uckfield's grotesque attempt to be gallant. Laura Rosewood seemed to like it though. More fool her, thought Horton.

She said, 'After I'd sold the business I was at a loose end, not sure what to do next. I don't like being idle. Then Terry Knowles mentioned that the European Commission needed advisers and my background and experience seemed ideal.'

'Their gain, Laura. I'm sure—' charmed Uckfield.

'To get back to Owen Carlsson,' Horton cut in tetchily, thinking they were wasting time. Uckfield scowled at him.

'Of course,' she said briskly. 'The results of the project will include a set of policy recommendations to deal with coastal erosion in a sustainable way, and, dependent on the findings, recommend how we should best deal with the increase of coastal storms and global warming. The Isle of Wight is one key area of this project. It has, as you might be aware, some serious coastal erosion problems, even where this house is situated. Owen was engaged on mapping the coastal erosion hazards, as well as providing an analysis of our shoreline, and an analysis of the sea around us.'

'How far had he got?' asked Horton.

'He started six months ago. It's a three-year project and Owen was going to move around Europe's coastline yearly to undertake studies in other key locations. There are some who would like to stall this report, however, others who might wish it never sees the light of day, and some who want to influence the policy recommendations for their own good, if it gets that far.'

'Like who?' asked Horton, more interested now there was a hint of a motive for Carlsson's murder.

'The marina development companies, the leisure boating industry, the fishing industry, property developers, and that's just for starters. There could be a great deal of money at stake if, for example, Owen's findings were to recommend no more marinas or property developments along coastal areas. Or that sea pollution and coastal erosion mean legislative changes and restrictions must be introduced in the leisure boating industry.'

'Can you be more specific? Company names would help.'

'Sorry, Inspector, I can't because I don't know exactly. I called Reg, the Chief Constable, when I heard about Owen's death because I was concerned that someone was determined to prevent this project from progressing. I've obviously had to report it to Brussels. The project's been put on hold and Europol have been notified, though I gather they're not going to investigate until they hear back from you.'

Now Horton could see another factor that had contributed to Uckfield's foul temper. If Uckfield had to hand this case over to the European Police, it would be a severe career blow for him and would really piss him off.

Laura Rosewood continued. 'It's been decided to keep any possible connection between Owen's death and the environmental project quiet for the time being until you've had time, Superintendent, to investigate it further. Owen's death might have nothing to do with the project and we don't want the alarmist press whipping up the story. You know how they love to dish the dirt on anything to do with the Commission.'

To Horton it made some sense, but if Owen had been murdered to prevent this project from progressing, they'd probably never discover his killer. The case would be too complex, with too many possible suspects, and the killer would have been professional and covered his tracks superbly.

With a sinking heart he said, 'And is the data Owen already collated lost because of the fire?'

'What fire?' she asked, alarmed.

Obviously hadn't heard about it on the local news then, but Uckfield said she'd only returned from London late last night.

'Owen's house was burnt down on Wednesday evening,' answered Horton.

'My God! And his sister? She wasn't . . . ?'

'No.' Horton didn't see any need to tell her about his or Thea's close encounter.

Uckfield said, 'But she is missing.'

Horton would have preferred to have kept that quiet. And he didn't like the undertone of Uckfield's statement.

Laura said, 'Perhaps she's returned to Luxembourg?'

Horton answered. 'How did you know she lived there?'

'I had a meeting with Owen on the twenty-second of December in Brussels to discuss the project and he mentioned he was spending Christmas with his sister who lives in Luxembourg. I think he would have preferred to be with Arina, especially as she was upset over losing her father. I knew Sir Christopher very well. He was a keen supporter of the environment, but I guess Owen had promised his sister and didn't feel he could let her down.'

Horton wondered why Arina hadn't invited both Thea and Owen to Scanaford House; it was big enough to accommodate a football team. But maybe Arina had had other friends to stay. Or perhaps she'd already met Thea and hadn't liked her, or vice versa. He frowned as speculations spiralled freely and didn't much care for where they were taking him.

Laura looked thoughtful for a moment. 'Thea Carlsson didn't set fire to the house by any chance, did she?'

'Why do you say that?' asked Horton sharply.

She shrugged. 'Anger at her brother's death? Despair? Who knows what people are capable of when they're distraught. When Jack died, I wanted to lash out at anyone and everything. It passes, but only to be replaced by other equally destructive emotions, like overwhelming sadness. Have you considered that Owen's sister might have been trying to kill herself by setting fire to the house and has now gone off somewhere to try again?'

They hadn't because Horton knew of the intruder, but he hadn't considered the possibility that Thea's grief over her brother's death might have led her to walk out of that hospital with the intention of committing suicide. For a brief and startling moment thoughts of his mother flashed into his mind. Could that have been her intention? No suicide note had been found in the flat, or at least had been given to him.

His neighbour had told him recently that his mother had been dressed up and happy on the day of her disappearance. But could she have been mistaken? He'd never once considered her suicide as a possibility. There was no time to analyse it further but he cursed his stupidity for not thinking it a possibility where Thea was concerned. If she had intended killing herself then he guessed she was already dead. His heart felt heavy at the thought.

Laura rose, looking worried. 'Does Terry know about the fire?'

'Not unless someone's told him,' answered Uckfield.

And Horton knew they hadn't because no one could find him. He hadn't known that the Shetland Islands was so big, but at the briefing this morning he'd learnt from Trueman that it was comprised of over a hundred islands, fifteen of them inhabited. That made it incredibly difficult to track Knowles down, especially when the man wasn't answering his mobile phone; maybe he couldn't get a signal.

Clearly agitated, Laura said, 'I hope to God that Owen emailed his report to Terry, or kept a back-up copy off the premises. I need to call Terry.'

She made as if to leave when Uckfield halted her. 'We can't get through on his mobile. Do you have another contact number for him?'

'I'll try his office; someone must know where he's staying.'

Horton said, 'We've already tried them. He only left them his mobile number because he was going to be moving about the islands.'

But Knowles had arrived there, Trueman had reported. He'd been on the eight forty-five flight to Glasgow from Southampton Airport on Wednesday morning and had checked in for the thirteen thirty flight from Glasgow to Sumburgh on the Shetland Islands. After that he had gone walkabout. Knowles' office had told Trueman that Knowles wasn't due to meet up with the people who had developed a new system to harness the wind for energy until Tuesday.

Horton said, 'Would Mr Knowles' secretary know if Owen had emailed his report to him before he went missing?'

'I'll get her to check his e-mails.'

'Before you do,' Horton quickly added, 'there are just a few more questions. We won't take up too much more of your time.'

She gave a brief tight smile but didn't resume her seat.

Horton said, 'Would Owen have sent his findings to the European Translation Centre?'

She looked hopeful. 'He might have done.'

And if Thea had been given Owen's findings to translate into Danish, Swedish or German, and her brother had been killed because of it, then so might she have been, he considered gloomily.

With a note of finality to her voice, Laura said, 'I'll check and let you know.'

But Uckfield was not to be hurried. He reached for the last chocolate biscuit. 'Do you know Jonathan Anmore?'

Laura Rosewood seemed baffled by the question. 'I've seen him once or twice at Scanaford House. He's the gardener. Why?'

'He's dead.'

Her eyes widened. 'You mean he's been killed?' She looked at each of them in turn with a bewildered expression. 'But this is dreadful. How?'

'He was stabbed.'

Horton studied her as she assimilated this new information. Clearly she was shocked and puzzled by it. Her expression serious, she said, 'And you believe there is a connection between his death and Owen's. But if that's so, then Owen's death can't have anything to do with the project.' Relief suddenly flooded her face. 'I'm sorry I can't be more helpful but I need to call Brussels.' This time she headed for the door with a purpose that not even Uckfield could ignore. He swallowed the remains of his coffee, rose and reached out a card to her.

'Call me personally as soon as you have any further information.'

And even if you don't, Horton interpreted Uckfield's gaze. She promised she would and judging by her expression Horton didn't think it would be a chore. But he hadn't quite finished yet. 'Do you know Bella Westbury?' he asked on the doorstep.

'Yes. She's very active on the environmental front, and she was Sir Christopher's housekeeper.'

'And Roy Danesbrook?' Horton thought he might as well ask. He expected Laura Rosewood to look blankly at him but she didn't. Instead, a flicker of distaste crossed her face before she answered with a tight smile.

'He runs a charity called Wight Earth and Mind. Sir Christopher was its patron.'

'It's an environmental charity?' asked Horton, surprised. From his brief encounter with Danesbrook he wouldn't have marked him down as a friend of the earth type.

'I believe so, though you'll have to ask Mr Danesbrook about it.'

'You don't like him?' probed Horton, noting her curt tone.

'I don't know him, but let's say that what I have seen of the man, which isn't much, doesn't exactly endear me to him. Over the last year he seemed to worm his way into Sir Christopher's life. I couldn't really understand what Christopher saw in him, and although that was his business, I couldn't help thinking that Mr Danesbrook was taking advantage of an elderly, sick man.'

And that, thought Horton with an inner nod of satisfaction, was his sentiment exactly.

CHAPTER TWELVE

'All we need to do now is prove that this Danesbrook has gone off his trolley again, and is running around killing anyone connected with the Suttons,' Uckfield said in the car.

We'll need more than that, thought Horton, *and so will the Crown Prosecution Service*. 'Owen's death could still have something to do with this project.'

'Yeah, and I'm Bugs Bunny. What she said was a load of old bollocks and the chief's got hold of the wrong end of the stick,' Uckfield continued. 'If you ask me the motive for Owen Carlsson's murder and Anmore's is much simpler, and closer to home, than some piffling European environmental project.'

Horton didn't think Laura Rosewood would go a bundle on the word 'piffling' but he agreed with Uckfield.

Picking a piece of biscuit from his teeth, while managing to change gear at the same time, Uckfield continued, 'I reckon Danesbrook had a thing for the old boy, Sir Christopher, and when he heard Arina Sutton plotting with her boyfriend, Owen, to kill off her old man — you know, easing his passing by putting a pillow over his head — Danesbrook flipped and killed them both.'

Horton didn't see Danesbrook as the caring kind, more the sucking-up type to gain some personal advantage. 'And what about killing Anmore?'

Uckfield shrugged. 'Maybe Danesbrook thought he was in on it too.'

Horton flashed Uckfield an incredulous look. 'Bit weak that, and it doesn't explain where Thea is or who set fire to her house.'

'You want sugar on it?'

No, just answers, thought Horton, falling silent as Uckfield drove more sedately back to the station. He didn't believe Uckfield's theory for one minute. OK, so he didn't know what Sir Christopher's sexual and personal tastes had been but he just couldn't see him falling for a weasel like Danesbrook. He wouldn't mind betting though that Danesbrook was involved somehow. And it was time to question him. It was also time to call his solicitor about Catherine proposing to send Emma away to school, but both would have to wait because Somerfield and Marsden were back from interviewing Charlie Anmore and Horton was keen to hear what they had to report.

Kate Somerfield said, 'The old man is pretty cut up as you'd imagine. Jonathan Anmore was his only child. Jonathan had been divorced for ten years. He's got two boys who his wife won't let him see, out of spite, Charlie Anmore claims. He says she took Jonathan for every penny he had. Jonathan returned to the Isle of Wight from the mainland ten years ago and took over his father's gardening business. Yesterday Jonathan came home at one o'clock for his dinner.'

That fitted with Horton seeing him at Scanaford House just after midday. He asked Trueman if he'd managed to trace the call Anmore had taken on his mobile phone as he'd left him.

'Still working on it,' came the reply.

Marsden took up the reporting. 'Jonathan then went out again just after two. Charlie hadn't heard Jonathan mention Owen Carlsson but he did know Arina Sutton was a customer of his son's.'

Uckfield said, 'Any special friends or girlfriends, rumours about his love life, grudges against him?'

'No.'

Horton asked, 'Did Anmore have any connection with environmental groups?'

'No. He liked sailing—'

'Yes, we saw the boat,' Uckfield said sarcastically.

'And he liked shooting,' Marsden added with a note of triumph. 'According to his father, Jonathan was a crack shot when he was in the RAF. He served six years as a mechanic before leaving to study landscape gardening at college on the mainland where he met his wife. Charlie didn't know where Jonathan kept his gun or what type it was. He said he'd never seen it. We searched the house and there was no sign of a gun or a licence.'

Uckfield turned on Trueman. 'Any gun found in the barn?'

'No.'

Horton could see what Uckfield was thinking, that it could have been used on Owen Carlsson and then discarded.

Uckfield sprang up. 'Right. Marsden, go back to the gun clubs and see if Anmore was ever a member or guest. While you're at it ask if Roy Danesbrook is too. Somerfield, get on to the Child Support Agency, find out if Anmore's behind with his payments. Talk to his wife on the phone and get the true story on the divorce. And then start going through the things you bagged up from Anmore's room. I'm going to report to the chief.'

Horton stepped out of the station and, sheltering from the rain in the doorway, punched in Framptons' telephone number.

'Andy, are you back from holiday?' Frances Greywell said moments later.

'No. I've got caught up in this case on the Isle of Wight. Catherine wants to send Emma away to school. Emma doesn't want to go. She rang me. I don't want her to go.'

There was a short pause. 'I'll speak to her solicitor.'

He rang off with the impression that whatever Frances Greywell said to Catherine's solicitors he'd somehow still fail his daughter. Staring at the rain he understood how and why some men were forced to kidnap their children, hang off tall buildings, climb bridges and throw eggs at politicians in Parliament for the right to have a say in their children's lives. Divorce was shit. He felt like shit. Would it matter if he walked away from this case now and went to try and reason with Catherine? He'd get a bollocking, but that was nothing. He could cope with that. And yet he didn't move. Part of him said that Catherine was beyond reasoning with, and that he'd achieve nothing by confronting her, while the other part said he should at least try. Then there was Thea.

A car drew up. Cantelli climbed out. The decision had been made for him.

'How did it go with Carlsson's solicitor?' Horton asked, noting but not wanting to acknowledge his relief.

'I'll tell you over a cup of tea, a bacon sandwich and chips. I'm starving.'

Cheered by Cantelli's breezy manner, and with the sudden realization that he was hungry too, Horton pushed aside his anxiety and melancholia and was soon tucking into a ham roll, chips and salad. Despite being impatient to hear what Cantelli had learnt, he knew that he'd have to wait until after the sergeant's first bite into his bacon sandwich.

'Owen Carlsson left everything to Thea,' Cantelli said with his mouth full. 'At a rough estimate he's worth about eight hundred thousand pounds which includes the house. It didn't have a mortgage. Carlsson and his sister inherited a substantial sum on their parents' death. Thea's was in trust until she became twenty-one. Now she'll get her brother's share.'

'If she's still alive.' Horton didn't like to think that was a motive for murder although he could see that Cantelli had considered it, and so too would Uckfield when he heard Cantelli's news. He told Cantelli what Laura Rosewood had said about Thea possibly being suicidal.

Cantelli said, 'With her parents dead, her brother murdered, and the house and belongings gone up in smoke, I'd say she had good reason to be depressed. Did she strike you as being the type?'

'Is there a type?'

'I guess not.' Cantelli took a gulp of coffee. Horton knew Cantelli was recalling the dark days of Horton's suspension. After Catherine had chucked him out he'd come within minutes of throwing himself off his yacht. It had been Cantelli's friendship that had been partly responsible for helping him through it. When he'd stopped drinking, anger had taken the place of self-pity. It had driven him to clear his name, but by then it was too late to save his marriage.

Stabbing a chip, he said, 'So what else did you get?'

'Arina Sutton made her last will at the same time as her father, which was in September. The solicitor, Newlands, says they had no relatives so Arina was happy to bequeath her estate to the same charities as Sir Christopher had made bequests to. He left most of his estate to Arina with four major bequests and there was quite a tidy sum to leave. The estate is worth over four million.'

Horton gave a soft whistle. 'So who now gets their hands on that lot?'

Cantelli consulted his note book. 'The Institute of Neurology, The National Hospital Development Foundation, The Hammersmith Hospital, and a charity called Wight Earth and Mind.'

Horton froze with what remained of his ham roll in mid-air. A slow smile spread across his face. Triumphantly he said, 'That's why the bastard was visiting Scanaford House. He'd come to eye up his inheritance.'

'Eh?'

Horton replaced the roll uneaten. 'Laura Rosewood's just told us that Roy Danesbrook runs a charity called Wight Earth and Mind with Sir Christopher as its patron, and now the shifty bugger inherits. He's got a damn good motive for killing Arina Sutton — money. Owen Carlsson must have recognized him, or worked it out, confronted him with it and Danesbrook had to kill him. No wonder he shot off so quickly when I mentioned Owen's death; the little bastard was guilty as hell.' But that didn't explain why Danesbrook hadn't reacted when Horton had first mentioned Owen's name. Then it clicked — of course! Danesbrook had an accomplice who must have killed Owen Carlsson without Danesbrook's knowledge. And that accomplice could have been Anmore who was in the churchyard waiting to rendezvous with Danesbrook, only Horton had scared him off. Then Danesbrook had gone to Anmore's barn and shoved a pitchfork into him, scared his part in Arina's death would come out. He said as much to Cantelli.

'Could Danesbrook be your arsonist?' asked Cantelli.

Horton thought for a moment. 'I'm not sure. I couldn't see who knocked me out.' And he didn't like to think that a weakling like Danesbrook could have got the better of him, though he'd had the element of surprise. Scraping back his chair, Horton said, 'But Danesbrook could have kidnapped and possibly killed Thea. Come on, Barney; time we had a word with him.'

'Shouldn't we tell the Super?'

'Later.' Horton was already steaming out of the canteen. He wanted all the answers neatly tied up before going to Uckfield. This was more like it. At last, they were getting somewhere. Their visit to Laura Rosewood had proved highly fruitful. This case was about good old-fashioned greed and not global environmental concerns.

Cantelli had Danesbrook's address from the vehicle check he'd done earlier. Horton only hoped Danesbrook was at home, perhaps working out how to spend his inheritance.

'There's more,' Cantelli said, on their way to Danesbrook's house in Ryde. 'Four days before Sir Christopher Sutton died he called his solicitor and said he wanted to change his will. Newlands had been due to see Sir Christopher on the day he died.'

It fitted. 'Sutton had discovered that Danesbrook was a fraud and wanted to cut him out.'

'We don't know yet that he is a fraud.'

'Take my word for it; he is,' Horton said firmly. He'd known there was something shifty about the man from the moment he'd set eyes on him, and Laura Rosewood had thought the same. For a year she'd seen him sucking up to Sutton and now they knew why. Horton wondered if Sir Christopher's death hadn't been precipitated by Danesbrook.

Cantelli said, 'Newlands had no idea what Sir Christopher was intending and he says Arina didn't know either, but she did say that her father was agitated and seemed to go downhill rapidly in the last few days. And there's another thing that's curious: Newlands told me that Owen Carlsson visited him three days after Arina's death.'

'To find out about Danesbrook?'

'No. He didn't even ask about the wills. He wanted a list of all the people who had attended Sir Christopher's funeral.'

Horton thought that odd too. 'And did Newlands give it to him?'

'Yes, and I've got a copy.' Cantelli pulled a piece of paper from his jacket pocket as they waited at a set of traffic lights.

Horton scanned it. There were some eminent people on the list judging by the Sir this and Doctor and Professor that. He wondered if Dr Clayton knew any of them, which reminded him about Anmore's autopsy. Had she completed it yet? He'd check after they'd seen Danesbrook. He glanced further down the list and saw Jonathan Anmore's name, along with Bella Westbury, Laura Rosewood and Roy Danesbrook.

Horton said. 'Ask Trueman to find out if Owen Carlsson contacted any of the people on this list, and when and why. Has Newlands given Danesbrook a key to Scanaford House?'

'No.'

'Good. Make sure it stays that way. His car's here,' Horton said, pleased, as Cantelli turned into the narrow street of tiny flat-fronted terraced houses just off the promenade in Ryde.

Cantelli squeezed his hired car into a space halfway up the steep incline and zapped it shut. The rain had ceased and the sun was making brief appearances in a cloud scudding sky. Walking back down the hill, Horton took a glance inside the dark blue saloon. It revealed only a screwed-up newspaper and some parking tickets. He could detect nothing from the dent in the front passenger door but he'd get Forensic on to it.

He pressed his finger on Danesbrook's bell and left it there. No one came. He swore softly.

'He can't have gone far if his car's here,' suggested Cantelli.

But that wasn't necessarily true, thought Horton, because Danesbrook might have caught the hovercraft or catamaran across to the mainland. Disappointed and frustrated he turned away and almost bumped into a lopsided elderly man with a bulbous, wart ridden nose.

'You looking for Roy?' the old man asked.

'Do you know where we can find him?'

'Not the bailiffs, are you?' He peered at them with watery eyes.

'No.'

'Then you must be police.'

Horton smiled to himself. Had Danesbrook already earned himself a visit from the local police? Or maybe he and Cantelli just looked like coppers.

'You'll find Roy in the bar of the Victoria Arms. Turn sharp right at the end of the road then along about two hundred yards. It's on the corner facing the kiddies play park and the seafront.'

'Thanks.'

'Don't tell him I sent you.' The old man put a key in the door of the neighbouring house and stepped inside.

Horton got the impression he didn't much care for Danesbrook. That made two of them. Three if he counted Laura Rosewood. Horton was looking forward to this official interview with the ponytailed man in the cowboy boots, and there would be no scuttling away and evasiveness. No, Horton thought determinedly, this time he'd get the answers even if he had to shake them from him.

CHAPTER THIRTEEN

'Why didn't you tell me you were the police?' Danesbrook demanded angrily, pushing away the half full plate of shepherd's pie after Cantelli had done the introductions and they'd seated themselves opposite him.

Horton could see Danesbrook's mind trawling through their previous conversation in search of anything incriminating he might have said. Not bothering to disguise his distaste for the greasy haired man beside him, Horton said, 'A man with your experience should have spotted one.'

Danesbrook bristled. 'You've been checking up on me. I only used violence for the sake of a cause.'

'Is that why you used it on Arina Sutton and Owen Carlsson? For the sake of your charity?'

'No!'

Horton ought to haul him in, charge him and then badger him into making a confession, but that wasn't his way. But if this man had kidnapped Thea, then every minute could count. 'You're now a rich man,' he said sneeringly.

Danesbrook shifted nervously. 'I don't personally benefit.'

'No?' Horton leaned forward and said in a soft low voice, 'You inherit a vast sum of money. I call that a very powerful motive for ramming your car into an innocent woman and killing her.'

'I didn't!' Danesbrook's restless eyes scanned the bar as though seeking help but the barmaid was reading a newspaper and the only other customers — two elderly men — were playing dominoes. 'I had nothing to do with Arina's death. And I had no idea what was in her will or Sir Christopher's.'

Horton pulled back, smirking. 'You expect us to believe that?'

'It's the truth and if you're going to make false accusations then you can charge me, and I want my lawyer present.'

'Know your rights, do you? But then you would, having been arrested and convicted for assault. Violence seems to be your style. Maybe you didn't mean to use excessive violence on Owen Carlsson but the gun went off, and he died.'

'This is ridiculous. I haven't shot anyone. And I didn't run over Arina Sutton.' Danesbrook leapt up.

Horton shrugged. 'If that's the way you want it. Charge him, Sergeant, then get a car to take him to the station where he can wait for his solicitor to arrive. Of course by then we might be out, and it could be some time before we get to question him. It could even be tomorrow morning . . .'

'All right, I get the message.' Danesbrook subsided into his seat. 'But I haven't killed anyone.'

'So you keep saying,' Horton said wearily. The man was nervous, and Horton reckoned guilty with a capital G. 'Where were you on the night of the third of January?'

'At home. And before you ask, I was alone. You can check with my neighbours; one of them should remember seeing my car parked in the street.'

'You could have used another car to run her down.'

'Well, I didn't. I mean I didn't use any car to run her down.'

'How did you get that dent in the passenger door?'

'A woman went into me in the supermarket car park.'

'You have her name and address?'

'Well, no. I told her not to bother.'

'That was generous of you.'

'I said the insurance could pay for it.'

'And lose your no-claims bonus! When did this happen?'

'I can't remember, a fortnight ago, something like that.' Danesbrook was sweating and the stench emanating from him was overpowering that of the smell of beer and food lingering in the pub.

Horton didn't believe him. 'Where were you on Saturday, Sunday and Monday?' Horton heartily wished they had a more definite date for Owen's death.

'I don't know. I can't remember.'

'Suffering from amnesia, are you? It was less than a week ago!'

Danesbrook licked his lips and fiddled with his ponytail. Horton felt like cutting the damn thing off.

'I was in here, having a drink, shopping, not doing anything special.'

Horton saw fear in his skittering eyes. The man was definitely hiding something. But without that time of death, it would be difficult to prove Danesbrook had been killing Owen Carlsson. At a sign from Horton, Cantelli took over.

'What exactly is Wight Earth and Mind?'

'It's a charity — well a project really.' Danesbrook wasn't sure whether to look relieved or scared at the question. 'It will help people suffering from mental illnesses by getting them involved in environmental projects. It was taking longer to set up than I thought.'

Yes, thought Horton, Danesbrook was waiting for father and daughter to die to get his hands on the money. And he'd got tired of waiting.

'Did you kill Sir Christopher?' he asked seductively gently. 'A pillow over his head to end his suffering? It would be understandable in the circumstances. Both his and his daughter's death could help many others.'

But Danesbrook wasn't rising to the bait. 'No! He was a good man. I wouldn't have done a thing like that. He understood how I . . . He understood things.'

‘Like your mental breakdown while in prison.’

Danesbrook sprang up and screeched, ‘I will not be tormented.’

The barmaid looked up and the two elderly men paused in their game of dominoes.

‘Sit down,’ Horton said firmly.

Danesbrook hovered for a moment then subsided. His shoulders slumped. *Here it comes*, thought Horton gleefully. Maybe they should caution him and tape this. But too late, Danesbrook was speaking.

‘I couldn’t stand prison,’ he said wearily. ‘Tending the gardens and growing things helped me to recover. I told Sir Christopher this. He understood.’

‘So much so that he bought you a new car and left you a huge sum of money.’

‘I’m not the only one,’ Danesbrook mumbled.

‘No, but you’re the only one with a fake project. The other beneficiaries are hospitals and renowned institutions. And you’re the only one who lives on the Isle of Wight.’

Danesbrook licked his lips again. ‘I can’t help that.’

Did Horton believe him? If he had killed Arina or been involved in her death then surely he would have thought of a better alibi for her time of death. It wouldn’t take much to break him, a couple of nights in a cell most probably.

‘Did you kill Jonathan Anmore to stop him from squealing about killing Arina for you?

Danesbrook’s eyes widened in alarm and horror. ‘You’re mad.’

‘Did you tell Owen about your project?’

Danesbrook blinked and wiped the sweat from his brow. ‘No. I met him once, at a talk that . . . was about wind farms.’

Horton knew that wasn’t what Danesbrook had been about to say, but had quickly covered his tracks. ‘Surely you would have bent his ear about your project?’

‘Well, I didn’t.’

This seemed to be getting them nowhere. Irritated, Horton gave Cantelli a nod to continue.

'How did you meet Sir Christopher?'

Danesbrook twirled his ponytail with nicotine stained fingers. 'He had a flat tyre on Brading Down. I offered to help him change it. We got talking. He invited me to Scanaford House; we exchanged ideas. Sir Christopher wanted his name to live on in a worthy cause. He'd seen how the combination of physical work, coupled with the power of nature, worked as a therapy. Things developed from there.'

Horton widened his eyes. 'Jesus! Next you'll be telling us that the earth is flat and that aliens have landed in Utah.'

'It's the truth!'

Danesbrook's indignant tone was genuine enough, but Horton knew it was a lie. The man was a con-artist and possibly a killer.

'Where were you on Wednesday night?' he snapped, referring to the night he and Thea had nearly been fried alive.

'Here. You can check with Maggie.'

Cantelli rose and crossed to the bar.

Danesbrook looked relieved that he had a firm alibi for at least one of the nights Horton had asked about. But there was still Thursday night and Jonathan Anmore's death.

'Where did you go yesterday after you left me at Scanaford House?'

'Home.'

'I thought you had a meeting to attend?'

'I got the dates muddled up. I was at home all afternoon and evening. I cooked something and watched the telly. Some stupid soap was on. I didn't take much notice of it. I fell asleep. Can I go now?'

'No, you can't. Not until we've checked your finances and searched your house.'

'You'll need a warrant for that,' Danesbrook said cockily.

'Then we'll get one while you wait in a cell.'

'Hey—'

'And before you say we can't do that either, I'll hold you on a charge of benefit fraud—'

'I want a solicitor.'

'Then you can call one when we get to the station. We'll also take your car in for forensic examination.'

Danesbrook looked like a cornered rat and well he should, thought Horton; he was far from satisfied with the skunk's answers. Leaning forward he said, 'What have you done with Thea Carlsson?' He scrutinized Danesbrook for his reaction. Disappointingly he could see his surprise was genuine.

'Nothing. I don't even know her.'

But Horton wasn't going to give up yet. They'd have another go at him in the interview room. He might crack then, and although Horton could tell by Cantelli's expression that Danesbrook had been in the bar the night of the fire, it didn't mean he hadn't killed or arranged to have killed Arina Sutton, Owen Carlsson and Jonathan Anmore. And that he didn't know where Thea was. And if the forensic team could prove Danesbrook's car had been at St Helens Duver, and near Anmore's barn, then they'd have him. Horton called Uckfield and quickly briefed him.

'I'll have a go at him,' Uckfield said with relish. Horton could almost see him rubbing his hands. 'You and Cantelli get down to the mortuary. Dr Clayton says she's finished the autopsy on Anmore. See if she can give us something that we can nail the bastard with, because he's the only suspect we've got.'

Horton was inclined to agree but he said, 'What about Terry Knowles?'

'His office confirms he was on a field study with a group of university students at the time of Owen Carlsson's death, all of whom could verify it if asked.'

'And when Arina Sutton was killed?'

'Why the hell should he want to kill her? He doesn't even know her.'

'We can't be sure of that.'

'OK, we'll ask him when he emerges from the mountains.'

Horton didn't know if they had mountains on the Shetland Islands. He guessed Uckfield was right about Knowles though. He doubted he had killed anyone.

Uckfield said, 'Laura Rosewood phoned to say that Carlsson hadn't sent any of his findings to Knowles' office by email, and neither had he sent them to the European Translation Agency.'

That meant Thea wasn't being threatened because of it. But there was still that link between Arina Sutton and the Carlsson parents being killed in the same place which troubled him like an itch that could not be scratched. For now though, he pushed it to the back of his mind and headed for the mortuary with Cantelli.

CHAPTER FOURTEEN

'Coffee?' Gaye Clayton said, meeting them in the corridor outside the mortuary. 'They've got a decent machine here.'

Horton agreed with alacrity. He felt in need of a caffeine boost and a desire to wash the taste of Danesbrook from his mouth. Eradicating the smell of his body odour might take longer, however. Danesbrook brought a whole new meaning to the term shit-scared — or was it bullshit Horton had smelt? Uckfield had better have the air freshener ready.

Gaye pressed some buttons on a machine. As the coffee beans were ground she continued. 'The victim died from stab wounds caused by the pitchfork. It penetrated the heart, and caused internal bleeding, and hence death. There was no evidence of the paint being in the stab wounds, which means it was poured over the victim after death. I've taken photographs both before and after I removed the pitchfork, which I had to do at the scene of crime, and the mortuary assistant is loading them on to the computer in the main office, as we speak. I'll then be able to study the images more closely.'

Cantelli took the paper cup from her. 'And the anti-fouling paint?'

'Interesting. From my examination — and it was a messy one — it was poured over him, starting from the back of the head and then down to the ankles. You might have noticed that there was less on his ankles and none, except splashes, on his outstretched arms.'

Horton had. As he took his coffee from her, she said, 'Come through to this cupboard they call an office.'

She waved Horton into a seat opposite the kind of desk he thought you only ever saw in furniture stores or advertisements: pristine clean and devoid of all paperwork. On it though was a laptop computer — Gaye's — and a telephone. Her own office in Portsmouth was probably groaning under the strain of paper, as his must be by now. He'd be back there on Wednesday unless this investigation dragged on. He was hopeful that later today, with some pressure applied, Danesbrook might confess to his part in the murders and give them the name of his accomplice.

Cantelli squeezed himself into the cubbyhole and leant against a filing cabinet to Horton's right. Slipping his chewing gum into a piece of paper and popping it in his pocket, he asked, 'Why pour the paint over him?'

It was a question that Horton had been asking himself. Somehow that didn't fit with Danesbrook, though it could fit his partner-in-crime, he supposed.

Gaye slumped into the swivel chair opposite Horton. He saw the dark smudges under her eyes. 'Some kind of gesture, I guess?' she said. 'Anger, jealousy. Perhaps after stabbing him, the killer picked up the first thing to hand. If your victim had been married, I might have said it was a jealous wife who resented playing second fiddle to the boat.'

Cantelli glanced at Horton. 'Does that mean we're back to considering the jealous husband or boyfriend of one of Anmore's clients out for revenge? Or could Danesbrook have got jealous?'

'You mean he's gay? You're the second person to suggest that.' Horton considered it briefly. 'I wouldn't have said he was, though who knows.'

'Danesbrook?' queried Gaye.

'Someone we've pulled in for questioning — and you were right about Arina Sutton, she was the daughter of Sir

Christopher Sutton, your neuropsychiatric consultant. He's dead. Cancer,' Horton quickly added.

She heaved a sad sigh, which turned into a yawn and was followed by a sip of coffee.

Horton again considered the paint and his and Uckfield's earlier conversation with Laura Rosewood. He had another theory. Admittedly it was a bit off beam but he might as well toss it in with everything else.

To Gaye he said, 'We've been told that Owen Carlsson could have been killed because he was working on an environmental project which not only involved mapping the coastal erosion hazards, but analysing the state of the sea around the Isle of Wight.'

Gaye eyed him keenly. 'You mean the anti-fouling paint was used as a kind of protest statement because it isn't environmentally friendly — well, not entirely,' she said, grasping his point at once. He should have known she would.

'What's wrong with it?' asked Cantelli.

'Shall I explain?' Gaye Clayton said eagerly.

'Be my guest.'

'Anti-fouling marine paint contains a biocide or poison held in the coating which, when on a boat's hull, leaches slowly from the paint straight into the marine environment. It's used to prevent larvae, barnacles, mussels and seaweed spores attaching themselves to a boat's hull, which would slow a boat down.'

She glanced at Horton who took up the explanation. 'Anti-fouling paint can have a harmful effect not just on the organisms trying to foul the hull, but on marine life. And that was Owen Carlsson's speciality.' He recalled reading somewhere how toxins from the paint can settle in the sea affecting a host of tiny creatures which made up the marine food chain. 'Owen Carlsson was studying the sea around the island for a European project. Maybe he discovered that a manufacturer of anti-fouling paint was using a new and more potentially harmful variety or one that hadn't been fully tested.'

'But why kill Anmore? He wasn't conducting a study,' said Cantelli, clearly baffled. He wasn't the only one.

Horton said, 'Perhaps Owen had uncovered fresh evidence that showed beyond all doubt this new paint was a major hazard to marine life, which if exposed would be a serious threat to sales, internationally. He's killed to silence him and then his house flashed up to destroy the evidence. Maybe Anmore witnessed Owen's death, or was involved in it. Or perhaps Owen told him when they got to talking about boats.'

Cantelli was looking at him as if he'd just read him a Brothers Grimm fairy tale. Horton shrugged and shaped a grin. 'Yeah, it's a bit weak.'

SOCO would have already bagged up the tin of paint and Horton made a mental note to have it analysed, but along with the theory that Owen had possibly been involved with a property development company or marina who wanted his findings stopped, it wasn't really a very strong motive. Danesbrook's greed was far more plausible.

Cantelli's phone rang. He ducked out of the office to answer it as Horton addressed Dr Clayton. 'What was the time of death?'

'Between six and eight p.m. last night.'

When Danesbrook had no alibi, thought Horton more cheerfully.

Gaye said, 'The victim didn't put up a struggle. I found a contusion on the back of the head. He was struck with some force, but the blow didn't kill him. He had a pretty thick skull. It would certainly have rendered him unconscious though. Studying the position of the body and my findings from the autopsy, I'd say he was kneeling down when he was struck.'

Mulling this over, Horton said, 'The body was found at the far end of the barn, so the killer would have walked the length of it. Anmore would have heard him coming. There was no other way in, which means that Anmore must either have known his killer and didn't see him as a threat, or our killer was already in the barn waiting for Anmore to arrive.'

Cantelli returned. 'That was Trueman. He says SOCO haven't found any additional tyre tracks around the barn other than Anmore's van, his father's car and our own vehicles.'

Horton considered this for a moment. 'Danesbrook could have parked his car further away and walked to the barn.' Though he couldn't see Danesbrook walking far in his pointed cowboy boots.

Gaye said, 'Perhaps the killer came in Anmore's van with him.'

And that didn't sound like Danesbrook's style either. And if he wasn't guilty then there was the other possibility which Cantelli had already voiced to him earlier: Thea Carlsson.

Reluctantly Horton now considered this. Had she been taken to the barn against her will and then killed Anmore? Or had she gone voluntarily and killed him? She could have thrown the anti-fouling paint over Anmore as a defiant gesture because Anmore had killed her brother. After doing so she'd left on foot. But why not come to the police? There were two possible answers to that question: because she was afraid of what she'd done or she, with Anmore, had killed her brother using Anmore's gun. Damn, that didn't sound good.

'Could a woman have killed him?' he asked Dr Clayton, hoping she'd say no.

'Yes.'

Shit. 'Must have been a fairly strong woman.'

'Not necessarily.'

Double shit.

Gaye said, 'The victim was struck with something flat and wide, a spade I think. Taylor found one and had it bagged up. There was no blood on it visible to me but something could show up under the microscope. I'd say your killer came up behind the victim; he might even have been talking to him while he walked across the barn. The victim turns back to his boat, or to look at something on the floor, the killer picks up the spade, whacks the victim on the back of the head, he falls forward then the killer picks up the pitchfork and plunges it into the victim's back.'

Cantelli shuddered. 'Must be a cold-blooded bugger to do that.'

'Or a very angry one,' Gaye added, disappointing Horton further. He guessed that Thea might be capable of such an act if she believed that Anmore had killed her brother. And, let's face it, he hardly knew the woman. He'd met her twice and they hadn't exactly had time for in-depth discussion. But he didn't want it to be her. He wanted it to be shifty-eyed Danesbrook with his greasy ponytail.

Gaye said, 'There's something else you might wish to consider. Your killer knew where to place that pitchfork for maximum effect in penetrating the pulmonary artery, which means he could have some medical knowledge, or maybe he was just lucky and your victim unlucky.'

Horton brightened up at that. As far as he was aware Thea Carlsson didn't have any medical knowledge, though they would have to check. And neither did Danesbrook, he thought disappointingly, but Dr Clayton's words reminded Horton about that list of names Cantelli had given him.

'Do you know any of these people?' he asked, handing her the sheet of paper that Cantelli had copied.

Raising a quizzical eyebrow, she studied it. 'I've heard of Joshua Viking, a highly accomplished neurosurgeon in his day. And Francis Grant, a radiologist, or rather he was, they must both be retired by now. Why the question?' Horton told her.

She looked at him, amazed. 'You think one of these people could have killed Owen Carlsson?'

'I didn't say that, but there must be a reason why he wanted this list.'

Before she could answer, his phone rang. It was Trueman. He excused himself and headed out of the mortuary into a windy, damp day which was rapidly darkening.

'We've found someone on that list who Owen Carlsson contacted.'

Great. 'Who?' Horton asked excited.

'Dr Edward Nelson. He's a retired GP, lives in Lymington.'

Even better, thought Horton, a man with medical knowledge.

Trueman added, 'Owen visited Dr Nelson on the ninth of January, six days after Arina Sutton died. I didn't press Nelson on the phone as to why Owen called on him. I thought I'd save that for you. I also didn't mention Owen Carlsson's death, but Dr Nelson asked me if that was why I was calling — he said he'd heard about it on the local news.'

'Then why didn't he come forward?'

'Because he didn't think Owen's visit to him had anything to do with his death.'

And it might not, thought Horton.

Trueman said, 'We've still got a couple of names to contact, but I reckoned you'd want to know about Nelson.'

Horton glanced at his watch. It was just after three. 'Call him back and tell him I'm on my way to see him, Dave.'

'I've already told him that.'

Horton should have known.

He got Dr Nelson's address and had just rung off when Cantelli emerged. Quickly bringing him up to speed on their way back to the station, Horton asked Cantelli to see if Danesbrook had confessed under Uckfield's questioning and to let him know immediately if he had. Then collecting his Harley, he made for Yarmouth and the car ferry to Lymington.

CHAPTER FIFTEEN

Friday, 5.10 p.m.

'My wife is at her art class and won't be back for a couple of hours,' Nelson said in a soothing voice, which Horton thought must have reassured his more nervous patients. He was a thin stooping man with sleeked-back silver hair, a prominent nose, kind and intelligent hawk-like eyes peering out from under bushy silver eyebrows. 'Do you mind talking in the kitchen?'

Horton would have talked in the garden shed if he thought he was going to hear something that might help him go forward with this tortuous case. He shook off his boots in the highly polished hall of the thatched house with mullioned windows that could have posed as an advertisement for Olde England. A grandfather clock ticked sonorously, and he half expected Miss Marple to appear from the sitting room as he followed Nelson into a kitchen, which oozed enough charm to make an estate agent wet his pants with excitement.

Nelson offered Horton a coffee. He shouldn't have accepted because his caffeine level was getting dangerously high, but he figured it was going to be another long night. Cantelli had rung through while he was on the ferry to say that Danesbrook's solicitor had arrived and that both he and Uckfield were about to interview Danesbrook after Uckfield's abortive attempt earlier to extract something from him. All he'd got were grunts. Birch's team had drawn a blank with any possible witnesses to Arina Sutton's fatality and the house-to-house near the barn where Anmore had been killed had come up with zilch.

'I was very sorry to hear about Mr Carlsson's death,' Nelson said, placing the kettle on a Rayburn built into an ancient brick fireplace and gesturing Horton into a seat at the big oak table straddling the centre of the kitchen.

Outside the wind was whipping itself into a fury and the rain was beating against the window. Thankfully the cottage didn't spurn modern comforts, and the central heating and thick curtains kept the drafts at bay. It was the type of kitchen Horton had imagined so often as a child, with a loving mother at the table, baking, and a father reading his newspaper. It was a childhood fantasy that still caused an ache inside him, exacerbated by the fact that it was the kind of home he'd like to have shared with Emma and Catherine — although in truth, Catherine would have run a mile from this. Her taste was minimalistic and ultra-modern, and, Horton thought, soulless, but he would have settled for a warehouse apartment or a shack in the Welsh hills if he could have saved his marriage and been with his daughter.

He brought his mind back to the job in hand as Dr Nelson continued. 'Mr Carlsson seemed a pleasant young man, though I suppose I could be wrong, hence your visit.'

'We're still trying to piece together the last days of his life and the reason for his death,' Horton explained, avoiding being drawn on Owen's personality, though — he thought wryly — they knew little about it anyway. He shrugged off his leather jacket, adding, 'And sadly there's been another death, which we believe might be connected, a Jonathan Anmore. Did you know him, sir?'

Nelson paused in the act of spooning coffee into two blue and white willow-patterned china cups complete with saucers. 'He's been murdered?'

'Yes.' Horton didn't see any need to tiptoe around Nelson. He held his gaze and saw curiosity and bewilderment. Then Nelson shook his head sadly.

'I met him at Christopher's funeral. He seemed such an amiable man.'

'Did you speak to him, sir?' Horton asked hopefully.

'Not much. After the committal we walked back to Scanaford House together. He told me he was Christopher's gardener; we discussed the weather, some plants, nothing more. He didn't come inside for the wake. I left him talking to Arina. She was understandably upset. And now you say he's also dead.' Nelson placed the coffee in front of Horton. 'And you think his death and Owen Carlsson's might be connected with Christopher's or Arina's, although I don't see how.' Nelson took the chair opposite Horton.

'How well did you know Owen, sir?' Horton asked, avoiding answering the question that Nelson had posed.

'I didn't know him at all, Inspector. I saw him walking into the church beside Arina at the funeral and then obviously with her at the graveside. He seemed to provide her with some comfort. She introduced me to him at the wake, but he didn't stay long.'

'How did she introduce him?'

Nelson frowned as if remembering. 'She just said his name and that he was a close friend.'

'And then he turned up here after Arina's death, why?'

'I must say I was surprised myself. He said he wanted to talk about Arina. He wanted to know anything I could tell him about her, and her mother and father. I think he was grieving for her and didn't know who else to turn to. He must have remembered that Arina introduced me as her father's oldest friend. Owen probably thought that meant I had seen Arina grow up. I hadn't though. I told him that Christopher and I had trained together at Guy's Hospital, London. But that I went into general practice and Christopher into neurology. We always kept in touch and used to meet up in London occasionally for dinner and a few drinks.'

'What sort of man was Sir Christopher?' Horton asked, interested, not having the faintest idea where his questions might lead him. The words 'time' and 'wasting' sprang to mind.

'Clever. Ambitious. Amusing. I liked Christopher very much but our friendship was always best served at a distance. He was a bit too ambitious and too overbearing for my tastes. I would say we were opposites, which was why the chemistry worked in small doses. Christopher had to be in charge. He was a dominant man but with a unique eye for detail that doesn't always fit with that type of personality. It was what made him a brilliant researcher though, and at the same time a risk-taker, a rare quality. But he'd never have made it as a GP, no bedside manner and not at all tolerant.'

In Horton's opinion that didn't stop many from becoming GPs.

Nelson added. 'However, what Christopher lacked in social skills with his patients he more than made up for by his skill as a consultant, and he was a pioneer in neuropsychiatry.'

'Did you tell Owen Carlsson this?'

'Yes. He seemed interested, but he didn't make any comment. I can see that I've disappointed you.'

Horton didn't think he'd shown any reaction but obviously had. He sipped his coffee thinking he'd need to be careful with Nelson.

Nelson gave a rueful smile. 'I've had years of reading patients' minds, Inspector. GPs are a bit like police officers; we learn to spot and interpret the smallest body language signals that show us discomfiture, embarrassment, worry, lies. And we're very adept at undertones. Owen Carlsson was anxious and upset. I thought it was because of Arina's death. Is her death now suspicious?'

Horton knew there was no point in lying or being evasive. Nelson by his own admittance would clearly see through it. 'I'm beginning to suspect it was.'

Nelson pursed his lips together as he considered this. After a moment he said, 'I can't think who would want to kill her.'

Only Danesbrook, thought Horton, but he'd ask Nelson about him in a moment.

'When was the last time you saw Sir Christopher?'

'Just over a year ago. My wife and I were in London. Iris went Christmas shopping with her sister while I had lunch with Christopher.'

'Did you arrange it or did he?'

'He did, though I can't see why that is important to you. He used the opportunity to tell me he had been diagnosed with cancer. I suspect it was why he wanted to meet.'

Horton drank his coffee wondering where next to go with his questioning. 'Did Owen ask if you or Sir Christopher knew or had ever heard of Helen and Lars Carlsson?'

Nelson shook his head. 'No. Who are they?'

'They were Owen's parents. Arina was killed in the same place as they were in 1990. Owen didn't mention that to you?'

'No.' Nelson's expression was one of genuine bewilderment.

'Did Owen ask you or did you discuss what was in Arina's will?'

Nelson's bushy eyebrows shot up in surprise. 'No.' He leaned forward with a faint flush on his thin face, his eyes shining. 'Now I see what you're driving at, Inspector. You think she was killed for her money.'

'We have to consider it,' conceded Horton. 'Have you heard of a charity called Wight Earth and Mind?' Nelson shook his head.

'Or a Roy Danesbrook?'

'No.'

'You didn't talk to him at Sir Christopher's funeral?'

'No.'

Horton studied the elderly man's face to detect a lie. He saw none, only interest. He would have thought that Sir Christopher would have mentioned his most recent passion to his old friend, but then Horton recalled that Nelson hadn't seen or spoken to Sir Christopher for a year.

Nelson said, 'Does this man Danesbrook inherit?' Then he held up his hands. 'It's not my business, I know. I'm just intrigued, and sorry I can't be more helpful. Owen didn't mention his parents, this charity or that man. He simply let me ramble on about Christopher and Arina although I could tell him very little about Arina or her mother, Nadia. I didn't really know either of them.'

Horton felt disappointment wash over him. He'd had a wasted journey. Owen Carlsson had come here for no other reason than to seek comfort for his bereavement. And yet Horton couldn't quite believe that. There was something he was missing, but he didn't have a clue what it was.

'Tell me about Nadia,' he asked, hoping he didn't sound as desperate as he felt.

'She was a fine lady from what I saw of her, which was only three times. She was Dutch and sadly lost all her family during the war. They were shot by the Nazis helping English airmen to escape. Young Nadia managed to hide and was helped to escape by one surviving airman who smuggled her back to England with him.'

'Who was the airman?'

'I've no idea. Arina was twelve when Nadia died in 1980. I remember that Christopher had bought Scanaford House a few years earlier after Nadia had fallen in love with the Isle of Wight. Who could blame her? It's a beautiful place, and Scanaford House is extremely splendid. Christopher kept an apartment in London to be near the hospital and his work. Christopher told me that Arina was a lot like her mother, who was a highly respected artist. She was quietly spoken and clever, artistic too. She worked as an interior designer. I'm not sure how any of this helps you find the killer, Inspector, but it's what I told Owen.'

'Why didn't you go to Arina's funeral?'

'I'd like to have done, but I had a hospital appointment and you know how long it takes to get one of those.' He smiled, but Horton couldn't help thinking that a doctor, who clearly had money, could surely have paid to go private and by-pass the National Health Service.

'Nothing serious,' Nelson said, and then as though once again reading Horton's mind added, 'I did think of cancelling it but . . . well, quite honestly, I didn't feel like facing another funeral or seeing Scanaford House again, after being inside it so recently with Christopher's funeral. I feel badly about not going, especially now you've told me her death might have been deliberate, but . . . well I can't undo what I've done.'

Horton left a short pause. 'Did Owen mention his sister, Thea?'

'No. I'm sorry I can't be more helpful. It sounds as if you've got your work cut out, Inspector.'

Horton scraped back his chair and pulled a card from his trouser pocket. 'If anything else springs to mind, sir, no matter how trivial it might seem, would you give me a call?'

'Of course.' Nelson took the card, whilst Horton pulled on his leather jacket. At the door Nelson said, 'Good luck.'

Horton thought he'd need more than luck to find out what the devil was going on with this case; he'd need divine inspiration. And clearly he wasn't going to get it or a confession from Roy Danesbrook, whom he saw leaving the station as he pulled into the car park just over an hour later.

Horton found a dejected team in the incident room.

'I see Danesbrook's been released,' he said, throwing his jacket and helmet on the desk in front of Cantelli.

'All we can charge him with is benefit fraud,' said Cantelli, looking as though he could do with a month's sleep.

'He's lying and a complete arsehole,' Uckfield said.

Horton was inclined to agree.

'Doesn't make him a killer though,' replied Cantelli wearily.

Uckfield snorted. 'I don't believe all that crap about chance meetings and changing tyres. He staked out Sir Christopher and then used him to wheedle his way into inheriting a ruddy great fortune. He has a perfect motive for killing Arina, and no alibi for Owen Carlsson or Anmore's deaths. But we can't prove he was involved in any of them.'

Horton fetched a plastic beaker of water from the cooler. His throat was still sore from the fire and the buckets of coffee he'd drunk hadn't really helped to ease it.

Uckfield glanced at his watch. 'I wanted to hold him but his smarmy solicitor objected.'

Horton drained the beaker and said, 'Danesbrook's the best suspect we have—'

'Unless we count the vanishing sister,' Uckfield said. 'I'll have to make her disappearance public. I'll put out a press statement tonight.' He scraped back his chair. 'I need a drink, and I don't mean water.'

Horton crushed the white plastic cup and tossed it in the bin. Nodding at Cantelli and Trueman to follow him, Horton headed out of the station after Uckfield, along the road to a nearby pub, leaving Somerfield and Marsden to hold the fort. He didn't know if Birch or Norris saw them. Uckfield didn't seem bothered if they did, so Horton too shrugged it off.

Once they were settled with their drinks, Trueman said, 'We've found the last customer to see Anmore Thursday afternoon. It was a Mrs Best who lives just outside Yarmouth. She says that Anmore was with her from just after two fifteen until three thirty. He seemed fine. She was very upset over his death.'

'And the call he took when I was with him?' asked Horton.

'Number withheld.'

'Just our luck.' Uckfield swallowed a mouthful of beer.

Horton agreed.

Trueman continued. 'Anmore is in debt to the tune of ten thousand pounds. He's run up a lot of expenses on his credit cards and owes child maintenance for a year, but there's no recent payments going into his account to suggest he was blackmailing anyone. I've got officers trawling through his customer records, and a list of his contacts and friends, but so far no one seems to have a grudge against him. On the contrary he was popular, especially with the ladies, though no one is admitting to having an affair with him—'

'Yet,' added Uckfield.

Trueman continued. 'Marsden also says there's no record of Anmore, Carlsson or Danesbrook belonging to a gun club on the island.'

Horton said, 'What about any known contacts of Owen Carlsson?'

'None have come forward on the island to say they were bosom pals. Seems he was a bit of a loner, though he had only been living here a year. And no sightings of him on the island from the Guv's press conference, though plenty in London, Liverpool and the Outer Hebrides.'

Horton gave a weary smile. 'Any sign of the rucksack or walking stick?'

'They weren't in the barn or anywhere near it.'

Horton told them about his interview with Dr Nelson. 'There must be a reason why Owen visited Nelson but I'm damned if I can find it. I don't believe he went there solely to seek comfort.' Three deaths: Arina Sutton, Owen Carlsson and Jonathan Anmore. What on earth was the common factor if it wasn't Danesbrook? Maybe there wasn't one and each death had nothing to do with the other.

Uckfield consulted his watch for about the fifth time in as many minutes. Perhaps he was expecting a call from his wife or the chief.

Abruptly Horton said, 'When are the police searching Thea's Luxembourg apartment?'

Trueman answered. 'Tomorrow morning. Inspector Strasser says the search warrant has come through. They've spoken to her employers and colleagues at the European Translation Centre where she's worked since October; no one knows why she left in a hurry, but the general view is that she seemed distracted on her return to work after the New Year.'

Was that hindsight talking, wondered Horton, as Trueman continued.

'She doesn't have any close friends that they can find who she might have confided in.'

Horton felt a stab of anguish for her as he was haunted by a vision of the thin, frightened woman he'd pushed out of the window of that burning house.

Trueman added, 'She spent Christmas with her brother in Luxembourg, as Ms Rosewood told us, but was here for New Year with her brother, returning the day before Arina Sutton was killed.'

Mrs Mackie hadn't mentioned that. Horton asked, 'Did they say what translations Thea Carlsson was working on?'

'Strasser says he'll e-mail us a list as soon as it's ready, which should be Monday, but they were told that she had documents to translate from the European Medicine Agency, the European Centre for Disease Prevention and Control, and the European Environment Agency.'

'But not Owen's findings,' Uckfield added pointedly.

Horton knew that Laura Rosewood had already confirmed that but he wondered if Thea could still have translated something that had made her rush home to her brother. Though what it could have been, and how it could have led to his death and Jonathan Anmore's, he didn't know. He reckoned he was on the wrong track with that one. But there was still the person who had broken into his boat, who they hadn't yet found, and he said as much.

'It's possible it could have been either Anmore or Danesbrook and if we can find a witness it might be enough to put a squeeze on the ponytailed little runt.'

Uckfield grinned. 'That would make me a happy man. I'll get Marsden on to it — and talk of the devil, look what the wind's blown in.' Horton looked up as the pub door crashed open. He saw DC Marsden's flushed face and his heart skipped a beat.

'You've found Thea Carlsson?' he asked, hardly daring to hope as Marsden joined them.

'No sir. I've just taken a call from Sweden.'

Horton felt torn between disappointment and relief. He gestured Marsden into a seat when Uckfield clearly wasn't going to.

‘It was from a Peter Bohman,’ Marsden continued, breathlessly. ‘He was Lars Carlsson’s business partner in 1990. He said he’d only just heard of Owen Carlsson’s death. He claims that Lars and Helen Carlsson were murdered and that Owen’s death must have something to do with it.’

Horton threw a quick glance at Uckfield.

‘Doesn’t mean to say you were right,’ Uckfield sniffed. ‘This Bohman could be nuts.’

‘He didn’t sound it,’ Marsden said defensively.

Barely containing his excitement, Horton said, ‘What makes him believe they were murdered?’

‘Because Lars knew something was going to happen.’

‘Not psychic, is he?’ Uckfield scoffed.

Horton stiffened as Cantelli shot him a glance.

‘Don’t think so, sir,’ Marsden replied. ‘But Helen Carlsson might have been. Bohman says the British police never believed him when he told them Lars and Helen’s death was no accident. Lars called Bohman two days before he was killed to say that Helen had had a premonition of danger.’

Uckfield rolled his eyes. Horton kept schtum. But Marsden’s words made him recall the book by Thea’s bed on the lost ghosts of the Isle of Wight that Helen had inscribed. Danesbrook and other events had pushed it from his mind. He also remembered what Jonathan Anmore had said about Scanaford House being haunted and cursed. Here was a link between the three cases, five if you counted Helen and Lars Carlssons’ deaths — which was now looking more like murder — but Uckfield would have him sectioned if he told him this case was about ghosts. And Horton knew that no ghost had killed these people — that demanded an earthlier presence.

‘What did Helen say was going to happen?’ he asked Marsden.

‘Bohman said that it might have been a presentiment about the accident or perhaps the break-in, but—’

‘Hold on. What break-in?’ Horton asked, suddenly very alert.

Marsden looked confused then crestfallen as he realized he'd overlooked a critical piece of new information. 'Apparently the day after Lars called Bohman to tell him about Helen's premonition, there was a break-in at the house they were renting in Yarmouth. Lars called Bohman again to tell him.'

Horton turned to Uckfield. 'The break-in's not on the file.' But then why should it be? The file contained a road traffic incident, nothing more. And what was one burglary amongst many others, and so long ago? Nevertheless, Horton was getting an uncomfortable feeling about this.

Trueman said, 'I'll track down the crime report.'

Horton wanted to talk to Bohman himself. Scraping back his chair, he said, 'I'll call him.'

Marsden looked disappointed but said nothing as they returned to the station.

In the temporary incident suite, Horton called Bohman, introduced himself and apologized for the lateness of the call. He started by asking if there were any living relatives of the Carlssons, wondering if Thea might have been in touch with one of them, or even managed to get out of the country and was with them now. But Bohman disappointed him.

'No. Helga, Lars's sister, is now dead. And, as far as I'm aware, Helen never had any relatives. At least none came to her funeral in Sweden.'

'Have you heard from Owen or Thea recently?' Horton asked casually though his body was tense with anticipation.

'Owen visited me the Christmas before last and told me about a project he was hoping to work on that would take him to the Isle of Wight—'

Horton interjected, 'Did Owen mention his parents' death there? Or did he seem worried or curious about it?'

'No. Owen was much like his father. He said it was the past, best to forget it. Owen was always focussed on the present.'

'And Thea?'

Bohman remained silent for a moment. Was he gathering his thoughts, wondered Horton, or was he steeling himself to say something Horton didn't think he was going to like?

'Thea is more like her mother, though much more sensitive than Helen was,' Bohman finally answered. 'That could be because she had no mother to bring her up, only Helga. Helga did her best but she was not terribly patient with children, having none herself. When Helen died, Thea needed love and understanding. Helga left her at boarding school. It was wrong.'

Bohman's words brought Emma to mind, about to be abandoned in that damn boarding school. Horton guessed that with Helga it was out of sight, out of mind. Catherine was probably thinking along the same lines. And Horton couldn't help feeling Thea's pain when he related it to his own abandonment.

Bohman said, 'I didn't know anything was wrong until Helga called me to say Thea was in hospital.'

Horton started. Had Thea tried to kill herself? Did that mean she'd tried again and recently? Would they find her body swinging from a tree in the woods? God, he hoped not.

'Anorexia,' Bohman said, 'brought on by the psychological pain of losing her parents and being left alone to cope with it. Helga wasn't the guilty type but she should have been. I blamed myself too. I should have done more to help Thea.'

So not a quick suicide but something that could nevertheless be fatal and a slow way of killing oneself. And how had Owen felt about his sister's illness? Horton wondered with a stab of anger. What had he done to help her?

He said, 'Did she get on with her brother?'

'Oh yes. They were very close.'

But not close enough for Owen to see how his sister was suffering. But then Horton told himself that Thea had been at school in Sweden and Owen at university in England. They couldn't have seen a lot of each other, and he knew that anorexia sufferers were highly accomplished at hiding their illness.

He said, 'Why do you think Lars and Helen were killed?'

'I've thought about that over the years. All I can say is that it must have something to do with Helen's work.'

'Not Lars's?' Horton asked, surprised.

'Lars was an architect, like me. Who would want to kill him?'

Horton thought he might have wanted to kill the sod of an architect who had designed the impersonal, bleak, urine-smelling, vandal-inhabited council tower block where he had once lived. Not that he remembered it like that when a boy. It had just been home. He was thinking more about the times he'd been called there as a police officer, and to other soullessly designed buildings that stripped the heart out of the community.

'Why do you think their deaths were because of Helen's work as a photographer?' Horton recalled what Trueman had said about Helen photographing the troubled spots of the world and the obituary he'd read on them.

'Because her camera was smashed. The next day she and Lars were dead.'

Horton knew this was significant by the edgy sensation crawling up his spine. He scrambled to connect this with the present murders. What had Helen photographed and where? Perhaps someone thought, or knew, that Owen Carlsson had these photographs and was threatening to show them, or tell someone about them. But why kill him now after all these years? Had Owen's keenness to get this environmental project on the Isle of Wight given him the chance to investigate his parents' death, despite what he'd led Peter Bohman to believe? Had he wittingly, or unwittingly, opened up the past, which had led to his and Anmore's deaths? Had Arina been silenced as a warning to Owen to stop his investigations?

'Go on,' he said eagerly.

'There isn't anything more to tell, Inspector. The police said that Lars lost concentration and skidded off the road. But now with Owen's death on the same island, there must be a reason.'

Oh, there was, and that wasn't the only death. Horton didn't know how Bohman was going to react to the news of Arina Sutton being killed in the same place as the Carlssons but he was about to find out.

Once he'd told the story, there was a silence that lasted for so long Horton was beginning to think they'd been cut off. Then Bohman said with a hard edge to his voice, 'That proves it. They were murdered. Now perhaps the police will find their killer.'

And that killer, thought Horton, *couldn't be Danesbrook*. He began to thank Bohman for his call when Bohman interrupted him. 'There's something else. Thea telephoned me.'

'When?' Horton's heart leapt several notches. If it was recent, it meant she was still alive.

'The day before Owen disappeared.'

Disappointment hit Horton in the chest. 'What did she want?'

'To know if her mother had mentioned a girl—'

'A girl? What girl?' Horton asked sharply, puzzled.

'I don't know.'

'And had she?'

'No.'

CHAPTER SIXTEEN

Saturday

Throughout the night Horton had racked his brains trying to think who this girl might be that Thea had asked about. Arina Sutton? Arina would have been in her early twenties in 1990. Was it possible she was connected with the Carlsson deaths? Had Owen cultivated her friendship because she had known something about it?

With sleep scratching his eyeballs, and no answers to his questions, he arrived at the incident suite to find Cantelli, Trueman and Somerfield already there. Trueman explained that Marsden was leading a small team of officers questioning the residents overlooking the Duver for sightings of the person who had broken into Horton's yacht.

He added, 'Birch's officers have finished checking with the owners of the handful of houses that are on the Duver and they all claim they haven't let their apartments over the last two to three weeks so not even a cleaner has been in them, and they haven't been there themselves since August. The café's been boarded up since the end of October and there's no link between the assistant in the marina shop and the harbour master with Carlsson. Neither claim to have heard or seen anything suspicious.'

Horton wasn't surprised. He hadn't thought they'd find anything from that line of questioning anyway. 'Where's Superintendent Uckfield?' he asked, eyeing the big man's empty office beyond the incident suite. There was also no sign of Birch, thankfully.

'Said he'd be in later,' yawned Cantelli. 'Didn't say why.'

No, but Horton could guess. The only thing that would keep Uckfield from his desk, apart from lunch with the hierarchy, was sex — and that meant Uckfield had made a conquest of the luscious Laura Rosewood.

'Any news from Luxembourg?' he asked, feeling bad tempered and frustrated. He had woken knowing that this was going to be one of those slow, wasted days in the middle of an investigation.

Trueman shook his head. 'But the file on the Carlssons' break-in should be with me later today.' The phone rang. Cantelli took the call.

Horton studied the crime board silently urging it to reveal some tiny scrap of information that could help with the case. Thea's employers had e-mailed a photograph of her taken from her personnel file. The serious pale blue eyes and thin face looked blankly at him. *Where are you? Are you alive or dead?* God, he wished he knew. He couldn't help thinking about what Bohman had told him about her illness triggered by the tragic events of her childhood. It didn't bode well for her current state of mind.

The thoughts jeered at him. There must be something that could connect and tie up all the loose ends of this case, but whatever it was remained tantalizingly out of his reach.

'That was the front desk,' Cantelli said, replacing the receiver. Horton spun round. 'They took a call early this morning from a woman who says she saw Thea Carlsson, but before you get your hopes up, Andy, this was before her brother was killed. She's a librarian at Cowes and she says Thea was in there on the Thursday before her brother's disappearance.'

Horton wasn't sure how this helped them. 'She could have gone to borrow a book or to look something up on the Internet,' he said grumpily. He didn't think Thea would have used her brother's computer and he'd not seen a laptop or any other mobile device in the house, and neither had she had a mobile phone on her when he'd found her at the Duver.

'I'll ask her,' Cantelli said, reaching for the phone.

Horton headed for the canteen after giving Trueman instructions to fetch him the moment he heard from Luxembourg. He hoped that breakfast might galvanize his sluggish brain and lift his mood. He ate mechanically, not tasting the food, going over all the facts of the case from that first moment on the Duver to the conversation with Bohman. Nothing clicked. All it did was make his headache worse. He had just finished eating when Cantelli breezed in.

'Thea asked to view the microfiche of the local newspaper coverage for 1990. And we know what happened then,' Cantelli said, taking a seat opposite Horton.

They did indeed. Maybe it was curiosity on her part, seeing as she was on the Isle of Wight for the first time. 'Did she copy anything down?' he asked.

'The librarian said she was too busy to notice, but Thea did ask for a local telephone directory.'

'Who was she looking up?'

'Don't know. Could it have been Terry Knowles?'

'No. You said he lives in Southampton, and he hadn't left any of his desperate sounding messages on Owen's answer machine then.' Horton thought back to his first conversation with Thea. She'd claimed not to know anyone on the island. If that was true then who could she have been trying to locate? Jonathan Anmore perhaps? Or someone from 1990?

'Get a copy of all the press cuttings on the Carlssons' accident, Barney. See who is mentioned in them, check who lives locally and contact them to find out if Thea got in touch.'

'The newspaper office isn't open until Monday, but I'll track down the editor to see if I can get hold of them today.'

Horton envied him his activity. He thought again of the girl that Bohman had mentioned, and the story that Anmore had told him about the ghost of Scanaford House. It reminded him of the book on ghosts in Owen's house with the inscription inside it. Horton didn't believe in ghosts except those of your own making, and he had a few of them haunting him. Nevertheless, was Scanaford House the link? Was it mentioned in that book?

He called Cantelli back. 'Find a copy of a book called *The Lost Ghosts of the Isle of Wight*. Track down the author, and if you find the book see if it mentions the ghost of Scanaford House.'

'Didn't know there was one.'

'Well, there is, and I'm getting rather tired of the wretched thing. According to Anmore a girl was murdered there by her father . . . At last!' he cried as Trueman headed towards them.

'Inspector Strasser's called. Thea's apartment has been broken into and ransacked.'

'When?' Horton asked sharply. Had it been immediately after Owen's death, or after Thea's disappearance?

'He doesn't know. The door wasn't forced so whoever did it must have had a key.'

Cantelli threw Horton a concerned glance. 'Did Thea give this person a key or—'

'Was it taken from her after she'd been killed?' Horton finished, his voice tight with emotion. Was the person who ransacked her apartment the same one who had attacked him and Thea, and set light to Owen's house? What was it that was so dangerously incriminating, that they were prepared to go to extreme lengths to destroy?

Trueman said, 'Owen could have had a key to his sister's flat and his killer took it from his body.'

Horton much preferred that version. Trueman continued. 'Strasser's got Forensic in and he's instigated enquires.

But there is something he thought we might like to see. He's no idea whether it's significant but there were some photographs in the flat.'

'Of what?'

'He didn't say. He's scanning them in and e-mailing them over.'

Horton thought they could hardly be relevant to the case otherwise the intruder would have taken them or destroyed them, as he'd done with Helen's camera.

Cantelli left to meet the editor of the local newspaper while Horton hung around waiting impatiently for the photographs to ping into Trueman's inbox. There was still no sign of Uckfield, neither had there been any further sightings of Thea Carlsson resulting from the press statement and photograph issued by Uckfield late last night. Monday might bring more response, Trueman said, but Horton wasn't optimistic.

Inactivity sat heavily on him. Pacing the incident suite he was half tempted to go and join Marsden in the search for his boat intruder — either that or ride around the island in the hope of finding Thea Carlsson, although he knew that would be a complete waste of time.

He was about to complain about Strasser's delay when Trueman cried, 'They're here.'

Horton rushed over to peer at Trueman's computer screen not daring to hope they might help with the investigation, and steeling himself for disappointment.

Trueman said, 'I'll print them off. They're all black and white photographs anyway.'

As they slid off the printer, Horton found himself staring at three pictures which, judging by the style and subject matter, were the work of Helen Carlsson.

Trueman said, 'Strasser says there was writing on the back of each one; he's copied it across in his e-mail. The first one is a demonstration in Kathmandu against the execution of Zulfikar Ali Bhutto. April 1979.'

And the authorities didn't much care how they crushed it, thought Horton. Helen Carlsson must have taken a hell of a risk to get in that close.

'The second,' Trueman read out, 'is of the demonstration by metal detectorists against a law to ban metal detecting in this country in December 1979.'

'They obviously won their cause then because I see them all over Southsea beach.' Horton had had no idea that metal detecting had caused such a stir. He studied the third photograph. It was of a woman standing at the top of the steps of a Royal Air Force aeroplane. Either side of her were a man and woman dressed in suits, while on the concourse below were men and women in uniform. 'I don't need you to identify her,' Horton said, pointing at the former Prime Minister, Margaret Thatcher. Then his eye lingered on the square-set woman standing to her right dressed in a smart suit, standing to attention, her eyes alert and hard. There was something familiar about her. He struggled to retrieve it as Trueman read from the computer screen.

'Twenty-ninth of August 1979, Prime Minister Margaret Thatcher visiting Northern Ireland, disembarking from the aeroplane at RAF Aldergrove.'

That had been when the conflict in Northern Ireland had been at its height, which explained Helen Carlsson's interest in taking the photograph. Margaret Thatcher hadn't long been in power. Then something registered in his tired brain. A snatch of conversation flashed into his head. *I will never forgive Margaret Thatcher and the Tories for their treachery . . . that mad woman.* Suddenly he knew without any doubt the identity of the young woman in the suit standing beside the Prime Minister.

'Well, well, well,' he expostulated, energized. 'Run me off another copy of this one, Dave. Then get me all the information you can on her.' Horton stabbed a finger at the sturdy figure.

'You recognize her?' Trueman asked, surprised.

Horton nodded. 'I do indeed. It's Bella Westbury. And I'd very much like to know what she is doing there and why before I ask her.'

CHAPTER SEVENTEEN

It was late afternoon and dark by the time Horton and Cantelli pulled up outside Bella Westbury's cottage. By then Horton had got some of the answers to his questions and Cantelli had managed to unearth the editor of the local newspaper who had generously opened up the office on the proviso that she got first bite of the news story.

Only police officers, the coroner and the relatives, such as they were — Helga and Peter Bohman — had been mentioned in the press reports of the Carlssons' road accident. The reporter had since married a sailor and moved to Plymouth. Horton couldn't see Thea being interested in any of them, but Cantelli had also discovered the author of *The Lost Ghosts of the Isle of Wight*, one Gordon Elms.

'He lives in Cowes,' Cantelli had reported. 'Two streets away from Owen Carlsson.'

And Horton's money was on Elms being the person Thea had been searching for in the library's telephone directory. He doubted now that it had anything to do with the case. It was just Thea's desire to meet the man who had written a much treasured book for her. But the librarian said she would get a copy of the book for them on Monday.

Horton detailed Trueman to check if Danesbrook, Bella Westbury, or Jonathan Anmore had travelled to Luxembourg at any time since Thea's arrival on the island. One thing, among many others, which troubled Horton, was if Bella Westbury had searched Thea's apartment, she wouldn't have left the photograph behind.

'No sign of life,' Cantelli said, peering at the small cottage opposite.

Which was more than could be said for Uckfield who had finally surfaced all smiles and rosy cheeks just after lunch. His mellow mood hadn't lasted long after Horton had briefed him. And his temper wasn't improved when Marsden had returned to say that no one they'd spoken to so far around the Duver recalled seeing anyone suspicious in the area around the time Carlsson's body was found.

'Better see if she's all right,' Horton said, climbing out of the car. 'You don't happen to have a ramming rod in the boot?'

'I never travel without one. No, of course I don't.'

'Then we'll ask her to let us in.' Horton nodded in the direction of a small dark-coloured car which had just pulled in further down the road. 'Mrs Westbury?' he hailed her as she was inserting her key in the front door.

She spun round with a frown. Even though she'd given no indication that she'd seen them waiting, he knew she had.

'Mr Horton.'

'Detective Inspector Horton and this is Detective Sergeant Cantelli.' They flashed their warrant cards. Horton doubted she could see them properly under the dim street lamp some yards away, but she pushed open the door and said stiffly, 'It's late for a police visit.'

'We're investigating the deaths of three people and time isn't a luxury we have.'

She flicked on the light and turned to face them in the small lounge. 'Why didn't you tell me you were a police officer when you were here before?' She didn't bother to hide her anger, but Horton could see it was false. She had known then exactly who he was. For someone who had been in the Army Intelligence Corps, as Trueman had discovered, and on protective security duty it wouldn't have been difficult.

'I was undercover,' he said, studying her closely, wanting to add, 'and I bet you know all about that from your career in British Army Intelligence', but he'd save that for later.

'Does that mean there is more to Arina's death than a hit-and-run, or is it Owen's death that sent you undercover?' she said with sarcasm.

'There's been another death—'

'I know. I've just come from Charlie Anmore's.' She closed the door behind them but didn't invite them to sit. 'Being undercover didn't help much, did it, Inspector?' she added acerbically, tossing her large canvas bag on the floor. 'What do you want? I'm tired and I'd like to go to bed.'

Horton could see the hostility in her green eyes. He wasn't sure if it was genuine or an act, but there was definitely something different about the tiny cottage. It took him a few moments to realize it was the cats. Where were they? If the kitchen door had been shut, he might have thought them inside, but that was wide open. And all was silent. Not a single meow and no furry friends had come rushing to greet her, which he found exceedingly strange. They couldn't all be out, surely?

'We won't keep you long, Mrs Westbury. Do you mind if we sit down?'

With ill grace she gestured them into the two comfortable and worn armchairs straddling the fireplace. Cantelli declined the invitation and waved Bella Westbury into the chair opposite Horton. He knew she would have preferred to stand to gain the advantage, but Cantelli was too wily to allow that. Once she'd sat the sergeant pulled up a straight hard backed chair and positioned it between them.

Horton asked, 'How well did you know Jonathan Anmore?'

'We used to talk about gardens, plants, the state of the nation, his father, that sort of thing. He'd come into Scanaford House for coffee on the days he was there.'

'Which were?'

'Tuesdays and Saturdays.'

Cantelli looked up from his notebook. 'Did he mention any girlfriends?'

'No, and before you ask Jonathan wasn't homosexual either.'

Horton said, 'When did you last see him?'

'At Arina's funeral.'

'How did he seem to you then?'

'Upset and angry.'

In the short silence that followed, Horton could hear the wind howling around the cottage. The rain had started up again, beating against the window, making him even more curious that not one cat had ambled in to settle in front of the fire.

'Have you been back to Scanaford House since Arina's funeral?' he asked.

'No. The solicitor took the keys.'

'But you had the keys after Arina's death.'

'Of course. Owen called me on Sunday morning to tell me about Arina's death. I couldn't believe it. I met him that afternoon at Scanaford House. He needed to talk to someone and so did I. We sat and had some tea. I called Mr Newlands, the solicitor, on Monday. He asked me to keep hold of my set of keys until after Arina's funeral and to organize the caterers for the wake. There was no one else to do it. Mr Newlands also asked me to sort through Arina's belongings. I packed up the clothes for the charity shop, and the personal items I boxed up and left for Mr Newlands.'

She brushed a stray strand of her brown hair behind her ears and held Horton's gaze, almost defying him to tell her she was lying. What Horton didn't like was the freedom of access she'd been given to the house since Arina's death.

'And what about Sir Christopher's things?' he asked.

'Arina hadn't touched them even though I volunteered to help her. So I cleared those out too. His clothes went to the charity shop and, again, I left the personal items for Mr Newlands.'

And he must still have those and Arina's. It was worth checking through them to see if there was anything that pointed to Arina's knowledge of Helen and Lars Carlsson. But if Bella Westbury had been involved in their deaths, then she'd had ample time to remove anything incriminating from Scanaford House.

'Did you know Helen Carlsson?' he asked, watching her carefully yet knowing that someone who had worked in Intelligence would be adept at disguising their real emotions and reactions.

'No, although judging by the surname I take it she must be a relation of Owen's.'

'His mother. She, and Owen's father, Lars, were killed in a car accident in March 1990.'

She didn't look surprised and neither did she look worried. 'Very sad, but I can't see what that has to do with any of the recent deaths.' She rose and reached for the poker.

'They died in almost the same place as Arina was killed.'

Holding the poker, she turned to stare at him before her eyes wandered to Cantelli and back to Horton. 'And you think there's some connection between that and Arina's death and then Owen's. And Jonathan's, I suppose. Well, I never heard Sir Christopher or Arina mention Helen and Lars Carlsson, and Owen never talked about them.' She opened the front of the stove and poked about inside it.

'Where were you in March 1990?' Horton said coolly.

She spun round with a wide-eyed look. 'I was in Wales, nursing my sick husband, who died in the August of that year.'

Horton left a moment's silence, holding her angry gaze before saying, 'Were you surprised that neither Sir Christopher nor Arina left you anything in their wills?'

'No. And before you ask, I wasn't disappointed either because I didn't expect anything.'

'Then you do know the contents of the will. You said before you didn't.'

'Mr Newlands told me on Friday.'

Horton could check that. 'And what about Roy Danesbrook: were you surprised when he was left what now amounts to a considerable sum?'

'No, why should I be? It was Sir Christopher's wish. He was a very charitable man. Now, if you've finished . . .'

Horton withdrew the photograph from his jacket. 'Is this you?'

She replaced the poker and took the photograph. He watched her as she studied it. There was the merest flicker of anger before she said, 'How did you get hold of this?'

She'd made no attempt to deny it was her because she knew they would check. He said, 'Helen Carlsson took it.'

Bella Westbury's surprise seemed genuine. 'Well, I don't remember her, or the photograph being taken.'

'I find that difficult to believe,' sneered Horton. 'A Prime Ministerial visit in troubled Northern Ireland and you on protective security duty, I hardly think you'd ignore a photographer. She could have been IRA.'

'She was probably one of the official press corps. That woman always wanted her face in the newspapers.'

Horton knew she meant Margaret Thatcher.

Bella added, 'Now I'd like to go to bed.'

But Horton refused to budge. 'Why did you change sides?'

'I don't know what you mean.'

Oh, she did all right. 'Army Intelligence and then rebel. They hardly seem compatible,' he scoffed.

She shrugged.

'I wonder what your ex-mining colleagues and former Greenham Common buddies would think of you if they saw this picture. They might not be happy about having a spy in their camp.'

'You're nuts.'

'Am I?' he said evenly, holding her steely gaze.

She eyed him with a confidence that bordered on smugness. 'I came out of the army and I changed sides. I didn't like the way the establishment and big business were always telling people what to do, what they should think and what was good for them. I'd had it with politicians' bullshit whilst working on protective security.'

It had the ring of truth about it, but he knew it was a lie. 'Where are your cats?'

'What? I don't know,' she said with exasperation. 'Out.'

'All five of them!' Horton said, surprised.

'A couple of them are probably upstairs asleep. You don't want to question them too, do you? I hardly think they'll be able to help. Now, if you don't mind . . .' She waltzed to the door and wrenched it open. A gust of damp chilly wind rushed in and rattled the wind chimes.

Horton rose, slowly. At the door he faced Bella and said evenly, 'How well do you know Roy Danesbrook?'

'I met him at Scanaford House a couple of times. Why?'

'Thank you for your co-operation, Mrs Westbury. We'll need to talk to you again, so please don't leave the island without telling us.'

The door slammed within an inch of his nose.

Cantelli exhaled. 'Funny sort of woman,' he said as they crossed to the car. 'Couldn't quite put my finger on what was wrong about her, but if pushed I'd say there was no warmth, or maybe I mean depth, to her. She said all the right things and showed anger in all the right places, even when she almost chopped your nose off, but it was like she was going through the motions.'

Horton climbed into the car and stared across at the house. A light had come on in the front bedroom. He watched as she pulled the curtains, pausing to look down on them.

'She's leaving.'

'How do you make that out?'

'No cats. She had five when I was here before and there wasn't a meow to be heard.'

'Perhaps they're all out chasing mice.'

'Have you ever known a cat to be out in this weather when it's got a nice warm comfortable bed or chair to sleep on?'

'I don't know much about cats.'

'Well, take it from me,' replied Horton, thinking of Bengal, 'given the choice at least one of them would have been in that lounge in front of the stove.'

'You reckon she's taken them to the RSPCA?'

'Either that or she's given them to a neighbour or killed them. Would you say she was capable of killing them, Barney?'

Cantelli peered at the house through the rain-spattered window. After a moment he said, 'Yes. I would.'

Horton shivered in agreement. 'I don't like the fact she had access to Scanaford House between Arina Sutton's death and the funeral. She could have removed anything incriminating, and helped herself to anything she liked. Newlands shouldn't have allowed it.'

'She could be leaving on the proceeds. There's no hint she left the armed forces under a cloud but perhaps she resigned before she was pushed and the army thought it best to hush things up.'

'Get a warrant tomorrow for Scanaford House, or better still see if you can get the keys from Newlands. That'll be quicker, though I expect we're too late anyway.' And that seemed to be the motto for this case. Everything they did or thought about was just that little bit too late.

'Do you want a warrant for here too?' Cantelli jerked his head at Bella's house.

'Might as well, though I doubt it'll yield much. But I want her watched. Call Marsden, he can relieve us. As soon as he arrives, we'll pay a visit to Roy Danesbrook. I have a feeling he might be closer to Bella Westbury than she claims.'

'It's late, Andy. He might be asleep.'

'Then we'll just have to wake him up.'

CHAPTER EIGHTEEN

'What do you want now?' Danesbrook demanded irritably.

He wasn't dressed for bed and Horton could hear the television blaring out in the back room. He pushed Danesbrook aside and marched down the narrow hall.

'Hey, you can't do that,' Danesbrook bleated, running after him.

'He just has,' Cantelli said wearily, closing the front door behind him.

Horton surveyed the untidy and shabby room with distaste. It stank of fish and chips, cigarette smoke and body odour. He picked up the remote control and killed the television.

'Who the hell do you think you are marching in here and messing about . . . ?'

Horton swung round, bringing the full force of his glare on Danesbrook. 'I'm tired, I'm angry and I'm sick of your lies. So sit down and answer my questions.'

Danesbrook sat. Cantelli took out his notebook and reached for his pencil from behind his ear. Horton could see him fighting off fatigue. He felt dead on his feet too. But he didn't have time to piss about being nice and waiting for 'office' hours, especially when he knew he was on the right track. The solution was within his grasp, he couldn't let go now. He would ride it until he got there; everything else was just wallpaper. And he knew that the thin man in front of him, in baggy jogging pants and an overlarge and grubby sweatshirt, was the key to the murders. How had an intelligent man like Sutton been taken in by this shyster? And why hadn't Arina Sutton seen through him? But then maybe she had, and it had cost Arina her life.

He said, 'If you tell me one more lie, I will charge you for murder. Is that clear?' His head was pounding. He knew he was out of order, but the only way to get the information he wanted was to scare this little runt shitless.

Danesbrook swallowed.

Horton took that, and the pungent smell emanating from him, as acquiescence. 'How long have you known Bella Westbury?'

'I—'

'Think very carefully before you answer,' Horton said menacingly. 'And ignore any telephone calls she's made to you in the last twenty minutes telling you to keep your mouth shut. We know she's clearing out. She intends to leave you to carry the can. Oh, I see she didn't tell you that.'

Danesbrook shuffled in his chair, considering it for a brief moment, then said with a resigned shrug, 'We met in 1996.'

'At the Newbury by-pass protest.'

Danesbrook nodded.

Horton had been right. In order to trust Danesbrook, Sir Christopher must have had some kind of testimonial or reference and the only person who could have given that was Bella Westbury, the trusted housekeeper, herself a veteran protester.

He said, 'She was a protester there too.'

Again, Danesbrook nodded. And that was one photograph that Bella Westbury hadn't hung on her kitchen wall for two reasons. One, because no wall would be big enough to take all of her protests, and two, because she'd rather keep that one quiet in case someone made the link between her and Danesbrook.

Danesbrook reached for a packet of cigarettes but Horton's glare prevented him from taking one out and lighting it. He said, 'We hit it off immediately.'

'You had an affair.'

'Yes.' Danesbrook fiddled with his ponytail. 'I was married and my wife found out. She slung me out after that. Not that it was a big deal; Valerie was never going to be able to do what she wanted with a bully of a father breathing down her neck all the time. I thought the protest would give her a chance to get out of his clutches but she scuttled back to him in the end, more fool her.'

Horton had difficulty seeing Bella Westbury fancying a weakling like Danesbrook, which meant she started the affair for a reason. She wanted something from Danesbrook and Horton didn't think it was sex. In fact, given her background he knew it wasn't. Sex had just been a tool to extract information.

He said, 'How long did the affair last?'

Danesbrook shrugged, 'A few months. We split up after the protest ended.'

I bet you did, thought Horton, drawing satisfaction from the fact he'd been right. 'And let me guess,' he sneered, 'you didn't meet up again until a year ago, here on the island.'

Danesbrook's eyes jumped to Cantelli and back to Horton. He swallowed hard but said nothing. Horton didn't need him to. A year ago, Bella had become Sir Christopher Sutton's housekeeper.

With a harder edge to his voice, Horton continued. 'Then you and Bella Westbury hatched a plan to screw the old boy out of a considerable amount of money. Whose idea was it, yours or Bella's?'

'It wasn't like that.'

Horton thrust his face close to Danesbrook's. 'No? I'll tell you what it was like. You met Bella, she told you about Sir Christopher's career and his interest in the environment, and then the two of you dreamt up the charity scam. Sir Christopher bought you that car and gave you money, but it wasn't enough, so you got him to include you in his will. Then Bella Westbury told you that Arina Sutton had also made a will after the death of her father and had bequeathed her inheritance to the same benefactors her father had given bequests to. The temptation was too great. You got scared that Arina might change her will later, so you and Bella Westbury decided to kill her.'

'No!' Danesbrook protested, alarmed. 'I haven't killed anyone and neither has Bella.'

'Are you sure about that?'

Danesbrook licked his lips, his Adam's apple jumped up and down as his eyes skittered around the room. The sweat was running off his forehead. 'She wouldn't.'

Horton ignored his pathetic denial. 'But Owen Carlsson guessed it was you, or perhaps he recognized that it was your car Bella was driving, as it slammed into Arina's body, so he too had to die.'

'This is crazy.'

'And then it was Jonathan Anmore's turn. Did he overhear you and Bella talking about it?' Suddenly, a worrying thought flashed into Horton's mind: Bella had called on Charlie Anmore. Was it to check that his son hadn't said anything about her and Danesbrook's scam? Was Charlie in danger? He almost broke off from questioning Danesbrook to get Cantelli to check the old man was OK, but then he thought it unlikely Jonathan would have said anything to his father.

'You have to believe me,' Danesbrook pleaded. 'We haven't killed anyone.'

'Get your coat.'

'But you said I could stay if I cooperated.'

'Did I? Sergeant, call a car to take him in.'

Danesbrook looked like a man who'd just seen his winning lottery ticket flushed down the toilet. 'You've got this all wrong, Inspector. We were going to get money from Sir

Christopher, I admit that. He had plenty and his daughter didn't need it all, there was no real harm in that, but we wouldn't and didn't kill anyone.'

Horton wasn't convinced. He thought they were both capable of murder and a million pounds was a powerful motive. Of course, that didn't fit with the deaths of Helen and Lars Carlsson. But that didn't mean there wasn't a reason. Only one he hadn't yet discovered.

As Cantelli stepped into the hall to call in, Horton said to Danesbrook, 'Where were you in March 1990?'

'I can't remember. Why do you want to know?'

Horton glared at him.

'All right. Let me think.' After a moment his haggard features brightened. 'I was in London, at the Poll Tax riots.'

'All month?'

'Pretty much. The riot was planned for the end of the month, the thirty-first of March, so there was a lot of organizing to do beforehand. That was one of my more successful demonstrations,' he added boastfully. 'It killed the tax dead. We showed the government they couldn't ride roughshod over us.' He gave a tentative smile.

'For someone who has spent most of his life on benefit and hardly paid a pound in taxes that's a bit rich,' Horton spat scornfully.

Cantelli led Danesbrook outside to a waiting patrol car. As he was giving instructions to the uniformed officers inside it, Horton's phone rang. It was Marsden.

'Bella Westbury's leaving home with a suitcase, sir,' he said excitedly.

'Follow her.' He rang off and said to Cantelli, 'Bella's on the move. She can't get far at this time of night. The only transport off the island is the car ferry. When she gets there, we'll bring her in.'

But they'd only just pulled into the station car park when his phone rang again.

'I've lost her,' Marsden relayed, dejectedly.

Horton cursed.

'She must have known I was tailing her,' Marsden said, 'because she timed it to perfection, slipping through on a red at a set of traffic lights. I couldn't follow, a damn great lorry was charging through. She was heading in the direction of Cowes so I thought she might have been taking the Red Funnel ferry to Southampton. But her car's not here.'

Horton quickly thought. 'Stay there, call me if she shows up and arrest her for the murder of Arina Sutton. I'll send a unit there to assist you.'

He rang off and speedily told Cantelli what had happened. 'Turn round and head for Cowes,' he ordered. 'The terminal's not the only place she could have been heading. There's a marina and that means boats.'

As Cantelli sped to the marina, Horton rang through to the station and told Uckfield what had happened.

'I'll put an alert out for her,' Uckfield said. 'Leave Danesbrook to me. This time I'll get him to talk, smarmy solicitor or not.'

Horton didn't know how he was going to find the boat Bella Westbury might be leaving the island on.

She'd given no indication that she could handle one, and neither had there been anything in her house to point him in this direction. But he had to be right. And he had a feeling that if they didn't catch up with Bella now then they never would. She would go underground again.

'Her car's here,' Cantelli said, sweeping into the car park.

'You take the pontoons to the right, I'll take these.' Horton set off at a fast pace to his left, knowing that Cantelli wasn't about to enjoy himself on the water, but he wouldn't shirk doing a thorough job nevertheless. He wondered if they were already too late. She could be halfway down the River Medina by now, or out into the Solent.

The rain bounced off the wooden pontoons and the wind whistled and clattered through the masts. He didn't even know where to start. He could be searching one pontoon only to see her boat slip past him having left another.

But, straining his eyes, he saw a figure step off a small yacht halfway down a pontoon to his right. His heart quickened but no, the build was wrong for Bella Westbury. Then there was the throb of a powerful engine. It was coming from the pontoon to his left. He spun round. It had to be her.

He sprinted back down the pontoon and up the other one with the rain bashing into him. A hooded figure was loosening the stern line. It spun round at the movement of the pontoon and the sound of his footsteps. There was no mistaking who it was this time.

Bella Westbury hesitated, dashed a glance at the boat, looked set to jump on board, and then changed her mind. She didn't have much choice; he could easily leap on before the boat pulled away, or, easier still, radio up and get the marine unit to pull her in.

'Tut, tut, you were meant to tell me if you were leaving the island,' Horton said with heavy sarcasm, drawing level with her.

'I didn't want to ruin your beauty sleep, Inspector.' Her expression remained impassive except, Horton thought, for a hint of scorn in the way the corners of her mouth turned down. She glanced away and retied the rope on the cleat. 'I expect you've taken Danesbrook in for questioning.'

'He said you were the brains behind defrauding Sir Christopher.'

She said nothing, simply raised her eyebrows.

'You'd better come with me to the station,' he said briskly, trying not to be irked by her arrogance.

'Then I'll need to switch off the engine and collect my things.'

Horton had no choice. Either he had to kill the engine or she did, and either way, if he let her out of his sight she could make a bolt for it. He wished Cantelli was here but there was no way of alerting him without phoning him and he didn't want to give Bella the slightest chance to slip away from him. He followed her on board and into the wheelhouse. The engine was silenced.

'My things are in the cabin.'

As he stepped down behind her he braced himself for a possible attack. He hadn't forgotten that pitchfork in Jonathan Anmore's back or the gunshot wound in Owen Carlsson's temple. He could be looking at a triple murderer who could be about to turn on him with a knife or gun.

'I'm not your killer,' she said, reading his mind.

'Why are you running away then?'

'My job's finished.'

Horton knew she didn't mean housekeeping. 'With Anmore's death?'

'No. Like I said, I'm not your killer, and neither is Roy Danesbrook. I didn't think there was any point hanging around any longer.'

Horton held her confident gaze. 'You didn't change sides, did you?' he said. 'In 1996 you were at the Newbury by-pass protest with Danesbrook. Your job was to infiltrate the protesters in order to tell the road contractor, or the police, or both, what the protesters were going to do. You also told Danesbrook's wife that you'd slept with her husband. Does Danesbrook know what you did to him, and that you were a spy?'

'I don't know what you're talking about.'

Oh, she did all right. And she didn't seem at all worried. That infuriated him. She was too complacent, too cocky.

Harshly he said, 'No doubt you also fed information to Intelligence on the Greenham Common peace protest and the miners' strike, and others I suspect. So who are you working for this time? And don't tell me you're not.'

She eyed him for a moment then said, 'Seeing as you're not recording this, Inspector, I work for whoever pays and needs me, private enterprise or the government, I'm not fussy. We both know there are organizations that will give handsome rewards for leaked information about their competitors. You can't get everything from the Internet despite what people think. Sometimes it needs a real live person to get into an organization undercover.'

'And that's your speciality,' he sneered. If she hadn't killed Arina Sutton for the money, and she was here undercover, then it couldn't have anything to do with the deaths of Helen and Lars Carlsson. So why else would she, or Danesbrook, kill Owen Carlsson? There was only one other motive — the original one: the environment. Laura Rosewood had said that there were powerful people who wanted to silence or delay Owen's findings and Bella Westbury had to be working for one of them.

He tried again. 'Who are your paymasters this time?'

She smiled her reply. 'You don't really expect me to go that far.'

'Then let's try Integrated Coastal Zone Erosion, Owen Carlsson's project.'

She looked startled for a moment before recovering her composure. Obviously, she hadn't been expecting that.

He said, 'The results of Owen's project are to include a set of policy recommendations to deal with coastal erosion in a sustainable way, so who wanted it delayed or stopped? Is that why you killed Owen?'

'I'm going to have trouble convincing you that I'm not Owen's killer or Jonathan's.'

'You had to be seen to be on the side of the environment, hence your interest in it and the friendship you cultivated with Owen. You also knew that Sir Christopher Sutton was a friend of Laura Rosewood, an adviser on the environment to the European Commission, so if you were friendly with Sir Christopher, you'd also be able to find out what Ms Rosewood was doing, regarding Owen's project. How did you wangle the job as Sir Christopher's housekeeper and cook?'

'He had a vacancy. I applied.'

He eyed her sceptically. 'When Arina arrived on the scene to look after her father you introduced her to Owen, and what a bonus that must have been for you when she and Owen fell for one another. Arina was another source of information on Owen's progress.'

She remained silent. Well, perhaps she'd change her mind when he charged her with murder.

'Did you set fire to Owen's house in the hope of destroying his findings?'

'No.'

'Did you search Thea's apartment?'

'No.'

'Did you kill Helen and Lars Carlsson in 1990?'

'No.'

She was staring at him with a slightly sardonic smile on her face that he would dearly love to wipe off. She said, 'As I've already told you, in 1990 I was with my husband, who was seriously ill.'

Horton felt frustration well up in him. His head was pounding with fatigue. Here was a woman who was highly trained and experienced in covert operations. And one who knew when to hold her tongue. If, as Laura Rosewood had suspected, Owen had been killed because of his project then there was no way this side of the century he was going to get Bella Westbury to admit to it, or admit to having a part in his death.

She said, 'Do you still want me to come to the station?'

'What do you think?'

'Then there is something you should know. I will deny your allegations about me spying at Newbury. And I shall deny having anything to do with these murders. So unless you have some firm evidence that can prove I killed Arina, Owen and Jonathan, I don't think you can charge me. And you certainly won't get a confession.'

'Then I shall try fraud.'

She laughed. 'I haven't committed any fraud, but if you insist then I also insist on calling a solicitor, who will insist that you formally charge me or let me go. Don't you think that's all rather a waste of time and you'd be better off catching a killer?'

'I've already caught one,' he said, but he knew his words fell on stony ground.

CHAPTER NINETEEN

Monday

She was as good as her word. Bella Westbury said nothing until her solicitor arrived from London mid-morning. Horton had tried to get her to tell him who her client was, and to admit to killing Arina Sutton, Owen Carlsson and Jonathan Anmore, but he knew even before he started that he was wasting his breath. He couldn't even get her on a charge of intent to defraud Sir Christopher Sutton's estate, especially when Danesbrook claimed the charity idea was his and he hadn't done anything wrong anyway.

Irritated and frustrated, Horton left her with Marsden to make her formal statement and found Uckfield, Cantelli, Trueman and Somerfield in the incident room.

'We'll have to let them go.' He threw himself into a chair. He felt exhausted, and clearly so did the others, judging by their faces. There were dark shadows under Cantelli's eyes whilst Uckfield's were bloodshot and his craggy face drawn and grey. Trueman's five o'clock shadow looked as though it had been around the clock twice without actually producing a beard. Only Somerfield looked relatively fresh as she placed a coffee in front of Horton, and he suspected that was some clever trick with make-up.

'Can't we even get Danesbrook for fraud and embezzlement?' Uckfield said in desperation.

Cantelli answered. 'Danesbrook claims he was in the process of setting up the charity and there's no one to say he wasn't. All we can get him on is not declaring any money that Sir Christopher gave him to social security.'

Uckfield snorted in disgust then winced. Horton wondered what was wrong with him. He looked ill.

'There's worse,' Horton said. 'Although Bella Westbury and Danesbrook have no alibi for the time of Owen's death, they have one for Arina's death, if we believe them. They now claim they were together that evening.'

'As in having a relationship?' Uckfield asked disbelievingly

'Apparently. Though they're probably lying to give each other an alibi. Danesbrook was in the pub at the time of Anmore's death and Bella says she was at home alone. We've got no proof to show that either she or Danesbrook were involved in Owen's and Jonathan's deaths, and we've got about as much chance of getting a confession as we have of walking on water. Bella Westbury is as tough as a cow's backside. Did you have a word with Charlie Anmore, Somerfield? Is he OK?'

'Yes. He said that Bella Westbury just wanted to pass on her condolences. They talked about the old days and that was it. He says it was kind of her to call.'

Horton remained sceptical about that. He doubted Bella Westbury did anything out of pure kindness. Horton had asked Trueman to email a copy of the photograph of Bella Westbury to Sweden to ask Bohman if he recognized Bella or had heard Lars, Helen or Owen mention her name. The answer had come back negative on all counts.

'So where does this leave us?' asked Uckfield, glowering at them all.

It was a good question. Horton swallowed a mouthful of coffee before answering. 'It leaves us trying to find enough evidence and a motive to convict her. Has Laura Rosewood had any joy finding out who Bella's paymasters might be?'

'She's making enquiries, but I can't see anyone owning up to it, can you?'

Horton couldn't.

'You've told Bella not to leave the island?' Uckfield's demand turned into a groan.

'For the second time,' Horton replied wearily. 'And I doubt she'll take any more notice of me this time than she did before.'

'Then put a watch on her.'

Trueman nodded.

Uckfield added, 'Isn't there any evidence in that barn to help us catch our killer?'

'The forensic lab is still testing various items,' Trueman said. 'There's no sign of Anmore's mobile phone, and he wasn't on a contract, but his phone company are seeing if they can list his most recent calls. We might get something from them later.'

'Might's no ruddy use to us,' grumbled Uckfield, frowning.

Horton said, 'What about the gun used to kill Owen, any more news on that?'

Cantelli answered. 'The lab has confirmed that the fragments of the bullets found in Owen's body match the gun you found Thea with.'

'Could it have been Anmore's?'

Kate Somerfield said, 'Charlie told me that his son often sailed to France. Perhaps Jonathan picked up the gun there.'

She had a point. Horton said, 'Anmore's boat is small enough not to draw too much attention from the Customs boys.'

'Why not simply register and buy a gun here or use one at a gun club?' asked Cantelli, folding a fresh piece of chewing gum in his mouth.

'Perhaps he didn't want to be bothered with the red tape?' suggested Trueman. 'Or he only wanted it for target practice in his barn.'

'Should have bought himself an air rifle then,' Horton added sourly.

Uckfield rose and immediately let out a howl of pain, clasping a hand to his back. They all stared at him, shocked.

'You all right?' asked Horton, concerned.

'Do I ruddy well look it?' Uckfield hissed through gritted teeth.

'Perhaps you've pulled a muscle.'

'Yeah, laughing at you clowns, who couldn't catch the clap in a brothel never mind a triple killer.' He flashed Horton a hostile look before trying to straighten up, decided it wasn't a wise move and made a vain attempt to hobble to the crime board.

Horton threw Trueman a look. *What's wrong with the Super?* Trueman shrugged. *No idea.*

Horton said, 'There could be another reason for Owen's death, which puts Bella and Danesbrook in the clear.'

'Then for God's sake tell us,' Uckfield snapped. 'Or do we have to play twenty questions?'

'Owen could have witnessed something when he was out gathering data for his survey.'

'Like what?' asked Trueman.

'He was on the coastline so it could be smuggling, boat stealing, or dumping waste in the sea or in a coastal stream.'

Cantelli looked up. 'He could have found something which incriminated someone—'

'Such as?' grunted Uckfield, screwing his face up with pain.

'A body, a treasure trove, guns. Owen Carlsson could have seen Anmore bringing in guns. He confronted him and — bang.' Cantelli made a shooting movement with his two fingers.

Horton addressed Trueman. 'When was the last time the boat was used?'

'I'll check with the lab.' He lifted the phone.

'And check if Customs have ever stopped him.'

Trueman nodded before speaking into the telephone.

Uckfield, with his hand on his back and clearly in some discomfort, said, 'We need to find out where Owen Carlsson went in the days before he was killed—'

'Before Arina was killed,' corrected Horton. 'Her death could still have been a warning for Owen to keep his mouth shut.'

'Yeah, and as we haven't got her diary, we're back to asking Joe public to help, which is about as much use as a split condom. No one's come through with a single sighting of him since that woman saw him on the Cowes chain ferry. And there's still no sign of Thea Carlsson.'

And that was worrying Horton. He hauled himself up with a glance at his watch. He wasn't going to find Thea by sitting round here discussing theories. Besides, he and Cantelli had an appointment. He nodded to Cantelli who unfurled himself from his chair.

'Where are you going?' demanded Uckfield, surprised.

'Ghost hunting.'

'What?' Uckfield's bellow turned to a yelp of pain.

'Gordon Elms is the author of a book that Helen Carlsson inscribed for her daughter and it's possible Thea went to see him.'

'And where the devil will that get us?'

Horton didn't know. Both Bella Westbury and Danesbrook had denied all knowledge of Thea's whereabouts but then they would if they'd killed her. 'You'd better see someone about your back,' Horton called out, not stopping to hear Uckfield's answer, which if true to his usual form would be a string of profanities.

'The super's obviously been overdoing it,' Cantelli said, pointing the car in the direction of Gordon Elms' house. 'Looks like he's taken on more than he can handle with this Laura Rosewood. What's she like?'

'Attractive, widowed and a friend of the Chief Constable's.'

Cantelli flashed him a look. 'He's playing a bit close to home. I hope his wife never finds out.'

Horton thought of Alison Uckfield, the Chief Constable's daughter, and agreed. It wouldn't do Uckfield's career much good either.

Cantelli said, 'Elms has got his own website and seems to be something of a celebrity in ghost-hunting circles.' He handed Horton a piece of paper.

Horton read aloud. '"The Isle of Wight is reputed to be the most haunted place in Britain. It is home to a medley of ghosts, spooks and spirits. Take a walk around Cowes with ghost hunter and popular author, Gordon Elms, and discover the mysteries of the old town. Sign up for a tour of the many houses and hotels on this mystical magical island where ghosts still haunt the halls and corridors."' He looked up. 'Scanaford House?'

'I can't see Sir Christopher Sutton opening his house to the weirdos of the world.'

And neither could Horton. Nor could he see Arina Sutton doing the same — but Roy Danesbrook as the owner? That was another matter altogether. Cantelli was obviously following his train of thought.

'Be a good money-spinner though. Especially for someone like Danesbrook. Spend a night in the haunted house and spot a spook.'

'Does Danesbrook know Gordon Elms?'

'He says not.' Cantelli yawned. 'I can't handle these late sessions like I used to. Must be getting old.'

'If it's any consolation I'm feeling just as rough.'

Cantelli dashed him a glance as if to check. 'Charlotte called this morning,' he added, pulling into the traffic.

'Anything wrong?' Horton asked anxiously, sensing Cantelli's concerns.

'She says Joe's missing the only male in the household, and with five women, three of them hormonal if you count Charlotte, I said who can blame him.' Cantelli smiled, but Horton could see he was worried.

Joe and his six-year-old twin sister, Molly, were the youngest of Cantelli's brood. Ellen, the eldest at sixteen, had caused Cantelli some sleepless nights recently and he guessed her sisters, Sadie, who was fourteen, and Marie now twelve were probably fast catching up on the worry front. Horton wondered if he'd be around to see his own daughter through troubled times. He had to be, there was no question of that.

'How are the girls?' he asked.

'Ellen's more interested in boys than studying, so nothing new there. Sadie's dancing her feet off, loves all that ballroom and Latin American stuff, and Marie's blossoming now she's started at that new school.'

Horton recalled that Marie had had the misfortune to be sent to one of the worst inner city schools in Portsmouth — the one he'd been condemned to spend some years at as a child — because all the places at the schools Cantelli and Charlotte had applied for had gone by the time the local education department had found their lost application papers.

Cantelli said, 'She's only been there a fortnight and loves it. I can tell you, getting her into St Crispins, and her winning that scholarship, is the best thing that could have happened even if I did have to promise to return to the fold of Catholicism. I'd have converted to Buddhism if it took that to make her happy. And I would have sold my soul to the devil to pay for her school fees if she hadn't got a scholarship, clever girl. Just to see her face light up every time she talks about it is worth . . . Sorry.' Cantelli flicked Horton a glance. 'There's me wittering on when you must be worried sick about Emma. Any news on that front?'

Horton found himself telling Cantelli about Emma's phone call and Catherine's plans to send Emma away to school.

'Why don't you visit the school?' Cantelli urged. 'It wouldn't do any harm to see what it's like. You've every right to do that, even Catherine can't stop you. And if you find you don't like it, and there are reasonable grounds, then you've got something solid to fight against it.'

Cantelli had a point. He should have thought of it himself but emotion and Emma's sobs had clouded his judgement. 'I'll call them.'

'And don't leave it too long. I know what you're like when on a case. That's not meant as a criticism,' he added hastily at Horton's dark look. 'Call that school as soon as we've finished with Gordon Elms — and talking of which, we're here.'

Cantelli indicated off the main road into a side street of stone bay terraced houses much smaller than the ones two streets away where Owen had lived. Convenient if you wanted to start a fire, Horton thought. But he had no reason to suspect Gordon Elms of anything let alone almost killing both him and Thea.

'It's not very impressive for a world-renowned professional ghost hunter.'

'Perhaps he's got a penthouse apartment on the south of France and this is his work base,' Cantelli joked.

The door was answered promptly. If Horton had expected someone dressed like Merlin, then he was gravely disappointed. Gordon Elms did, however, resemble a gnome. He was small with a little round pot belly protruding over a pair of camel corduroy trousers that came just an inch short of being the right length. Beneath them, Horton caught a glimpse of fluorescent pink socks above shabby white trainers. In his fifties, with greying hair and a little grey goatee, Elms waved them into a small sitting room and offered them refreshments, which they both refused.

Horton noted there was no television. Above the fireplace was a sinister-looking painting of a large house, which he didn't recognize, though it bore a faint resemblance to *Manderley* before Mrs Danvers had set fire to it, according to the Alfred Hitchcock version. As he took the seat Elms gestured him into, Horton thought it a gloomy picture to hang in this room, it being executed primarily in shades of grey, while the room was decorated in red and gold, as if it had overdosed on Christmas and was reluctant to let go of the festive season. He noted the candles on the mantelpiece along with a couple of photographs of a younger version of Elms with an older woman, whose facial qualities and age paraded the fact that she must be Elms' mother.

Cantelli opened the questioning. He showed Elms the photograph of Thea and asked if he had seen her recently. Clearly by Elms reaction he had. 'Why yes! She came here some days ago.'

They'd been right then, thought Horton; this had been the address Thea had been looking up in the library.

'When exactly?' pressed Cantelli.

'It was a Thursday. I know that because I hold an evening class on Thursdays. I lecture on the paranormal at the community centre. I was preparing for it when she arrived. Yes, it was the fifteenth.'

Two days later Owen Carlsson left his house and never returned.

'She'd read my book,' Elms said proudly. Maybe he didn't get many admirers, thought Horton.

Cantelli said, '*The Lost Ghosts of the Isle of Wight*.'

'Yes. She was very complimentary. Said it had been given to her as a present. I said that must have been at birth.' He smiled. 'I wrote it years ago and it's long been out of print though I am considering updating it and publishing it myself. Publishers these days only seem interested in you if you've been on the telly. And, as you can see, I don't even have a television set, and I wouldn't appear on one if you paid me. I'm not into cheap magic tricks. I'm a genuine ghost hunter and medium.'

'I'm sure you are, Mr Elms,' soothed Cantelli. 'When did you write the book?'

'Let me see. It was published in 1985, which means I wrote it in 1983, but I remember researching it for a year before that. In fact, I began as soon as I moved here in 1982, a year after I first came here with my mother on holiday. I knew immediately this was the place for me, so when my mother died, I sold up and moved from London. Never regretted it either.'

Cantelli nodded and jotted this down in his notebook.

Horton said, 'Are you a full-time ghost hunter and medium?' If his voice held a note of scepticism, Elms didn't seem to notice it.

'Yes. I took early retirement from the council where I worked in the planning department. Why do you want to know about the book and this woman?'

Horton was tempted to say, 'Psychic powers deserting you?' But he held his tongue and instead asked, 'What did Thea Carlsson ask you?'

'She said her mother had given her the book,' Elms continued, with a slight frown at not having his question answered. 'She showed it to me and asked if I recalled selling it to her mother.' He gave a little laugh. It sounded as if his underpants were too tight, thought Horton.

'I told her I was a writer, not a bookseller, and that her mother could have bought it in any number of bookshops. She showed me a photograph of her mother, a blonde, good-looking woman, but I didn't recall her . . .'

Suddenly Elms looked uncomfortable, almost embarrassed. Horton wondered why, but it was Cantelli who beat him to the question.

'But you remembered something.'

'I felt something.'

Horton tried not to snort with derision. He was getting the impression that Elms was a bit of an actor, and the word 'ham' sprang to mind.

Earnestly, Cantelli continued. 'Like what, sir?'

Elms drew in his breath, closed his eyes, and steepled his hands in front of his chest. Cantelli flashed Horton a glance. Horton raised his eyebrows and rolled his eyes in response. He'd almost had it with this little squirt, but Cantelli, with a nod of his head and a steadying hand, urged patience. Horton waited. After a moment Elms threw open his eyes.

'Evil. I felt evil.'

'In what way, sir?' asked Cantelli chirpily, drawing a slight narrowing of eyes from Elms.

'In the danger kind of way,' he snapped. 'Is there any other kind of evil? You of all people should know it exists. You see it daily in your professional lives.' He had a point, thought Horton.

Cantelli said solemnly, 'And evil seems to have befallen Miss Carlsson. Her brother was killed shortly after her visit here.'

'Good grief!'

'You didn't see, feel or smell that?' Horton sneered, drawing a flash of hostility from the little gnome.

'The evil wasn't specific, and it wasn't directed at Miss Carlsson,' Elms replied tight-lipped. 'I would have warned her otherwise.'

Horton considered this. Was Elms really psychic or had Thea told him about her mother's death and Elms was making this up as he went along? Horton wouldn't mind betting that was so. Behind Elms' angry eyes Horton saw his dislike of him, but then he was used to that.

'Did you tell Thea Carlsson of this evil?'

'Yes. She said she already knew about it. But I didn't pick up any vibes of her being a kindred spirit, so to speak.'

If he believed Elms was a genuine medium or spiritualist, or whatever you called them, then maybe he hadn't detected the vibes because Thea wasn't in danger, and neither was she psychic, but had colluded in the killing of, or had killed, her brother. Dr Clayton's words returned to haunt him. *This is a clever killing by a clever killer*. But no, he refused to believe it of Thea. They'd got their killers — Westbury and Danesbrook — even though they couldn't prove it yet. Elms was the phoney.

'Who was the evil directed at then?' he snarled, tired of the gnome and not wanting to waste any more time on him.

'I'm not sure, but as Miss Carlsson handed me the book, I felt it.'

He wanted to say 'bollocks'. Maybe Cantelli felt this because he quickly interceded.

'Did she ask you about ghosts mentioned in the book or any specific ghosts?'

'No.'

They hadn't yet seen a copy of the book and Horton now doubted that it mattered anyway. There was a brief silence in which Horton strained for any sounds in the house. All he could hear was the whirring of the central heating. What was Elms not telling them? Horton felt sure there must be something, or was that just desperation on his part? Probably.

Elms asked, 'Who is her mother?'

'Was,' corrected Horton. 'She died in 1990, along with her husband, in a car accident at Seaview.'

Elms looked surprised but that could have been faked.

'Tragic. But why was their daughter . . . ?' Elms paused.

Cantelli prompted him. 'You've thought of something?'

'Just the accident you mentioned in Seaview. There was a hit-and-run there about three weeks ago.'

'Arina Sutton.'

'That's right. Such a nice lady.'

Horton resisted throwing a glance at Cantelli. Keeping the excitement from his voice he said, 'You knew her?'

'Yes. Well, not exactly, but I'd met her.'

'When?' asked Cantelli casually, pencil poised.

Elms thought for a moment. Horton wasn't sure if it was for show or he really was trying to remember. After a moment Elms said, 'It was just before Christmas. Would you like the exact date, Sergeant?'

'Please.'

Elms rose. 'I'll check my diary.'

He left the room. Horton swiftly and silently crossed to the door to make sure Elms wasn't hovering outside. He saw him disappear into the back room. 'What do you think?' asked Cantelli.

'He's a phoney, but this link with Arina Sutton could be interesting.'

Horton could hear Elms moving about. 'Hope he's not hiding anything in there.' Like something of Thea's. But why would Elms want to kidnap and kill Thea? No, he was miles off beam with that one.

He said, 'Did you get a search warrant for Scanaford House?' He'd forgotten to ask earlier.

'Yes. It should be through this afternoon along with the warrants for Danesbrook's house and Bella Westbury's cottage.'

Horton doubted they'd find anything though. Bella was too wily for that. This case was really getting to him now. He was sick of it and he was desperate to find Thea Carlsson.

Elms entered with a frown and a diary. 'I went to Scanaford House on the sixth of December.'

'You had an appointment there with Ms Sutton?' Cantelli asked.

'Yes. I'm researching for a new book—'

'*Lost Ghosts of the Isle of Wight Part Two*,' posed Cantelli.

Elms smiled. 'Something like that.'

Horton scoffed, 'The father who murdered his daughter and threw her body in the lake.'

'You know about it?' Elms said, surprised.

'I thought everyone did. Why the interest now?' Horton saw Elms start slightly at the sharpness of his tone.

'I don't know what you mean by now,' he said haughtily.

Horton laughed derisively. 'Oh, I think you do.' He held Elms' stare, saw him flush and look away.

Picking at a corner of the diary and avoiding eye contact, Elms said, 'Sir Christopher Sutton would never let me in or near the house.'

And I don't blame him, thought Horton. He wouldn't have let the likes of Elms within spitting distance of his boat.

Wriggling up his nose, Elms added, 'He said he didn't want it becoming a spectacle for all the . . . ghost hunters in the UK.'

And I bet he expressed his opinions more vehemently than that, thought Horton, seeing Elms' discomfort. 'So, why the change of heart?'

'His daughter must have persuaded him, and besides Sir Christopher was dying of cancer.'

Cantelli said, 'You knew that?'

'Not until I arrived.'

'But what sparked you to telephone Miss Sutton after having been refused a visit for so long?' asked Cantelli, bewildered.

'I read an article in the local newspaper about the public meeting on the wind farms. There was a photograph of Sir Christopher Sutton with a group of people and one of them was his daughter, Arina. I didn't even know he had a daughter until then, so I thought I'd try her. She might be more sympathetic to my needs. I telephoned the house. She answered. I explained that all I wanted to do was to see the lake and the house and, if permitted, take some photographs for my new book. She agreed and we made arrangements for me to call round on the sixth of December. She told me her father was terminally ill and wasn't to be disturbed, but he must have got wind of me being there because he came onto the terrace; or I should say staggered. Miss Sutton was pointing out the lake to me.'

Elms fell silent. Horton could see by Elms' expression that something had happened there and it had been unpleasant. He hoped it didn't have anything to do with ghosts. He prompted, 'And?'

Elms shifted. 'He went white, and I mean white. He couldn't speak. He just stared at me as if he'd—'

'Seen a ghost, sir?' suggested Cantelli.

'Well, yes, since you put it like that. He looked as though he was about to collapse when Miss Sutton rushed to his side and so did I. We got him into the house and onto the sofa. I left immediately. I could see that Miss Sutton was extremely worried and upset. And now the poor woman herself is dead.' He sighed, a little theatrically Horton thought.

He left a short pause before asking, 'Did Sir Christopher say anything?'

'No.'

'And Miss Sutton?'

'Just that she would call me. She didn't, of course, and then I read about her father's death.'

'You didn't attend their funerals.'

'I didn't want to intrude on the family's grief. And I didn't really know them.'

It was said genuinely enough but Horton wondered why he hadn't. It would have afforded him the perfect opportunity to nose around the gardens and the house, something he, by his own admission, had yearned to do.

'Did Miss Sutton call the housekeeper, Miss Bella Westbury, to help with Sir Christopher?'

'No.'

'Did you see her there?'

'Can't say I did. I didn't know he had a housekeeper, though I'm not surprised considering the size of the place. Do you know what will happen to it now? I wonder if the new owners would let me have a look around the place. Or perhaps I could call there before it's sold. That way I won't inconvenience anyone.'

Cantelli said, 'You'll have to talk to the solicitor, or perhaps Mr Danesbrook will tell you.'

'Who's he?'

Horton studied Elms' expression. He didn't appear to be bluffing.

'A friend of Sir Christopher's,' Cantelli added, as Horton rose.

'Thank you, Sergeant, I will.'

On the threshold Horton said, 'Do you know Jonathan Anmore?'

'No. Should I?'

'Did Thea Carlsson say anything to you, or ask you about a girl.'

'What girl?'

Horton thanked him.

'Was he telling the truth?' Cantelli asked as they pulled away.

'About his visit to Scanaford House or not knowing anyone connected with this case except for the Suttons and Thea?' Horton sighed. 'Probably. But I want a copy of that newspaper article he mentioned, just to make sure he really did see it.'

CHAPTER TWENTY

While Cantelli stopped off at the newspaper office, Horton rang directory enquiries and asked to be connected to Northover School. A woman answered. He had wanted her to sound unfriendly so he could have good cause to dislike the school from the start, but she wasn't.

After he'd introduced himself as a prospective parent, he was whizzed through to the head teacher faster than a Japanese bullet train. He made an appointment to view the school in a week's time. That would give him a chance to conduct some research when he returned to his office. He learnt that the earliest his daughter could start there would be at the beginning of the new term, after Easter.

Cantelli climbed in and handed Horton a photocopy of the press cutting. 'Elms' story checks out with this at least,' he said.

Horton saw the group just as Elms had described it. It was the first time he'd seen Sir Christopher Sutton, who was hollow-cheeked with illness but still a commanding presence with his piercing eyes and slightly superior smile. Beside him was an attractive woman with mid-length dark hair and a shy smile: Arina Sutton, and next to her Horton couldn't mistake Owen Carlsson and Bella Westbury.

Cantelli added, 'Trueman phoned while I was waiting for the photocopy. He's got the crime report on the Carlssons' break-in. It confirms that Helen Carlsson reported her smashed camera.'

'Was that all that was wrecked?'

'It's all that's mentioned in the report.'

Cantelli swung the car around and headed back to the station. Horton said, 'Why didn't they steal her camera and sell it? And why did Helen leave the camera in the house? Surely a professional photographer always takes her camera with her.'

'Perhaps she was going somewhere she couldn't take it, or didn't want to,' Cantelli replied.

'Even if she was going out to eat why not lock it in the boot of the car?'

'She could have had more than one camera.'

Horton threw Cantelli a glance. He'd hit on something there. 'You could be right. If she and Lars Carlsson were killed then it could be because the killer discovered that Helen Carlsson had another camera in her car, and there was something on that film that he didn't want developed, which means we're looking for someone who Helen unknowingly photographed here on the island in 1990.'

'Bella Westbury?'

Horton considered it. 'Possible. I don't for a moment believe all that stuff about nursing a sick husband.' Then he frowned, puzzled. 'But why didn't she take or destroy that photograph of herself in Northern Ireland?'

'Because she didn't break into Thea's apartment but got lover-boy to do it for her and he cocked up.'

Horton cheered up at that. 'Danesbrook probably wouldn't have recognized her in that photograph. Though Trueman can't find any record of either of them travelling to Luxembourg.'

'Danesbrook probably used a false ID. Fixing something like that would have been child's play to Bella Westbury.'

Cantelli was right and that posed a problem. Gloomily, Horton said, 'If it is Bella Westbury then I doubt we'll ever be able to confirm what she was doing here in 1990; it'll be hushed up.'

He fell silent, seeing the case slip through their fingers. Europol would be called in, which would make Uckfield livid. Horton would be too. And he doubted Europol would get any further forward than them. Slowly and quietly the case would be side-lined and Thea Carlsson would remain 'missing', just like his mother, until her body turned up somewhere — if it ever did.

Cantelli said, 'Maybe Owen discovered who his mother photographed. It would explain why he was killed. But not Jonathan Anmore.'

'Anmore's death could still be unconnected with the others. If only we could find out where Helen Carlsson went and what she did while on holiday here, unless . . .' Horton swivelled his gaze to Cantelli. He wondered. 'Barney, what do you do when you're on holiday?'

Cantelli flashed him a glance before putting his eyes back on the road. 'Eat too much, drink too much and—'

'Apart from that,' Horton said impatiently. 'You're away in sunny Italy, or in Blackpool, and you want to tell your sister you're having a great time—'

'I'd text her,' Cantelli said with a grin. Horton knew he was being deliberately obtuse. He'd got the point all right.

'In 1990?'

'Yeah, I know. How on earth did we manage? I'd send a postcard,' Cantelli grinned.

'Precisely. And Helen could have sent a postcard to her son and daughter; here we are having a great time at The Needles type of thing.'

'So what if she did? That doesn't tell us anything. And Owen was at Southampton University so she'd hardly send a postcard to him when he was just across the Solent.'

Cantelli was right. The postcard idea was crap. But Cantelli had sparked another idea. He said, 'Owen could have travelled here to see his parents, or even to stay with them.'

‘And? I don’t get what you’re driving at, Andy.’

‘Neither do I,’ Horton said, deflated, but for a moment he felt there was something there. Something his subconscious had caught, but had slipped away. He tried again. ‘Let’s say Owen was told about the break-in by one of his parents. He comes rushing over here after it had happened to console them.’

‘I doubt a twenty-year-old student would have given it a second thought.’

‘OK,’ Horton grudgingly admitted. ‘But his parents didn’t live in England and they were practically on his doorstep. Even if he didn’t come because of the break-in, he wouldn’t have missed the opportunity of seeing them.’

‘Maybe not. But the Carlssons could have visited their son on their way here, in Southampton. You’re not thinking he could have something to do with their death?’ Cantelli said, clearly bothered by the thought.

Horton hadn’t but now that Cantelli had mentioned it, he said, ‘Children have killed their parents.’ The thoughts tumbled their way through his mind like leaves in a hurricane and he didn’t much like where they were taking him.

Cantelli said, ‘Why would Owen do that?’

After a moment Horton answered. ‘Money. Perhaps Owen was in debt and saw an easy way out. Or perhaps he’s mentally disturbed.’ The picture of Owen’s house flashed before Horton’s eyes, the neatness of the place, all except for that chaotic study. Did that portray a personality in conflict? He said, ‘We don’t know enough about Owen Carlsson. In fact, we know nothing.’ But that wasn’t true. He recalled what Peter Bohman had said about Owen. Owen had never asked Bohman about his parents’ death or had seemed worried or curious about it. *He said it was the past, best to forget it. He was like his father, focussed on the present.* Maybe he’d never asked because he already knew what had happened. He said as much to Cantelli.

‘If Owen did have a hand in his parents’ death and Thea found out then she—’

'Could have killed him, or arranged to have him killed, yes.' Horton's heart sank. He knew it was highly probable given Bohman's information about Thea's disturbed background. And that was one more feather of doubt fluttering down on the scales against her. He much preferred Bella Westbury and Danesbrook as their killers.

Quietly Cantelli said, 'So we could be back to thinking Thea got Anmore to kill Owen and then she killed Anmore.'

Horton gazed up at the black-clouded sky through the windscreen, not wishing to examine his feelings. This was looking bad. If Thea had sought revenge on her brother, then where was she now? How had she known about Owen's part in his parents' deaths, if he had killed them? Had he finally told her? Horton recalled what Strasser of the Luxembourg police had said about Thea being distracted on her return to work in the New Year. And who had ransacked her apartment? Had she done that herself to make it look as though an outside force was at work? Did it mean Arina Sutton's death was an accident? Why had Owen visited Dr Nelson?

There was an answer to that last question at least. Nelson could have been Owen's GP in Southampton, and all that stuff he'd spun Horton was a lie. They needed more information on Nelson's background, and they needed to dig deeper into Owen's past employment record, university career and medical background.

Depression settled on Horton and stayed there while he briefed Uckfield. He could tell instantly that Uckfield warmed to the idea of Owen being involved in his parents' death and Thea's subsequent quest for revenge.

Uckfield sat forward but a cry of pain stalled his further comments.

'Back still giving you jip?' asked Horton.

'Yes, and so are you,' Uckfield gasped. 'I've already asked to see Thea Carlsson's medical records, which after what you've just told me sounds like a smart move. I'll request her brother's. Even if Owen Carlsson didn't kill his parents, Thea could still blame him for neglecting her after their parents' death. That architect man in Sweden, Bohman, said as much.'

'She's had a long time to think about getting even,' Horton growled.

'Yeah, and maybe hearing her brother singing Arina Sutton's praises over Christmas and New Year really got up her nose. Then, seeing how upset he was following her death, Thea feels rejected once again when he won't let her comfort him. Especially when she's come home to take care of him.'

Despite not wanting to believe it, Horton knew that it sounded plausible.

Uckfield said, 'DCI Birch is looking for a past connection between Anmore and Thea Carlsson.' Uckfield held up his hand to staunch Horton's reply and winced as he did so. 'It's possible that Owen told Thea at Christmas that he was planning to marry or live with Arina Sutton, which was why he went to Luxembourg on his own leaving his newly bereaved girlfriend in that big house. When Thea Carlsson came here to stay with her brother over New Year she could have met up with Jonathan Anmore while visiting Scanaford House with Owen. If we can establish a link between Thea Carlsson and Anmore then it's possible that she could have arranged for Anmore to kill Arina in the place her parents died—'

'Why would she do that?'

'Because she's sick. She's got a warped mind. Then she rushes home to comfort her brother.'

'That's a damn big if.' But even as he said it, Horton knew he had been thinking the same and had said as much to Cantelli earlier.

Uckfield continued, 'Anmore kills Owen after Owen rejects Thea. Then Anmore and Thea Carlsson arrange that neat little performance at the Duver that you happened to stumble upon.'

Horton didn't like this one little bit. In fact, he hated it and judging by Uckfield's expression he had been considering this for some time.

Eagerly Uckfield went on. 'Anmore tries to kill Thea Carlsson by setting fire to the house because he's scared she'd confess. Then Thea gets out of the hospital, finds Anmore and plunges a pitchfork in his back.'

'So where is she?'

'That's what I want you to find out.'

Dismissed, Horton headed for the canteen tormented by the knowledge that the woman he had thrown from that burning house could have killed her own brother and Jonathan Anmore.

'Any news on Anmore's boat?' he asked, sitting between Cantelli and Trueman.

'It hasn't been in the sea for some months,' replied Trueman, shovelling fish and chips into his mouth as though he'd not eaten for days. 'So he couldn't have been meeting gun runners or drug dealers.'

'He could still have met them on shore,' Cantelli said stubbornly.

'He could,' agreed Trueman, 'but if your theory that Owen killed his parents and Thea killed her brother with Anmore's help is correct then it's of no significance anyway. At least not to this case.'

Cantelli had obviously been updating Trueman while Horton had been in with Uckfield.

To Trueman, Horton said, 'I want you to look into Dr Edward Nelson's background. He could have known Owen Carlsson professionally when he was at Southampton University.'

'I know where he was during his National Service.'

'Not sure that helps us much,' Horton said with sarcasm.

'You never can tell,' Trueman replied solemnly. 'Nelson and Sutton were both in the Royal Army Medical Corps from 1956 to 1959, based at the British Military Hospital in Tripoli. Or at least Nelson was in Tripoli until 1959. Sutton left there a year earlier but there's no trace of where he went. He next shows up as a registrar at Guy's Hospital in 1960.'

'Don't the army records tell us what he was doing?'

'Not the ones I've had access to. But I've asked a mate who works there to have a nose around.'

'Where haven't you got mates?' Horton muttered.

'It pays to keep in touch. He doesn't know why Sutton's records are missing from 1958 to 1960.'

'Could he have been abroad on another posting?'

'Probably, but the records should show that.'

Cantelli said, 'Perhaps it was hush-hush.'

Trueman shrugged. 'Could be, which means that someone's conveniently lost that information or destroyed it. Or it could just be incompetence and someone forgot to fill in where Sutton was between September 1958 when he left Tripoli until he was discharged from the army in November 1959 and showed up for work at Guy's in January 1960.'

Horton could feel his curiosity rising. He didn't like gaps of any kind, although Trueman could be right and this was probably just a piece of slipshod work. Even if it weren't, he didn't think it had any bearing on the case, except for one thing that still irked him: Owen's visit to Nelson.

He stretched and rubbed his face. 'What was going on in the world in 1958 and 1959?'

'The Cuban crisis,' Trueman said, promptly. 'Fidel Castro took over as Prime Minister on the sixteenth of February 1959 and brought the world to the brink of nuclear war as his alliance with the USSR provoked a missile crisis.'

'*Our Man in Havana*,' muttered Cantelli.

'It's a book,' confirmed Trueman to Horton's raised eyebrows.

'And a film,' added Cantelli. 'By Carol Reed, starring Alec Guinness and Maureen O'Hara. 1959.'

'If you say so,' Horton said. Cantelli was an expert on these things. 'But I can't see Sutton being in Havana or anywhere else in Cuba.'

'Probably not,' Trueman agreed. 'But *Our Man in Havana* is a good book.'

Suddenly something connected in Horton's tired brain. 'Book . . . Sutton . . . Of course! Trueman, you're a genius.'

With a smile, Trueman said, 'I know that.'

Horton leant forward. 'Bella Westbury, ex British Army Military Intelligence, shows up on the Isle of Wight and becomes housekeeper to Sir Christopher Sutton just when the man has been diagnosed with terminal cancer. And what do some people do when they discover they haven't got long left for this world?'

Cantelli said, 'They confess.'

'There's a Catholic for you.'

Trueman caught on. 'Or they write a book — their memoirs.'

Horton smiled triumphantly. 'Exactly! Bella said to me that she was leaving because her job was done. I thought she meant killing Arina, Owen and Jonathan Anmore and maybe even Thea Carlsson, but that wasn't her job, and neither has it anything to do with Owen's environmental project. Bella Westbury was here to stop Sir Christopher blabbing about where he was and what he was doing during 1959. My God, it makes sense.'

He threw himself back in his seat and watched the expressions on Trueman's and Cantelli's faces before adding, 'By being in Scanaford House as housekeeper, she was able to field Sutton's calls, sift through his post and his possessions and make sure he wasn't about to break the Official Secrets Act, which he must have signed when doing National Service. She was also able to conduct a thorough search of Scanaford House after Arina Sutton was killed in case Sutton had left a written confession.'

Cantelli said, 'So she did kill Arina.'

Horton chewed it over. 'Only if Sir Christopher had told his daughter his secret on his deathbed.' And he could have done. Confession being good for the soul and all that. But he still couldn't see where Helen and Lars Carlsson came into it. Maybe they didn't and the fact that their deaths had occurred in the same place as Arina's had been just one of those weird coincidences. Or perhaps Owen had killed his parents and Arina really had been killed by a hit-and-run driver. Her death in Seaview had been the catalyst which had unlocked Owen's secret and set up a tragic chain of events ending in his death and Anmore's.

He leant forward. He didn't much like what he had to say but there was no way round it. 'OK, theory number one. Bella Westbury is here to stop Sutton from blabbing about where he was in 1959 and to make sure he's left no written evidence when he dies. She can also check that Arina knows nothing about her father's secret, whatever it is. By some strange and tragic fluke Arina gets killed by a hit-and-run driver in the same place as Owen killed his parents. Because Owen loves Arina and was planning to marry her he believes her death is a punishment for him killing his parents. He calls on Dr Nelson because he saw him at Sutton's funeral and is now worried he might have recognized him from 1990, when Nelson had treated Owen Carlsson, or knew something about his medical background. Thea comes home to comfort her brother. Owen by now is filled with guilt and remorse, and confesses to her what he did in 1990. She kills him, either with a gun Owen had, or she's teamed up with Anmore and used his gun. Then Thea kills Anmore and has gone into hiding.'

'Or killed herself,' added Cantelli sorrowfully.

Horton took a breath. He had to admit it was possible.

'What's theory number two?' asked Trueman, pushing his plate away.

'Bella Westbury is here to stop Sir Christopher Sutton's secret from coming out, but Sutton says something to his daughter before he dies. Arina tells or hints at this secret to Owen. When Arina is killed by Bella Westbury or someone working with her, Owen gets curious, concerned and angry. He starts to investigate if there is any truth in what Arina's told him, which takes him to Edward Nelson GP, Sir Christopher's old friend and colleague. Nelson tips Bella the wink, or someone who is working with her, so Owen Carlsson too has to be silenced.'

'And Anmore?' asked Trueman.

'Maybe he overheard something, or saw Bella talking to a colleague.'

'Danesbrook?' suggested Cantelli.

'I doubt he's got the intelligence to be working with a sharp operator like Bella, but we might as well haul him in again just in case he's brighter than he looks.' Horton scraped back his chair. To Trueman he said, 'Tell Marsden and Somerfield to pull Bella Westbury in. She could still be our killer.'

'And you?' asked Trueman.

'We're going to talk to Dr Edward Nelson.'

Cantelli looked alarmed. 'We? I'll be no good to you, Andy. If I have to sail anywhere I'll be throwing up all over the place.'

'OK. Interview Bella. See what you can get out of her.'

Cantelli heaved a sigh of relief. To Trueman, Horton said, 'Dave, check out when Sutton was diagnosed with cancer. Has the warrant come through for Scanaford House?'

'Yes.'

'Then get a team in there even though we're too late. And another team into Danesbrook's place and Bella Westbury's cottage.'

'How does this fit with the photograph and Helen and Lars Carlsson's death?' asked Cantelli, following Horton out of the canteen.

Trueman said, 'Sutton was working in London at the Hammersmith Hospital as a consultant surgeon in 1990.'

'Yes, but he owned Scanaford House then.' Horton saw it all in a flash. 'It has a ghost and Helen Carlsson was reputed to have been psychic, or at least interested in ghosts, hence the book she bought and inscribed for Thea, which went up in smoke in Owen's house. Maybe Helen went to photograph Scanaford House and saw Sir Christopher Sutton talking to someone from British Intelligence.'

'Could it be this "girl" that Thea asked Peter Bohman about?'

'Maybe, Barney. Or it could have been Bella Westbury.'

Uckfield looked up from the crime board. 'My God, it's the three musketeers. I thought you lot had gone home.'

'No, but I am going out,' Horton replied, picking up his helmet.

'Where?'

'Sergeant Cantelli will explain; I've got a ferry to catch.'

Uckfield looked about to explode but Cantelli quickly interjected. 'I'll tell Dr Nelson you're on your way.'

'No. I want to surprise him. I might catch him off guard. He must know more than he's told me.'

'What if he's not in?' said Trueman.

'He will be,' Horton replied with conviction.

CHAPTER TWENTY-ONE

Nelson showed no surprise as he opened the door. This time Horton was shown into a comfortably furnished lounge where a gas fire hissed incongruously in a large brick fireplace. There was no sign of Mrs Nelson and no explanation of where she was.

Horton took a seat on the floral patterned sofa wondering if Nelson had been warned by someone that he was on his way. He didn't for a moment suspect either Trueman or Cantelli of going against his instructions, which meant he could have been followed, though he hadn't noticed anyone as he crossed on the ferry. And he'd seen no one watching Nelson's house.

On the crossing, Horton had received a call from Cantelli. Despite Marsden and Somerfield's surveillance, Bella had somehow contrived to give them the slip. Horton wasn't really surprised. He didn't think Marsden and Somerfield had been incompetent but an old professional like Bella Westbury had probably already worked out an escape route. He suspected that she'd climbed over the garden wall into neighbouring properties until she could call a taxi, or meet up with someone ready to help her disappear.

He told Cantelli to get Marsden to check the boat at Cowes, though he knew she'd be long gone, and to alert

Sergeant Elkins of the marine unit to look out for it. Elkins would contact the harbourmasters and marinas around Portsmouth and along the south coast. He gave Cantelli the name of the boat, knowing that Bella Westbury could pull into any harbour, or even motor to London and up the Thames.

'So how can I help you, Inspector?' Nelson said, switching off the television news and settling himself in the armchair to Horton's right.

'Did you know Owen Carlsson before he came to visit you here?'

'I met him at Christopher's funeral.'

'I mean before then. Was he ever a patient of yours?'

'No.'

'Are you sure?'

'I may be old but I am not senile, Inspector,' Nelson replied somewhat tartly. 'My memory is still good.'

'I'm glad to hear it, sir, because in that case you can help me with another matter.' Nelson had played right into his hand. 'National Service,' he said flatly.

Nelson raised his bushy eyebrows. 'What of it? I told you that Christopher and I served together in Tripoli.'

'I don't think you did, sir,' Horton replied politely, knowing full well Nelson hadn't mentioned it.

'I could have sworn I did. Maybe my memory is fading, after all.' Nelson's lips twitched in a sad smile, but the play-acting at dementia wasn't going to wash with Horton. There was nothing senile in Nelson's sharp gaze or behind the intelligent blue-grey eyes. Nelson saw he couldn't fool Horton and gave a small smile before adding, 'Christopher and I were both in the Royal Army Medical Corps and stationed at the British Military Hospital in Tripoli.'

'Did you tell Owen Carlsson this?'

'I don't recall mentioning it.'

Nelson was stalling, waiting to see why Horton wanted to know and how much he already knew. Was he in the pay of British Intelligence? Could he have informed them that Sutton had terminal cancer?

'Why do you want to know about our National Service time?' Nelson pressed when Horton remained silent. 'It was years ago.'

Horton wasn't going to give him the full story, but he saw he would have to impart some of it, and a version of the truth, to gain his co-operation.

'We believe that something happened then that has had repercussions recently.'

'You mean resulting in Owen Carlsson's death?'

'And others.'

'Arina's? No, I can't believe that.' But Nelson was looking worried.

'What happened in Tripoli?' Horton pressed. He could see Nelson weighing up how much to tell him. He held his breath waiting for it, but Nelson rose and crossed to the sherry decanter on a small table behind the door.

'Drink, Inspector?'

Horton declined, wondering if Nelson was preparing himself for the ordeal of revealing something from his and Sutton's past, or perhaps it was a diversionary tactic designed to give himself time to concoct a lie. Nelson poured himself a small sherry and returned to his seat before speaking.

'Christopher and I were in National Service from 1956 to 1959 and stationed at the hospital in Tripoli for most of that time, that is to say I was, Christopher left the hospital in 1958.'

Horton already knew this. 'Where did he go?'

'I don't know. Oh, you can look sceptical, Inspector, but I genuinely don't know where he went from the time he left Tripoli to when I bumped into him again in 1960 at Guy's Hospital.'

'Didn't you ask him?' Horton said, irritated, and not bothering to hide his exasperation.

'No. It didn't seem relevant. Besides I sensed that Christopher didn't want to talk about it. He was never one for looking back anyway, and we were both keen to get on with our lives and our careers. After I completed my time as a registrar I decided to go into general practice and Christopher, as you know, rose to the dizzy heights of consultant surgeon and finally as an adviser to the government on mental health law. Ah, I see you didn't know that.'

Nothing got past this man. Nelson would have made a good copper. Perhaps he should put him on to interviewing Roy Danesbrook who, Cantelli had said, had protested vehemently at being dragged in for the third time. Well, tough. But Horton wondered if Danesbrook had known about this government advisory position of Sutton's. He wouldn't mind betting that Bella had told him. It would have given Danesbrook further ammunition to use when selling the idea of his charitable project to Sutton.

Nelson said, 'After Christopher retired in 1992, he was attached to the Neurological Unit of the Behavioural and Clinical Neuroscience Research Institute. From there he was appointed to the expert committee to advise ministers on mental health law.'

With bitterness Horton said, 'The committee that let out all the psychopaths and paedophiles for us to locate and bang up again after they had destroyed more lives.' There had been a furore over it a few years ago and rightly so. Suddenly, heavy with fatigue, Horton wondered if Nelson had given him yet another reason why Arina had been killed. Maybe this case had nothing to do with Sutton's National Service or Helen and Lars Carlsson. They could be looking at a whole new spectrum of suspects — an avenging father, brother or uncle. Someone who had killed Arina because her father had been on a committee that had recommended the killer's release. But no, he was complicating things, or at least he hoped he was.

Sharply he said, 'So what happened in Tripoli?'

Nelson's lips twitched in a kind of smile and Horton saw at once that Nelson had been trying to side-track him with that mental health committee stuff.

'Before I answer that, tell me one thing.'

Horton nodded though he had no intention of bargaining or keeping his promise. He was getting rather fed up with Nelson.

'What did Christopher's will say?'

Horton narrowed his eyes. 'Why do you want to know that?'

'I'll tell you if you answer my question.' Nelson tossed back the remainder of his sherry, keeping his eyes on Horton all the while.

Horton didn't see any need for secrecy. The will would probably be public knowledge soon anyway. But why was Nelson interested in Sir Christopher's will and not Arina's?

'He left most of his estate to Arina with generous bequests to charities and hospitals.'

'Not to any particular individual?'

'No.' *Not unless you count Roy Danesbrook*, Horton thought, growing more curious.

Nelson nodded slowly. Carefully he set his glass down on the small table beside him. *Here it comes,* thought Horton, with a flutter of anticipation. He only hoped it had been worth waiting for.

'I shall of course deny what I am about to tell you, Inspector, if asked to repeat it.'

Not another one acting like Smiley in a John Le Carré novel, thought Horton exasperated, but he nodded. He would have agreed to sell the Elgin Marbles to the biggest crook this side of the English Channel if it meant he'd get some fresh information to help solve this case.

Nelson said, 'In September 1958, Sir Christopher Sutton was found in bed with a nurse.'

Jesus! Was that it? Horton could hardly contain his frustration but then he told himself that 1958 standards of propriety were a million miles away from where they were now. Even his own illegitimacy had been something to be ashamed of when he was a child, and that wasn't so long ago. He knew that his mother had probably been disowned by her family when they had discovered she was pregnant because he had never seen, heard or spoken to any of them.

Nelson said, 'That sort of behaviour was not expected of nurses.'

'And what about doctors?' said Horton scornfully.

'Ah, those were the days.' Nelson smiled. 'We were unchallenged. Gods. We could do as we liked.'

'So the nurse got the sack, or dishonourable discharge, and Sutton got posted away,' Horton declared, seeing the picture.

'Spot on.'

Bit hard on the poor nurse. This then was the gap in Sutton's career which Trueman had discovered. 'Where did Sutton go?'

'I don't know.'

'Oh, come on, you must have swapped tales when you met up again.'

'We didn't. As I said, Christopher was not one to reminisce.'

'And it never came up in all the years you knew him?'

'No. I don't know where he went after Tripoli or what he did.'

Horton didn't believe him. Nelson was closing ranks even now after Sutton's death just as they would all be doing. He could take Nelson in for further questioning but he had no real cause to and he doubted Nelson would say more. In fact, he'd say less, as he'd already intimated.

'Three people dead,' Horton declared coldly, 'five if we include Helen and Lars Carlsson. Don't you think the time for secrecy is past?'

'I can't see how their deaths can have anything to do with where Christopher was during his time on National Service.'

'Then let me explain.' And Horton did. He told Nelson that Sutton could have been working for the government during that missing year on something secret and in 1990 was seen talking to someone whom Helen Carlsson, because of her job photographing many of the trouble spots around the world, recognized and photographed. So she and her husband were killed. Then the dying Sir Christopher confided something to Arina, setting up a chain reaction of more murders.

Nelson's expression remained studiously neutral. So much so that Horton felt like shaking him. Anyone else and he might have shoved the photographs of the deceased under his nose. But a doctor wasn't going to be fazed by pictures of dead bodies or of a post-mortem. He wondered if Gaye Clayton might be able to find out more about Sutton's missing year. Perhaps her father, the eminent Home Office pathologist Dr Ryedon, might help.

'I think your imagination is running away with you, Inspector. There must be a far more logical explanation for these deaths. The Carlssons were killed in a road accident, Christopher died of natural causes and Arina in a tragic accident.'

'And Owen Carlsson and Jonathan Anmore? Not to mention that Thea Carlsson, who is missing, is probably dead by now,' Horton snapped, though he was getting the feeling that Nelson might be right. What had sounded so plausible at the station less than two hours ago now, even to him, smacked of that John Le Carré novel. But he wasn't beaten yet.

'What happened to the nurse?' he asked tersely.

'I have no idea.'

Another lie? 'Did Sir Christopher ever talk about her?'

'No.'

'What was her name? And don't tell me you don't remember because I won't believe you.'

Nelson sighed wearily. 'It was all a long time ago and I can't see that it has any bearing on your case.'

'Maybe not, but you told me to look for a more logical explanation for these deaths and if I discard the Carlssons' car accident as being murder, but not Arina's, then I'm back to the question you asked me earlier.' Horton drew some satisfaction at Nelson's surprise. Was that because he had remembered what Nelson had said or because Nelson hadn't expected him to reason it out? A little smugly, Horton added, 'You asked if Sir Christopher Sutton had left anything in his will to an individual. You were thinking of an illegitimate son or daughter.'

Nelson eyed him with interest. After a moment he said, 'Her name was Elizabeth. She was a tall, slim woman with fair hair. I can't remember her surname.'

'Try,' Horton said harshly.

'No, it's slipped my mind,' Nelson smiled politely. 'But I'm sure it will come back to me, eventually.'

'Then I'll just have to wait until it does.' Horton glanced at the clock on the big oak mantelpiece. 'What time did you say your wife would be home?'

'I didn't,' Nelson said slowly. 'Now I come to think of it, Inspector, maybe I have an old photograph that might jog my memory. She might just be in one of them. If you've got a moment, I'll dig them out.'

Horton had several moments, though he would have preferred not to spend them in the sitting room listening to that grandfather clock in the hall, soberly ticking away the minutes while Nelson went through his old photos and extracted any he didn't want him to see. What's the betting he'd find none of this nurse? But Horton was wrong. In less than three minutes Nelson was back with a triumphant look on his face and with two photographs in his hand.

'Here's two of a group of us outside the hospital.' He handed them to Horton. 'There's Christopher.' Nelson pointed to a tall, good-looking, dark-haired man with an aristocratic face. 'And here's me.' But Horton wasn't interested in either of them. Instead, he was staring at the tall, slender woman whom Sir Christopher had his arm draped around and who was laughing into camera. With a shock he realized he'd seen that face before. He didn't need Nelson to tell him her surname now. He already knew it. And although the passing years had obliterated most of the likeness there was no mistaking the shape of the face, the wide, slightly protruding eyes, because less than six hours ago this woman had smiled down at him from a mantelpiece underneath a painting of what looked like *Manderley*.

Nelson eyed him keenly. 'Her name was Elizabeth Elms. I told you I'd remember. But I can see you already knew that.'

'Not until you showed me this.'

'She's alive? You know her?'

'No, but I know her son.' And he also now knew the reason why Sir Christopher had been so shocked and upset when Gordon Elms had turned up at Scanaford House to research the ghost. Sutton had just seen one. His illegitimate son.

CHAPTER TWENTY-TWO

'I was just going out,' Elms said, clearly not pleased to receive another visit from the police, and so soon after the first. 'I've got a meeting with my paranormal group.'

The mind boggled, thought Horton, envisaging spooks, ghouls and ghosties sitting (or should that be floating) in a semi-circle, bemoaning the state of the nation and deciding where best to haunt.

'This won't take a moment, sir,' he said with a tight smile, stepping into the red and gold room. If Elms was a triple murderer, then he could kiss goodbye to his meeting tonight, and for the next twenty-five years, a good judge and a fair wind willing. But Elms hadn't inherited his late father's fortune, so what other motive could he have for killing Arina Sutton? Revenge on the family that had deserted him and his mother? Yes, that was possible.

Horton hadn't mentioned Gordon Elms to Uckfield on his way back to the Isle of Wight from Lymington because Cantelli had told him that Uckfield had got an emergency appointment with a chiropractor. His back had got so bad that he could only just about hobble and Cantelli had added, 'You can imagine the temper he's in.'

Horton could. Best to stay clear. He'd asked Cantelli to meet him outside Elms' house and before knocking had quickly briefed him.

Elms stood, trying to glare at them, but it just made him look as though his truss had slipped. Clearly he was not going to offer them a seat. Glancing at his watch, Elms said, 'I can only give you a few minutes.'

You'll give me a lot more than that, sunshine, if I think you're guilty of murder, thought Horton, but arranging his features into a suitably civil expression he said, politely, 'Do you own a car, Mr Elms?'

'Yes. Why?'

'What kind, sir?' asked Cantelli.

Elms looked baffled. 'A Ford. It's taxed and insured and has a current MOT if that's what you're after.'

'It's colour?'

'Blue. But what's that got to—?'

'Where were you on the third of January?' Horton said briskly. Now let's see what the little gnome comes up with as an alibi for the night Arina had been killed.

'I can't remember.'

'It was the Saturday after New Year's Day, if that helps,' Horton said. Elms bristled at Horton's sarcasm. He looked set to make some smart remark but Cantelli quickly intervened.

'Perhaps consulting your diary will help, sir?'

Elms considered this for a moment, then replied stiffly, 'I'll fetch it.'

'I'll come with you.'

'There's no need, Sergeant.' But Cantelli ignored him.

As soon as they had left the room, Horton crossed to the mantelpiece and studied the photographs of Elizabeth Elms. Elms had said that his mother had died in 1981. How old had she been then, he wondered, picking up the gold-effect frame and peering more closely at her. She looked to be about forty when this picture was taken with Gordon, and if she had been in her twenties when working as a nurse at the military hospital in Tripoli then she had died young. Certainly before she had reached fifty.

He could still see traces of the attractive young woman in the photograph that Dr Nelson had shown him, but whether life, betrayal, desertion, disappointment, or all four had made her mouth tighter and her eyes harder he couldn't say and would never know. And neither would he know whether his own mother might look the same if she were still alive, which he doubted. Or maybe he wanted to believe she was dead because that was easier to cope with than acknowledging the fact that he'd been deliberately ignored for years. The only photograph he'd had of her had been burnt when his beloved boat *Nutmeg* had been torched by a mad killer. That reminded him that soon he'd have to give up living on the boat borrowed from Sergeant Elkins' friend and find a new home for himself. It was something he had been putting off in the hope of a reconciliation with Catherine, which was now completely out of the question. New Year, new decisions, he thought, pulling himself up. Get somewhere to live, sort out your life.

He turned his mind to Elms. Had Elizabeth Elms told her son who his father was? Did Gordon Elms know what his father had been doing during that missing year? Trueman had confirmed that Sutton had bought Scanaford House in 1976 and that his wife had died in 1980. It was possible that Elizabeth Elms had returned to nursing in London where Gordon Elms had told him they had lived. Maybe she had kept her eye on Christopher Sutton's career and, hearing the news that his wife had died in 1980, had come here in 1981 hoping to rekindle some of the passion or love between her and Christopher Sutton but it had never materialized.

Horton couldn't help his thoughts flitting back to his own mother. Had she done the same on that fateful day in November when she'd left their council flat dressed up in her best clothes, according to the only witness he'd managed to find? Was his father someone like Christopher Sutton, an eminent man, who didn't want his affair acknowledged? Or was he the powerful underworld figure that only recently the Intelligence Directorate had claimed was possible? But perhaps her disappearance had nothing to do with either of these — quite the opposite in fact. He felt a stirring of excitement that told him he could be right before a reality check said it was more likely he was the result of a one-night stand. He told himself he didn't really care or want to know, but as he heard footsteps in the hall, he guessed Gordon Elms had said much the same over the years. And Horton knew it was a lie.

Brandishing the diary, Elms said, 'On the evening of the third of January I was at a private meeting with a client in Newport.'

'Doing what?'

'Helping her to communicate with a loved one.'

'A séance.'

'You can scoff all you like, Inspector, but there are powers out there you can't even begin to imagine.'

And there are powers I've got that you don't need to imagine, he felt like saying, but didn't. 'What time did you leave your client?'

'It was late, about eleven thirty.'

After Arina had been killed. But Horton would check.

'I'll need the name of your client.'

Elms drew himself up. 'That information is confidential. And I don't see any reason to breach that confidentiality.'

'I'm going to have to insist.'

'You can insist until you're blue in the face; I am not giving it to you.'

'Then we'll just have to take you to the station.'

Elms looked alarmed. 'On what grounds?'

'Murder.'

Elms made to laugh, then seeing that Horton was serious, his face fell. His eyes flitted nervously between Horton and Cantelli. 'You can't mean it? Who am I supposed to have murdered?'

Cantelli answered, 'Arina Sutton, Owen Carlsson and Jonathan Anmore.'

Elms' protruding eyes widened so much that Horton thought they'd pop out of their sockets. 'This is ridiculous,' Elms declared.

Horton said smartly, 'Unless we can confirm with your client where you were on the third of January how do we know it's ridiculous?' Before Elms had a chance to reply, Horton swiftly continued. 'And what were your movements between Saturday the seventeenth of January and Monday the nineteenth of January?'

Elms shuffled. 'I was here.'

'Can anyone confirm that?'

'No.' He shifted nervously.

'And last Thursday between six twenty p.m. and ten twelve p.m.?'

Elms brightened at that. 'I was at the hospital all day Thursday until just after nine o'clock—'

'You're ill?' Horton asked so sharply that Elms jumped.

'No. I'm a volunteer with the League of Friends.'

Horton's mind whirred. St Mary's Hospital was almost the size of a small town. Elms could have been working anywhere within it but what if he'd seen Thea Carlsson there during that Thursday morning and, recognizing her as the woman who had come asking questions, and ones he didn't want to answer, he'd disposed of her? But why should he? the silent voice inside him nagged. It didn't stop him asking though, 'Where is she, Elms? What have you done with Thea Carlsson?' Horton stepped forward.

Alarmed, Elms took a step backwards towards the door. Cantelli quickly slid between Elms and the exit.

'I haven't done anything with her,' Elms cried, crashing into a small table and spilling its contents.

'You saw her in the hospital. She thought you were a friend. But you weren't, were you? Did you tell her you'd take her out of there? Or did you just lie in wait until she came out then offered her a lift?'

'I don't know what you're talking about.' Elms swivelled round, appealing to Cantelli.

But Horton knew there was something Elms was not telling him. Time to frighten him into revealing it. 'Gordon Elms, I'm arresting you on suspicion of the abduction of Thea Carlsson and the murders of—'

'I haven't killed anyone, I swear it.' He spun round to Cantelli and back to Horton. 'I didn't abduct her, she came willingly.'

Horton felt as if time had stopped. His fists clenched. If Elms had harmed her . . . He wanted to grab Elms and shake the hell out of him. He saw Cantelli's warning glance — go easy — but he was prepared to ignore it.

Elms couldn't get the words out quick enough. 'I was leaving the hospital Thursday morning. I'd promised Mrs Westleigh — she's elderly and frail — that I'd fetch her husband — he's blind — and that I'd take him to the hospital to visit her. I saw Miss Carlsson walking across the car park. I was just climbing into the car and I asked how she was. She asked if I'd give her a lift.'

Horton stared at Elms. 'I don't believe you.'

'It's the God's truth. I swear it.'

Cantelli quickly stepped round to the side of Elms. 'Why didn't you tell us this before? You know we've been looking for her.'

'Have you?'

'Don't give me crap,' blazed Horton. 'We came here asking about her.'

'Yes, but I didn't know you were looking for her.'

Horton did a rapid replay of his previous conversation with Elms, looking for a fault in the man's statement and sadly found none.

Cantelli asked the question that was on Horton's lips.

'But you must have heard the appeal on the radio and television.'

'I don't have a television or a radio. The news depresses me, so I decided a long time ago to stop listening to it. Please, you must believe me, I had no idea she was missing. I simply dropped her off.'

'Where?' rapped Horton, making Elms jump.

'Yarmouth.'

Horton opened his mouth to call him a lying little shit when he saw it could be true. Apart from the fact that Thea could have been visiting the place her parents had stayed she could have been intending to leave the island from there. Did she have a boat? Or perhaps someone had collected her by boat. Maybe she'd bought a ferry ticket by cash as a foot passenger, though the ticket office staff hadn't recognized her when one of Birch's offices had visited them to ask. But perhaps she'd managed to disguise herself, or the staff simply weren't observant. Horton wondered where she had got her money from with no credit or debit card and everything in the house destroyed. He also wondered if she could have been planning her escape while in the hospital. If that was so then there was only one reason why she should: Thea Carlsson must have killed her brother. But why go to Yarmouth when Jonathan Anmore's barn was in the opposite direction and several miles away? Then he recalled what Trueman had said — Anmore's last call on the Thursday of his death had been to a Mrs Best in Yarmouth. His shoulders sagged with the realization of what that meant. But still he clung on to the hope that Elms might be their killer.

He said, 'We'll need you to come with us to make a statement.'

'I will, but please tell me why you could even think I could have killed these people.'

'Revenge,' answered Cantelli.

'For what?' His eyes widened, his brow puckered.

Horton answered, 'For not being acknowledged by your father and sister. For being ignored for years. For what your father did to your mother. You discovered who your father was, but he rejected you again at Scanaford House that day you visited there and so too did your sister. So you decided to get even. You deliberately ran over Arina Sutton. But Owen Carlsson saw you so he also had to die. You enlisted the help of Jonathan Anmore, who could have witnessed your little scene at Scanaford House while he was there as gardener, and you got him to dispose of the body and to frame his sister, Thea Carlsson. Offering him money. Then you killed Anmore and abducted and killed Thea Carlsson.'

Elms looked deeply confused. 'I've no idea what you're talking about.' He appealed to Cantelli, whose gaze remained impassive. Elms' protruding eyes swivelled to Horton. 'You're saying that Miss Sutton was my sister and that Sir Christopher was my . . .' His voice faltered. He staggered back, pale and shaking, and sat down heavily.

Horton could see that Elms genuinely hadn't known. And although Elms could be the best actor since James Stewart, in his heart Horton knew that he was no killer, just a man who had finally discovered his past. The lucky bugger.

Elms' breathing became laboured and he raised a hand to his chest. Cantelli threw Horton a worried glance.

'Are you all right, Mr Elms? Do you need a doctor?' Cantelli asked, concerned.

Elms managed to shake his head.

'I'll get some water.'

Horton studied Elms with a feeling of envy. Over the years he'd told himself that he didn't care who his father was, probably much as Elms had done. But Horton knew he did, and a hell of a lot.

Cantelli quickly returned. Elms took the glass and drank from it as though he'd been living in a desert for a week. The colour slowly returned to his face and his breathing eased. The first shock was beginning to wear off. Looking up, he said with a tremor in his voice, 'How do you know this? Is it really true?' All thoughts of attending his paranormal meeting seemed to have vanished.

'It's true,' Horton replied firmly.

'That explains why he looked so shocked when he saw me.' Elms' eyes flicked to the photograph of his mother. 'My mother and I were very much alike; Sir Christopher . . . my father . . . must have seen the resemblance immediately. My God, if only I'd known.' The tears began to run down his face. 'I'm sorry,' he blabbed, trying to dash them away. 'After all these years . . . You must excuse me.'

He staggered up and stumbled from the room. Horton jerked his head at Cantelli to follow him and pulled his mobile from his pocket. He quickly briefed Trueman. Uckfield hadn't returned to the station. Horton asked Trueman to get a list of the boat owners for Yarmouth Marina and get someone to check with them and the harbourmaster for any sightings of Thea. Then he rang off and stared out of the window seeing nothing but the years of his lonely childhood and wondering if there would ever come a day when he'd experience what had just happened to Gordon Elms.

He was glad when a few moments later Elms returned with his composure recovered. Horton handed across the photograph that Dr Nelson had given him. Elms took it with a trembling hand.

'I've never seen her like this. She's so young and beautiful.' He looked up. 'She was a bitter woman. I know she tried to do her best by me, but she would never speak of my father or her past.'

Horton was tempted to ask if she hadn't communicated with him after passing over or under or on, or whatever these people said. Elms read his mind.

'I didn't attempt to get in touch with her on the other side because she was sceptical. We didn't really get on that well. The regrets I have . . . But you don't want to listen to that. She told me my father was in the army and had died on National Service. As I got older, I knew that wasn't the truth, but she would get so angry when I asked her questions so I finally stopped asking. We came here on holiday in 1981. It was her suggestion. I didn't want to come, I was young — twenty-two — I thought the Isle of Wight was the back of beyond, full of retired people waiting to die, but when I arrived it instantly felt like home.'

'Did you go to Scanaford House?' asked Cantelli.

'No. But we went there.' He jerked his head at the painting on the wall that had reminded Horton of *Manderley*.

'They had a summer fête in the grounds. Whitefields, it was called. They pulled it down in 1986 and built new houses on it. Mum was happy then. The happiest I'd seen her in years. I bought it to remind me of my mother, laughing.'

Horton thought the painting didn't exactly inspire jollity, but there was no accounting for taste.

Elms sat forward and eyed Horton steadily. 'I don't know whether my mother was a saint or sinned against, and I doubt Sir Christopher would have told me the truth anyway, even if I had managed to speak to him. But I'm sorry I didn't make my peace with either of them before they went.'

'Maybe you'll be able to in the next world,' Horton said with an element of cynicism. Elms took it as genuine.

'I hope so.' After a moment he added, 'Does this mean . . . ? No, I can't say it.'

'That you inherit,' Horton helped him out, noting that basic human nature had quickly reasserted itself. 'You'll need to talk to the Suttons' solicitor.' Horton wasn't going to give him that information. Let him discover it for himself. Though he knew that Elms was not their killer he still said, 'We need you to make a statement, and confirm where you were at the time of Arina Sutton's death and for the deaths of Owen Carlsson and Jonathan Anmore.'

Elms nodded and rose. In the hall as Elms reached for his coat from a peg, Horton said, 'We'll also need to take your car in for forensic examination and talk to the League of Friends. Who's in charge?'

'Mrs Mackie.'

Horton halted. 'Evelyn Mackie?'

'Yes. We're not always on the same rota but she organizes them.'

And that meant she could also have seen Thea in hospital on the day Gordon Elms gave her a lift. Then why the blazes hadn't she mentioned it?

CHAPTER TWENTY-THREE

'I thought you knew I worked there as a volunteer,' Evelyn Mackie said brightly, as soon as Horton was seated in the stuffy, over-furnished front room. Cantelli had taken Elms to the station.

Horton felt like asking, how? He wasn't psychic. 'Did you see or speak to Thea in the hospital?' he asked, curbing his irritation and impatience.

'Oh, yes. I wasn't working on her ward but I made a point to see how she was. I told her Bengal was fine and that he could stay with me as long as she liked. I even offered her my spare bedroom but she refused. Then the nurse came over to tell her about the phone call.'

Suddenly every nerve in Horton's body tingled. This was news to him. Why hadn't Somerfield discovered this when she questioned the staff after Thea's disappearance, he thought with a flash of anger? He'd bawl her out for this. It had cost them four days of delay, which they could ill afford.

'Do you know who was calling Thea?' Horton prayed she did, but she shook her head.

'No. The nurse asked Thea if she was up to speaking on the telephone. Thea nodded and the nurse wheeled the phone over. I left then.'

Horton cursed silently. He had to speak to the nurse. 'What's the nurse's name?'

'Vanessa Tupper, but she's on holiday. Tenerife. She told me she was flying out late that night, Thursday.'

He cursed silently. But it explained why Somerfield hadn't discovered this. Just their luck. They'd have to try and reach her in Tenerife. He wondered if Thea had left the hospital in response to that call. It seemed likely. Perhaps it was to meet someone who told her they had information about her brother's death. But if that were so then why the hell hadn't she called him? Surely she would have known that she might be in danger after being knocked out and nearly fried alive. And that left him with three possibilities: she trusted the caller implicitly, which meant that it couldn't be the same person she'd admitted to her house; the caller was Thea's accomplice in murder, the person who had nearly killed her, who said they would try again, so she had gone on the run to escape him; or she'd agreed to meet him and then killed him. If the latter, then the caller could have been Jonathan Anmore and Thea had cadged a lift from Gordon Elms to meet him in Yarmouth, returning in Anmore's van to the barn where she'd killed him.

Then another thought struck Horton. There was a possibility she might not have known who the arsonist was because he'd let himself in using Owen's key. No key had been found on his body. And had that person been Bella Westbury or Jonathan Anmore? Horton felt sure it couldn't have been Danesbrook; he'd have smelt him.

Horton asked Mrs Mackie if she'd known that Gordon Elms had given Thea a lift from the hospital that morning. Clearly she hadn't, but she confirmed that Elms had been working that morning, and that he'd told her he was going to pick up Mr Westleigh and bring him to the hospital.

He had one question left to ask. 'Why didn't you tell me Thea stayed with her brother over the New Year?'

'Did she? He never said. My husband and I were in Scotland, visiting his family. We always see the New Year in with them.'

There didn't seem much more he could gain here. Outside, he stared at the boarded-up, blackened remains of Owen Carlsson's house, hoping that it might stimulate his thoughts, but nothing new occurred to him.

At the station, Marsden confirmed what Horton already knew — that there was nothing in Scanaford House to tell them what Sir Christopher Sutton had done during that missing year, or anything to reveal he had been in contact with Elizabeth Elms or her son. In fact, Marsden claimed there was remarkably little correspondence for either Sutton senior or his daughter and, Horton thought, they all knew who had taken and probably destroyed what there had been.

Horton found Uckfield in his temporary office in a foul temper, his frowning face grey with pain.

'Couldn't the chiropractor fix it?' Horton asked.

'The stupid man's made it worse. Quacks, the lot of them. I'll sue him if he's injured me for life.'

'What does he say it is?'

'A severely pulled back muscle. All I did was bend down to tie my shoes.'

A likely story, thought Horton. Uckfield's sexual exploits with Laura Rosewood were more likely the cause. He said, 'Shouldn't you be lying down?'

'And shouldn't you be catching a killer?' Uckfield's phone rang and he reached for it with a grimace of pain.

Horton joined Trueman and Cantelli in the incident room, dashing a glance at his watch. It was almost ten p.m. It had been a long day and he felt exhausted. Tomorrow, Trueman would talk to Vanessa Tupper. Fortunately, he'd managed to get her mobile telephone number from a colleague, but it was too late to call her now, though she could still be awake and partying in Tenerife.

Trueman said, 'The forensic team have found gun oil on some rags in Anmore's barn.'

'But no guns?'

'No.'

Which meant Anmore's gun could be the one that had killed Owen. 'Any evidence of Thea Carlsson having travelled in the van?'

'There are some hairs. The lab is matching them with the DNA swab taken from Thea Carlsson when she was first brought in.' And that would take time. If they matched, it wouldn't prove she had killed him but it would be one more factor to weigh against her.

The door of the incident room burst open and Horton looked up to see DCI Birch eyeing them with a cold gleam of victory in his granite eyes.

'The Chief Constable has just sanctioned me to take over this investigation from Superintendent Uckfield,' Birch said crisply, striding in. 'He can't run this case incapacitated.'

Horton's heart sank. He should have known that Birch would find a way to get even. His eyes flicked to Uckfield. He was still on the phone and Horton didn't need second sight to know who he was talking to or what about. Judging by Uckfield's expression his protest was falling on deaf ears.

Addressing Horton, Birch said, 'If I recall correctly, Inspector, you are officially on holiday. So you can get back to your boat and your holiday. I'll handle this now.'

The door crashed open and Uckfield stood, or rather crouched, on the threshold. He made to straighten up when a roar escaped his lips and his hand grasped his back.

'I'll call an ambulance,' Horton said, reaching for the phone.

'No,' Uckfield whispered urgently, trying to glower at Birch at the same time, but it only made him look like he was severely constipated. 'Cantelli can take me back to the hotel.'

'You need some pain killers and anti-inflammatory drugs.'

'I'll take you to A & E,' Cantelli said.

Clearly Uckfield didn't have the strength to protest. Eyeing Horton as he passed him, he only managed to growl, 'Keep me informed.'

But Birch clearly had no intention of letting him do that. 'Still here, Inspector?' And turning his back, he said to Trueman, 'Sergeant, put out an all-ports alert for Thea Carlsson, wanted in connection for the murders of Owen Carlsson and Jonathan Anmore.'

'You've got no evidence,' Horton declared.

Birch spun round. His eyes narrowed with spite. 'This is evidence,' he declared triumphantly, waving a manila folder at Horton like Neville Chamberlain declaring 'Peace for our time' in 1938. 'It's Thea Carlsson's medical history and it makes exceedingly interesting reading. She was committed to a mental hospital three times between 1994 and 1995 for anorexia, psychological problems, hallucinations, and depression. And she attempted suicide in 2002. Clearly the woman is unbalanced.'

Horton's jaw tightened. 'Her parents were killed, how do you expect her to react?'

'She's unstable. She faked the break-in at her flat before walking out on her job. She killed her brother, most probably with the help of Jonathan Anmore, who she then stabbed with a pitchfork before making off. She was jealous of Owen Carlsson falling in love with Arina Sutton; her notes tell of an unhealthy relationship with her brother—'

'Unhealthy? What do you mean?' snapped Horton, going rigid with fury.

'It's not your case, Inspector.'

Horton stared at Birch's hard, malicious eyes and felt afraid for Thea. Birch would show no mercy with her, if he found her. He would smirk, sneer, ridicule and belittle her. And for someone whose confidence and self-esteem were already at rock bottom it would be the end for Thea.

Horton left the station, boiling with fury. Birch's anger and jealousy must have been bubbling underneath the surface ever since he had found him at the scene of the crime. It had been exacerbated when Uckfield had left Birch at the scene of Anmore's death, and when Uckfield had taunted the DCI with the fact that he'd been negligent over the Carlssons' car accident. But Uckfield had played right into Birch's hands by having an affair with Laura Rosewood and getting a pulled back muscle as a result. He was a fool. Horton cursed them both as he rode his Harley back to the boat.

He wondered if Birch had told the Chief Constable about the affair. If so then Steve Uckfield was really in trouble. But no, Horton guessed that Birch had simply put his evidence to the chief about Thea Carlsson and shown that he'd got further with the investigation than Uckfield. Birch must also have told the chief that he was officially on holiday. That, coupled with the fact that he'd found Thea leaning over the body of her dead brother, and had been at her house when the fire had started, had probably been enough to make the chief think he was involved with Thea and could therefore compromise the investigation — at least that was probably what Birch had told him.

There seemed little more he could do for Thea. But there had to be. Even if she had killed her brother and Anmore he still felt he should do something to help her.

It was late. He was tired. He took a shower and lay down on his bunk. Tomorrow he'd have to return to Portsmouth. Best to put the case and Thea Carlsson out of his mind. He had a divorce to get through and a daughter to save from a boarding school, which only made him think of Thea again.

He went over the facts of the case. Owen had last been seen by Evelyn Mackie crossing the chain ferry on the Saturday before his disappearance. But no one else had seen him either then or since that time. Was Mrs Mackie telling the truth, or had she said that to throw them off the scent? Perhaps Owen had been nowhere near the ferry. Perhaps he'd gone somewhere else that morning. But why would Evelyn Mackie want to lie?

Then she'd been in the hospital the morning Thea had disappeared. Evelyn Mackie knew that Gordon Elms was collecting Mr Westleigh to visit his sick wife, and she also knew about the telephone call. But why would she want Thea out of the way and Owen and Jonathan Anmore dead? No, he was running up a blind alley with that one. The nurse, when Trueman spoke to her, could confirm the telephone call. Horton knew it hadn't been Peter Bohman because he'd called him earlier, despite the late hour.

Then there was Bella Westbury. They knew what she had been doing on the island and why, although they didn't know all the facts of the case. Owen could have discovered this and been killed to silence him, ditto Jonathan Anmore. Bella had disappeared. She certainly wasn't crossed off Horton's list yet.

And Danesbrook? They knew he had been out to get money from Sir Christopher Sutton while he was alive, and that he could have killed Arina Sutton so that he could inherit through his charity. His only alibi for when Arina was killed was Bella Westbury. Yes, Danesbrook was definitely still in the frame.

Thea had visited the library to check the press cuttings of her parents' accident and to get Gordon Elms' address, which led Horton to thoughts of ghosts and Scanaford House. Gordon Elms was Sir Christopher's illegitimate son, but not his sister's killer. And neither was he Owen and Jonathan's murderer. Sir Christopher's affair didn't explain what he was doing during that missing year, only why he'd been sent away. Horton doubted if they'd ever discover where. Was that the key to all these deaths? Then there was the 'girl' Thea had mentioned . . .

However much he considered matters he wasn't going to get the answers. Not now. Not ever. On or around the high tide tomorrow, at one o'clock, he would sail out of the harbour and head for home, returning later to the island to collect the Harley, and be at his desk bright and early Wednesday morning.

Was Birch right? Was Thea their killer? Perhaps she hadn't planned to kill her brother. Maybe she'd just lost control. But the gun made that impossible. That stuff about being told by some psychic power where she would find her brother was rubbish. For a moment he wanted to believe that she might have killed Owen in a trance or some kind of blackout, except that Owen Carlsson had been dead for some days. How long, Dr Clayton had said was difficult to diagnose because of the weather conditions and where the body might have been kept, but there was no disputing that Carlsson had been killed some days earlier and his body taken to the Duver and deposited in the sand. And Anmore had to be her accomplice. Anmore was the person who had searched his boat, and Anmore had tried to kill Thea because Thea said she was going to tell the police what she'd done.

So it was over, he thought wearily. Birch was right. He wished he'd never come here. He told himself that his memory of her would fade over time. But he would never forget her expression as she'd spun round to face him, nor the look she'd given him before she went to the police station. Neither would he forget her stricken expression during the fire and the feel of her slender body in his arms as he'd thrown her from the window.

He closed his eyes, hoping to sleep. Eventually, when it came, he dreamt of her.

CHAPTER TWENTY-FOUR

Tuesday

Charlie Anmore looked tired and incredibly old. He hadn't shaved and he was wearing a red and cream striped pyjama top under a frayed and grubby rust-brown cardigan. Horton felt sorry for troubling him, but one thing had surfaced in his mind after a restless and lustful sleep and that was the fact that Bella Westbury had called on Charlie Anmore. Why? Was it just to offer her condolences as she'd claimed? He doubted it. Not with her history. And once the question had formed, Horton knew he couldn't ignore it. It nagged and gnawed at him as he went for a run early that morning. It niggled at him as he ate his breakfast, and it burrowed and chewed at him as he made his boat ready for sailing. Had Charlie been gardener to Sir Christopher Sutton at Scanaford House in 1990 when Helen might have taken a photograph there? Was that what Bella Westbury had wanted to find out? Had she been trying to establish if Charlie Anmore had made the connection between Helen Carlsson and the secret that Sir Christopher Sutton harboured? Horton had to know before heading for home.

Charlie Anmore's eyes lit up for a moment when Horton introduced himself; obviously he'd been hoping he had brought him news about his son's killer. Horton shook his head and said gently, 'I'm sorry, Mr Anmore.'

'Aye, so am I, son. I doubt you'll get who did it anyway.' He waved Horton into a seat in the small living room which smelt of sorrow and whisky.

Horton felt saddened that Charlie had so little faith in the police. He said nothing about DCI Birch believing he knew who the killer was. He began. 'When Bella Westbury came to visit you what did you talk about?'

'This and that, how the island's changed since Jonathan was a boy, that sort of thing.'

Horton felt disappointed. So it was Jonathan's childhood days in the seventies that Somerfield had meant by 'the old days'.

'She didn't ask you about 1990 when you were the gardener at Scanaford House?' probed Horton.

Charlie looked confused. 'No. I was never a gardener there. That was Jonty's client.'

So that was it. Horton's final attempt at trying to find the reason for Owen's death had fallen flat. He'd listen politely for a while then make his way home. There was nothing more he could do and, though he felt frustrated, he saw that he had no option.

Charlie continued. 'Bella and I talked about all the building that's going on. They call it progress but it doesn't look much like it to me.'

Horton nodded sympathetically while steeling himself for a diatribe on the planning authorities. Then he wondered why Bella Westbury would want to talk about building. But of course, she was on the environmental bandwagon . . . only she wasn't. That was all a sham. Part of her cover. So if she wanted to talk to Charlie about building, he damn well wanted to as well.

'Any building works in particular?' he asked politely.

'Just here and there, though we did chat about the site of the old mental hospital. I said I wouldn't fancy living there myself, too many ghosts.'

And there was that word again — ghosts — only this time coupled with another word that made him think of Danesbrook and his charity, and Sir Christopher Sutton and his specialism: mental hospital . . . neuropsychiatry. Horton felt a quickening in his pulse.

'Ghosts?' he prompted.

'Aye. Poor souls. Beautiful grounds though,' Charlie said wistfully. 'I was a gardener at the old asylum in the 1950s and 1960s.'

Horton was even more interested now. He nodded encouragement at Charlie, who didn't need much; Horton could tell his mind was back in the past in probably happier times.

'Most of the patients were harmless. You'd see some of them in the gardens with a nurse. Others were locked away in the main house. We had our own lodge in the gardens, me and Dickie Jones along with Harry Makepeace; he was the boss. We kept our tools there, and made our tea and ate our dinner. They're both dead now.'

'And you chatted about this to Bella?'

'Oh, yes. She was very interested. Probably only being polite.'

I doubt it, thought Horton. And he knew why Bella had been so interested. Calmly, though his pulse raced with excitement, he said, 'Did you know any of the doctors there?'

Charlie eyed him as if he were mad. 'Gawd, no! They wouldn't talk to the likes of us or us to them. Things were very different in those days, not like now where everyone says we're all on one level, but we aren't. Maybe it was different for Jonty.' A cloud crossed his face. 'I left Whitefields in 1969, worked for the council as a gardener for fifteen years and then started my own little business in 1984 before Jonty took it over.'

But Horton had stopped listening after Charlie had said 'Whitefields'. A dark, intimidating painting of a big house flashed before his eyes and Gordon Elms' words sprang to mind. *They had a summer fête in the grounds. Whitefields it was called. They pulled it down in 1986 and built new houses on it.* And

Gordon Elms and his mother had visited there in 1981, the year after Sir Christopher's wife had died. Gordon had bought the painting because it reminded him of his mother being happy. And Horton would stake his last penny that Sir Christopher Sutton had worked at Whitefields at some stage in his career as a neuropsychiatric consultant. He'd need to check with Trueman, but Horton was convinced it hadn't shown up on Sutton's employment records. Of course, Sutton could have spent a short spell there, which didn't warrant recording, but Horton didn't think so. His money was on 1959.

'Was there ever any hint of anything not quite right happening at Whitefields?'

'Like what?'

Horton had no idea, but something the Intelligence Service didn't want exposed. He shrugged.

Charlie said, 'I wouldn't know if there was. I just worked in the gardens. Funny you should mention that though because Bella asked me if Jonty and I had ever heard rumours about the place. I said only that it was supposed to have been haunted.'

That clinched it for Horton. Sutton had been there all right, and Horton wouldn't mind betting doing something with those poor inmates that the government and medical council desperately wanted to keep quiet, such as experimenting with new and potentially dangerous drugs. If he recalled correctly, and from what Trueman had said earlier, this was at the height of the Cold War, when anything was possible. And, if he was right, Bella and her paymasters, whoever they were, would be very eager to keep any such confession from Sutton's dying lips, and from the public gaze. Eager enough to kill for? He reckoned so.

Charlie said, 'It was pulled down in 1991 and Cawley's began building all those houses on the land a year later—'

'Hold on,' Horton said. 'I thought the houses had been built on it in 1986.' Surely that was what Gordon Elms had said.

But Charlie was shaking his head. 'No. It was closed in 1986 but they didn't get round to pulling it down until 1991, and building on it a year later. The big house was grand, but it wasn't listed. There were a lot of people who wanted to save it, but that didn't count for much in the end. Who would want to live in a flat converted from an insane asylum? Can't say I blame them, all those ghosts.'

Which brought Horton right back to Helen Carlsson. Could Helen have visited Whitefields because of the stories about ghosts? It was possible given the fact that Bohman had told him she had 'the gift'.

Horton talked to Charlie a little longer out of politeness, but was impatient to get away. When he did, ten minutes later, he immediately called Cantelli.

'Can you talk?'

'I'm in the canteen.'

'How's Uckfield?' Horton asked.

'Fuming and supposedly resting in his hotel bedroom where I left him last night. He's been on the telephone to Trueman half a dozen times this morning and me about the same.'

'What's Birch doing?'

'Still trying to find a past connection between Thea and Jonathan Anmore. He's matching their employment and medical histories, looking for a link. Nothing so far but he's not that concerned as he claims they must have met up when Thea was over here at New Year. Trueman spoke to the nurse, Vanessa Tupper, in Tenerife this morning. It's not good news, Andy. The call Thea received in the hospital was from Jonathan Anmore.' Horton swore softly.

'It looks as though she could have gone to meet him in Yarmouth. Birch thinks she returned with him to his barn where she killed him, and then made off on foot. She doesn't drive, remember.'

'Convenient then that Gordon Elms happened to be driving to Yarmouth,' Horton said cynically.

'Birch reckons she must have overheard Elms saying he was collecting Mr Westleigh from Yarmouth and that was why she said she'd meet Anmore there.'

'He's got an answer for everything,' Horton quipped.

'There's something else, Andy.'

Horton braced himself for more bad news. His heart felt like lead.

'DCI Birch is so certain Thea killed her brother and Anmore that we're not looking for anyone else. He's making a press statement later this morning. I'm taking Uckfield home later this afternoon, against his will, may I add, along with Somerfield and Trueman. Chief's orders. Marsden's staying behind to help Birch. Sorry, Andy. The evidence is beginning to look overwhelming.'

It was and Horton didn't like it one bit. Birch might be winding down the case but Horton still had a few hours left to follow up the lead Charlie Anmore had given him. And he was damn well going to.

'There's something I need you to do for me, Barney, and without Birch shoving his oar in.' Horton quickly told him about his interview with Charlie Anmore. 'Check Sir Christopher's employment record, see if you can find any note of him ever having worked at Whitefields. Call Dr Nelson and ask him about the place. Did Sutton ever mention it? If Nelson's involved with Bella, and whoever she's working for, then you might have the funny buggers come down on you after speaking to him. Ask Dr Clayton if she can find out anything through her contacts. I'm heading for the library.' It would be quicker than returning to his boat and using his laptop, and he would also have access to other information like press cuttings or reference books that might give him some idea what all this meant.

In Newport library, Horton logged on to the computer and trawled the Internet for references to Whitefields. Soon he was reading how the mental hospital had been built on farm land during the 1890s as the Isle of Wight's first County

Asylum and officially opened on 13 July 1896 with the first patients transferred from the mainland a few days later. By the 1980s the hospital was outdated and ill-equipped for modern needs so it was gradually shut down until, as Gordon Elms had said, it had closed in 1986. After that it had lain derelict until Cawley Developments had purchased the land from the National Health Service Trust in 1990.

Horton read about the ghosts that were supposed to have haunted the hospital, which made him wonder why Elms had never mentioned them. And then he came across some other more unusual websites where people had posted their photographs of derelict buildings, including Whitefields before it had been demolished. As he viewed the sad pictures of the deserted ablutions rooms, broken-back doors hanging off their hinges, rotting balustrades and iron beds in tiny cells, he shivered. Words flitted through his mind. Ghosts . . . Sutton . . . Whitefields . . . photographs . . .

He sat back and stared at the screen. Sutton would have been long gone from Whitefields by 1990 when Helen might have shown up there to take her photographs, *if* he had worked there in the first place. Had Helen Carlsson stumbled on some old documentary evidence, *if* she'd been photographing the place? Given her interest in ghosts and photography maybe she had.

Judging by the pictures on the Internet it had certainly been a splendid building. But why would someone have killed her and her husband because of that? And who was this girl Thea had mentioned? Had Helen Carlsson met a girl in the derelict building who had told her about Sutton's work there? But no, the girl wouldn't have been a girl in 1990 if she'd known Sutton; she'd have been well into her sixties, unless she was a ghost . . . He smiled at the stupidity of that theory. This seemed to be getting him nowhere. He needed air and space. He needed to think. He stepped outside. His phone rang. He hoped it was Cantelli but it was Uckfield.

'Where the hell are you?' But before Horton had a chance to answer, Uckfield went on, 'What's Birch doing to cock up my case?'

'No idea. I'm not working on it anymore.'

Uckfield scoffed. 'That's never stopped you before.'

Horton told him what he'd discussed with Cantelli and his conversation with Charlie Anmore. He also told him his theory that Helen Carlsson might have been photographing the derelict Whitefields.

'And where does that get us?' Uckfield growled.

Precisely, thought Horton. But it had to mean something. He heaved a sigh of relief as Uckfield rang off and tried to get back to his thoughts about Helen and her photographs. What was it that had cost her her life and the lives of the others?

Whichever way he looked at it he couldn't come up with a reason. There was nothing more he could do except return to the boat. It was too late now to ride the Harley back to Portsmouth via the ferry and then return to sail the boat across. He wondered if he would ever see Thea Carlsson again.

The wind was rising with every passing minute, howling through the masts, building itself up for storm force six, or seven by the sound of it. Maybe even stronger, which meant the Met Office had been wrong and the front they had predicted had rolled in quicker than anticipated. It also meant that if he didn't start soon, he'd never get the boat back to the mainland. Even in the shelter of the harbour the waves, flecked with white horses, were bashing against the sea wall, the spray dancing in the air before splashing over the top.

There was still no word from Cantelli. He should head for home before it was too late, but he made no attempt to do so. Horton told himself not to be so stupid — he was due back in Portsmouth CID tomorrow — but he found himself locking up the boat and striking out across the abandoned golf course. The wind was tossing the grass and bending the branches of the shrubs and trees landwards so that they looked like thin old men with lumbago.

He stopped at the place where he had found Thea huddled over the body of her brother and tried to recall every detail. How did Owen's body get here? Anmore's van, of course. Together they'd hauled Owen out of the van and dumped it here. But no, recalling her expression and her shivering body when he'd found her, he refused to believe she could have done that.

He walked on up to the holiday centre, where Anmore with binoculars must have been viewing the scene. Anmore must have seen him talking to Thea and watched him go to his boat which he had then searched. This was futile. Time to forget Thea Carlsson, forget this case and go home. His phone rang. It was Cantelli.

'Well?' he asked sharply, hoping.

'There's no record of Sutton having worked at Whitefields in 1959. I called the editor of the local rag, Sonia Belman, and asked her what she knew about Whitefields. She said there was quite a furore over demolishing the old house. Jack Cawley, the developer, was set on pulling it down. That way, he said, he could build more houses. And he got his wish. The NHS Trust was glad to get shot of it. The land was contaminated, some kind of chemical was found underground in places.'

'Chemical? What chemical?' Horton had read nothing on the Internet about that.

'I don't know.'

'Find out who handled the sale on behalf of the Trust.'

'Already have. It was a man called Noel Halliwell. And before you ask, you can't talk to him unless you enlist the help of Gordon Elms. He died not long after, in 1993. Suicide.'

'Why did he kill himself?'

'No idea. Sonia says that no note was found with the body. He hanged himself.'

Horton frowned in irritation. 'What about the developer, Jack Cawley?'

'He's also dead.'

So that was it. Another dead end, unless . . . 'Hold on — Jack?'

'Yes. It's a fairly common name.'

It was but Horton's mind quickly trawled through a previous conversation '*I ran a property development company, with my late husband, Jack, for fifteen years.*'

Had this Jack Cawley been Laura Rosewood's husband? Did she know anything about the land being contaminated? If so, then why should it matter? How could it have any connection with Sir Christopher Sutton? And how could it be connected to Helen Carlsson's death? Horton watched the seagulls dive over the area where Owen Carlsson had been found. He didn't know but he needed to find out.

CHAPTER TWENTY-FIVE

Laura Rosewood wasn't at home. Instead, he found the silent Julie, her hired help. This time she spoke.

'Laura's on her way to Brussels. You've only just missed her. Can I help?'

Horton doubted it. Annoyed at missing Laura, and frustrated that he couldn't get the answers to the questions bugging him, he stepped inside the hall at Julie's invitation, and thought, what the hell, he might as well ask. 'Was Jack Cawley Ms Rosewood's husband?'

'Yes.'

'Why doesn't she use her married name?'

'I don't know. You'd have to ask her that. Not every businesswoman does.'

He guessed not.

'Why do you want to know?' she asked, eyeing him curiously and a little suspiciously.

Horton didn't see any harm in telling her. 'I'm interested in the development of Whitefields, the old mental hospital.'

'That was a long time ago. Is it important?'

'It could be.'

'And something to do with these murders?'

'Possibly.'

'Then you might catch Laura at the cottage.'

Horton didn't bother to hide his surprise. Uckfield hadn't mentioned any cottage, but then why should he? Maybe he didn't know about it.

'She's got a house near Northwood Abbey on the north coast,' Julie explained in response to Horton's baffled expression. 'It's called *Tideways*. It's not far from the old church near Binstead Hard. Laura said she was calling in there before catching the ferry to Portsmouth. Do you want me to phone and see if she's there?'

'No,' Horton said quickly. 'I'll take a chance on finding her in.' If she was, then fine, if not, then it would be time to go home and ask Marsden to follow up the lead he had uncovered once he was back in Portsmouth. He knew DCI Birch would prevent that, however, especially when Horton couldn't say exactly what that lead was. Helen *might* have gone to Whitefields in 1990, she *might* have taken photographs, she *might* have been killed because of it. But why? He still had no idea.

Horton found *Tideways* without too much difficulty. It was at the end of a quiet, narrow lane that led towards the sea. Turning the Harley into a twisting driveway bordered by naked trees, he pulled up outside a substantial house built in grey Isle of Wight stone. It looked to be about a hundred years old, was solid, with a square stone porch and three storeys high. He guessed that the low-slung sports car with a suitcase on the back seat belonged to Laura. Thank God he had caught her.

'I have a boat and plane to catch,' she said, letting him in and dashing a glance at her watch. He might be pleased to find her in, but clearly she wasn't too thrilled to see him. Neither was she surprised. Despite asking Julie not to alert her boss, she had obviously done so. Perhaps he should be grateful otherwise he might have missed her.

'I won't keep you a moment, Ms Rosewood. I just need some information.'

'Is it about the murder? Only Steve — Superintendent Uckfield — has told me that Thea Carlsson killed her brother and Jonathan Anmore. I feel sorry for her. She's obviously unbalanced.'

As she spoke, he followed her through to a lounge with wide patio doors that gave onto a broad sweep of grass and beyond it a substantial log cabin facing a pontoon and a grey turbulent Solent.

He wondered at Uckfield's change of heart when not long ago he was bellowing down the telephone wanting to know what was going on. But then Birch must have told Uckfield that Anmore had called Thea in the hospital. And that had clinched it.

'Whitefields,' he said. 'I understand your husband, Jack Cawley, developed it.'

'He did,' she answered, surprised. 'Why the interest?'

'What can you tell me about the contaminated land?'

She frowned, clearly puzzled by his line of questioning. 'Jack had it cleaned before developing it, but what has this to do with Thea Carlsson?'

He didn't know. Probably nothing but, reluctant to give up on it, he asked, 'What was the land contaminated with?'

'I've no idea.' She was eyeing him as though he was slightly mad. After a moment she gave a small sigh and her expression softened. 'You don't believe Thea is the killer, do you?'

'No.'

She looked at him sadly. 'Why?'

He wasn't going to tell her that. Instead, he said, 'Did Jack ever talk to you about Helen or Lars Carlsson?'

'No.'

'Did Owen mention them to you?'

'No.'

But Horton knew immediately that was a lie. And she saw that he knew it.

She held his gaze. He could see she was deciding on a course of action. He hoped it was to tell him something that would help him prove Thea was not a killer, but he wasn't holding his breath.

After a moment she said, 'I'm sorry, that wasn't the truth.' She crossed to the glass doors and stared out for a moment before turning back with a troubled expression. 'I don't think you're going to like what I'm going to tell you, Inspector. It concerns Thea.'

'Go on,' he said stiffly, steeling himself for the worse.

'Owen did talk about his parents. He told me how their sudden death had affected his sister — mentally. He said he was very concerned about Thea living alone and so far away. He wanted to bring her to the island, to live with him and Arina. Arina told me that she and Owen were getting married and that's why Owen visited his sister alone over Christmas to break the news to her. He wasn't sure how she would take it.'

'And how did she take it?' Horton stiffened.

'Badly. You see, she was extremely jealous of Owen showing affection to anyone else. You can understand it with her parents' tragic death.'

And this was what Birch had meant by his comment about Thea's 'unhealthy' relationship with her brother. Somewhere in her medical notes there must have been a note on it. And now it seemed even more likely that Thea had arranged for Anmore to kill Arina when she had been here over the New Year.

'Why didn't you tell us this before?' Horton said bluntly, watching her reaction.

'I should have done. I know. But I genuinely thought Owen's death was concerned with the project. I only told Superintendent Uckfield a short time ago.'

And that was why Uckfield had lost interest in the case. As far as he was concerned it was solved. Horton fought desperately to fight off his anger and disappointment.

She said, 'How could I believe Thea could have anything to do with killing her own flesh and blood? I didn't think she was capable of such a terrible thing until . . .'

'What?' he asked sharply. With each passing word from Laura Rosewood he felt more and more despondent.

'She came here and told me.'

'When?' he cried, surprised.

'About an hour ago. Thea called me and asked to meet me.'

'She's here now?' he asked, straining for any sound of her but hearing only the wind and rain and the pounding of the blood in his ears.

Laura shook her head and appeared worried. 'No. When Julie phoned to say you were on your way she left. I don't know where she went.'

Horton cursed Julie vehemently and silently. He stared beyond Laura to the summer house.

'I thought that I might be able to get Thea some professional help,' Laura added. 'But I knew that if I called the police or told Steve she was here, he'd tell Birch and I've met him once or twice and don't much care for him. It would mean hanging on for someone to arrive and then making my statement. So I decided I'd leave for Brussels and call Reg, the Chief Constable, when I got there and tell him everything. Only now you've shown up, I can tell you. I know you'll see that Thea is treated properly, and besides,' she shrugged, 'I've missed my flight.'

Horton felt relieved she hadn't called Uckfield or Birch. 'Have you any idea where she might have gone?'

'I doubt it would be far.'

'Like your summer house?' he said, interpreting her earlier nervous glances towards it.

There was a frightened pause. Then, resigned, she said, 'I'll take you down there.'

She brushed past him into the hall and through to a large gleaming modern kitchen at the rear of the house. Taking an ankle-length raincoat from the hook in an adjacent utility room she shrugged it on and slipped her feet into Wellingtons. Then ramming a waterproof hat on her blonde hair, she opened the door and the wind rushed in.

Horton had abandoned all thoughts of getting his boat back to the mainland ages ago. The tall pampas was bucking in the gale and he could hear the booming of the waves as they crashed and burst on the shore, filling the air with the taste of salt. As he accompanied her down the long stretch of grass, the rain bashing into his face, his motorcycle boots squelching in the water-logged grass, his brain was whirling with the events she'd just described to him, trying to fit it with everything he'd seen and heard over the last week. He tried to calm himself. Soon he would see Thea. And soon he'd be able to help her.

Laura Rosewood pushed open the door and flicked on the electric light. They were standing in a sturdy single-storey, timber-clad building. Glazed doors with windows either side of it opened onto a decking area and a jetty at the end of which Horton could just about see a RIB, tossing wildly in the waves and wind. There was no sign of Thea inside or out. Damn. He needed to find her. He reached for his mobile but Laura prevented him.

'There's something you should know before you call for help.' She sat down and gestured Horton into a seat. When she saw he was reluctant to take it, she said, 'Thea couldn't have got far in this weather. And it's probably best you hear it all now before DCI Birch catches up with her.'

Reluctantly he perched on the edge of the wicker chair opposite.

She wrenched off her hat and with an anxious expression said, 'Owen confided something in me and Thea's just told me the rest. It's not a very happy story.'

'Go on,' he prompted when she stalled.

Taking a deep breath she said, 'Owen killed his parents. And Thea found out.'

It was just as he and Cantelli had worked out! He had hoped it wasn't true. He nodded at her to continue.

'Thea discovered that when Owen was a student at Southampton University, he got a girl into trouble.'

This must have been the 'girl' that Thea had asked Bohman about.

Laura said, 'But it wasn't a simple case of pregnancy; the girl claimed that Owen had raped her. And before you ask, it never got as far as the police because Owen asked his parents to help him out. He wanted money to pay the girl off, a tart I believe, but one who had her head screwed on and very believable. You probably know the type, Inspector.'

Oh, he did. Lucy Richardson, who had accused him of rape, had been believed in all quarters, even by Catherine.

'Owen's parents refused to pay up though,' Laura continued. 'They said they would see her in court first. And Owen knew that it would ruin his life and his career.'

'And Owen confided this to you?'

She fiddled with her hat. 'Only about getting the girl pregnant. He said she had died in a road accident shortly after their affair but Thea told me the real story.' She looked up defiantly. 'Owen and I had a brief affair before he met Arina. That's why Thea came to me. She knew Owen and I had been close, and there was no one else she could turn to.'

She could have come to me. But then he was a policeman. He felt bitterly disappointed.

Laura continued. 'Thea told me that her brother had confessed to her that he couldn't let this girl destroy his life so he killed her in a hit-and-run accident. Yes, the same way that Arina died.'

'But Owen didn't kill Arina.'

'No, Jonathan Anmore did.'

Horton could see now the pattern of events.

Laura continued. 'I didn't know this of course until Thea told me an hour ago. You see, Owen thought Arina had discovered his secret, the one he'd do anything to protect. And though he loved her, he couldn't let her live knowing what he'd done — and besides, he knew she would no longer love him when she discovered the truth. He couldn't face that kind of rejection. Jonathan told Thea this at Arina's funeral—'

'Thea wasn't there,' Horton said quickly.

'She was, but not in the crowd of mourners. She kept her distance. I saw Jonathan cross to talk to her after the committal. I doubt he told her everything, probably because he didn't know it, but he must have said enough for Thea to become curious and concerned.'

Which was why, thought Horton, Thea had gone searching for answers in the library. It all added up.

He said, 'Did you get close to Steve Uckfield because you wanted to know how the investigation was progressing?'

'I was worried my affair with Owen would come out. I didn't want the newspapers to get hold of it so I called Reg and told him that Owen's death might have something to do with the environmental project he was working on. Well, it was a possibility,' she added defensively. 'Reg said Steve Uckfield, his son-in-law, would be in charge, and I guessed he'd keep me informed.'

He eyed her keenly. There were still some questions he needed answers to before calling Uckfield. He couldn't bring himself to tell DCI Birch about Thea.

'Why did Owen kill his parents?'

Laura rose and crossed to the patio doors. Ramming her hands in her pockets she turned back to face him. 'I only have Thea's version of it but this is what she says Owen told her. His father heard about the girl's hit-and-run accident and accused Owen of killing her. They were highly principled people and he said he was handing Owen over to the police, just what Owen didn't want. Owen smashed up their house and fixed their car to make it look as though they'd had an accident. I'm not sure how he did it and neither is Thea. Maybe he didn't really mean to kill them, just to warn them, but . . .' She shuddered and drew her coat tighter around her.

Horton thought the summer house felt a few degrees colder. The wind howled around them, searching for gaps to squeeze through and chill them further. He recalled that cheerful voice he'd heard on the answer machine message, and found it hard to believe Owen Carlsson had ruthlessly killed a girl and his parents, though sadly as a police officer he knew those things happened.

Laura continued. 'Owen then had the girl off his back and his parents' money to help him through university. But poor little Thea was scarred for life by her parents' tragic death. After Jonathan had told Thea that Owen had paid him to kill Arina, Thea confronted her brother who, distraught over Arina's death — even though he'd caused it — and guilt-ridden, told Thea everything, including how he'd killed their parents. Thea flipped, understandably so after the traumatic childhood she'd had. Filled with anger and hatred, she arranged for Jonathan to kill her brother, promising him half her inheritance. She said that Jonathan jumped at the chance.'

Horton knew the gardener had had financial difficulties.

'Then she killed Jonathan.' Laura shook her head sadly. 'Poor Thea is as mixed up as her brother clearly was. It's a mess and a tragedy.'

'What about her apartment? It was ransacked.'

'She did that to throw the scent off her.'

Horton rose and crossed to the window. Where was Thea now? Where had she been these last six days before showing up here? Had she returned there? Did Laura Rosewood know?

He turned back, his foot crunching on something as he did. Flicking his eyes down to see what it was, he heard Laura say, 'I thought I heard a noise outside. Thea must be trying to get away on the RIB. She's mad. She'll drown.'

She pushed past him, wrenching open the door, but Horton didn't follow.

'Why did Owen visit Dr Nelson?' he asked.

'Who? I don't know. Did he? I'm sure Thea is there.' And before Horton could stop her, she was hurrying down the jetty.

Horton quickly moved after her. The sea was crashing onto the shore, spraying them both as it splashed over the jetty. He could hear it sucking up the stones underneath them as it retreated. The light from the summer house showed the waves breaking over the RIB. He could see no sign of Thea.

'Thea's not here,' he shouted above the roar of the sea and wind. 'She's never been here. Everything you said was a lie. It was convincing, Laura, I'll give you that. And I nearly fell for it. It will probably be enough to convince DCI Birch and maybe others, but not me.'

She halted and turned. He could see her wary expression.

'You killed Owen Carlsson,' he said. 'You shot him through the summer house window. There's glass on the floor, probably left from when you or Jonathan Anmore mended it. I take it Anmore helped you move the body. I can't see you managing that yourself. How did you get Owen to the Duver, Laura? Was it in Anmore's van or did you use your RIB?'

She stared at him amazed and bewildered but he knew it was an act. With the rain and sea lashing at them he held her gaze. Then her expression cleared. A cold gleam came into her eyes as her mouth tightened and her body stiffened. Evenly she said, 'You're right, of course, which means I'll have to kill you.' And before he could blink, he found himself staring at a revolver aimed steadily and directly at his chest.

CHAPTER TWENTY-SIX

It was a different make to the one which had killed Owen Carlsson, but it was no less deadly, and Laura Rosewood knew how to handle it. He considered rushing her before discarding the idea; he'd only end up with a bullet in his chest. She had killed three people; she wouldn't hesitate to kill him. She had tried to throw him off the scent with her lies about Owen Carlsson. For a while he had believed her, but even before he'd seen the fragment of glass certain things had troubled him. One of them was his refusal to believe Thea had killed her brother.

Horton stared at Laura Rosewood's cool and determined expression and said, 'Helen Carlsson took photographs of you, Cawley and Noel Halliwell at Whitefields, didn't she?'

Laura said nothing. It didn't matter. He knew most of it anyway.

'The land wasn't contaminated,' he shouted above the crashing waves. 'You, Cawley, and Noel Halliwell concocted that tale between you in order to profit by the sale. What was it you told me and Steve at our first meeting? That you'd been a surveyor. You surveyed Whitefields and said it was contaminated. Did Noel Halliwell, the planning director of the NHS, kill himself because he couldn't live with the guilt of what he'd done?'

'I never promised him undying love.'

Horton saw at once how she must have seduced and sexually blackmailed Halliwell into defrauding the NHS. He wouldn't mind betting the whole scheme had been Laura's idea.

Tautly he said, 'Which of you killed Helen and Lars Carlsson?'

'Jack,' she replied coolly.

His jaw tightened in anger. 'And was that because you asked him to?'

'No. I had no idea what he'd done.'

Horton didn't believe her. She was a heartless, scheming bitch.

She said, 'Jack said he'd get the film and scare her into keeping her mouth shut. Then I heard they were dead.'

'Oh, yeah,' Horton said sarcastically. Laura Rosewood was poisonous.

She said, 'Whitefields was a prime site. There was a lot of money at stake. Noel Halliwell steered other potential buyers away from purchasing it by telling them it was contaminated and showed them my report. Phoney, of course. They thought it would cost thousands of pounds to clean up before any kind of building work could commence and no one wanted to take that on. Jack bought the land for a song, and Halliwell and I got a generous pay off. I eventually married Jack, and inherited his estate when he died of a heart attack two years later.'

Horton wondered if Jack Cawley's death had been down to natural causes after all. This explained a great deal, but there were still elements that were puzzling him.

'Owen found out, so you killed him?'

'Yes.'

And there it was: a confession, and one she thought no one would ever hear. Perhaps they wouldn't. Not if she killed him, and she had every intention of doing so. He didn't doubt that.

'How are you going to explain my death?' He kept his gaze on her but at the same time his mind was working overtime to find a way out.

'I won't have to. The tide is on the turn; it will take your body miles away from here. There will be nothing to connect your death with me.'

Clever. Which was why she had wanted him out here on the jetty. And what about Julie, the hired help, was she in on this too? Was that why she had called Laura and told her he was on his way and that he'd been asking questions about Cawley and Whitefields, to give Laura time to concoct or put the finishing touches to a story she'd already worked out?

He said, 'Steve Uckfield will never believe that.'

'Why not? He doesn't know you're here. You could have slipped and fallen anywhere along a coastal path, or even killed yourself, depressed over your divorce and not being allowed access to your daughter.'

Horton stiffened. What the hell gave Uckfield the right to talk about his private life? He imagined them in bed and Laura teasing out all kind of personal information from Uckfield. God, the man had been an idiot.

With barely concealed anger, he snarled, 'What about the bullet in me?'

She lifted one shoulder in a shrug. 'The sea life will have seen to that. If, of course, your body is ever found.'

She was ruthless as well as clever. Cantelli knew where he was. But wait — no, he didn't. Horton, as usual, had dashed off without saying where he was going. The gun came up. He had to think of a way to stall her. Not without desperation he said, 'How did Owen find out about Whitefields?'

'Arina told him. I don't know how she knew but I overhead her talking to Owen at her father's funeral. She said she'd discovered something awful that had happened at Whitefields and that if it ever came out, there would be major political repercussions.'

Thoughts and ideas flashed through Horton's mind. Amongst them was Bella Westbury. But he had no time to consider that now. Survival was his priority.

Laura Rosewood was saying, 'I tried to get more from Arina, but she was very distant with me. She knew. She told me that she and Owen were dining at the Seaview Hotel on Saturday night so I went there and waited. I parked the car not far from the hotel. I saw Arina leave. I drove into her.'

'Whose car did you use, Laura? It wasn't yours.'

'I borrowed Julie's. I told her mine wouldn't start and that I had a dinner engagement the other side of the island, which I did have only I left there early on account of a headache. Julie offered me her car for the evening, as I guessed she would. Julie worships me. She's very loyal.'

Yes, thought Horton, loyal enough to lie for her employer about the times she was actually in London.

'Now, I hate to do this, Andy, because I quite fancy you, but—'

'Before you shoot me,' he said quickly, 'at least tell me how you killed Owen.'

She seemed to consider this for a moment. Horton held his breath, while uttering a silent prayer for a giant wave to swamp the jetty and sweep her over the side. The swell was growing, along with the wind, but was it enough? He doubted it, though the thought had given him an idea. Maybe there was a way out of this.

She shrugged as if to say a few more minutes wouldn't make much difference. 'When Terry Knowles put Owen forward for the project I agreed. Carlsson is not a common name. I wondered if he was a relation of Helen and Lars Carlsson. When he mentioned that his parents had once holidayed on the Isle of Wight and had died here, I knew he was Helen's son. I needed to find out if he, or his sister, had ever suspected that his parents' death had been anything other than a tragic accident, hence the affair, and to ensure that he hadn't come here to investigate it. He hadn't.'

Horton was looking at a callous woman. Uckfield had been playing with fire, and might still be when all this came out, if he lived to tell the tale. And he had to for Thea's sake, even though he knew Laura must have killed her. But the gun was steady, and she showed no signs of weakening.

'After Arina's death I arranged to meet Owen in the summer house that Saturday, hinting that I might have some information about Whitefields but that we had to keep our meeting a secret. He agreed eagerly. I knew he'd come by the coastal path and then climb up onto the decking because I'd told him it would be better that way. I waited until he was almost in front of the window; he turned to look along the shore and I shot him through the glass in the left temple. I'm an expert shot. My father was in the services and we used to belong to a gun club when we lived in Europe. I've always had guns and they're so easy to pick up on the continent. This was Jonathan's. I took it from the barn. I guess he picked it up on one of his sailing trips to France. I dragged Owen inside the summer house and left him there, covered with a blanket, of course.'

As if that made any difference, thought Horton with disgust and anger.

She said, 'I thought I'd be able to take him out to sea and dump his body overboard. My RIB was on the pontoon. But the weather was atrocious and I had an early-morning meeting to attend in London on Monday, which meant travelling on Sunday evening, and then a two-day conference, so I wouldn't be back until late Thursday evening. But when I heard that the weather forecast for early Wednesday morning was calm, I came back late Tuesday evening by train and ferry, using cash to buy my ticket. Jonathan picked me up.'

Leaving no trace of her movements.

'I knew Jonathan fancied me. I told him here was his chance to do me a favour, and in return I'd do him one.'

'Like shoving a pitchfork in his back.'

She ignored the remark. 'Jonathan and I came here very early Wednesday morning. The stink was appalling and the body disgusting.' She wrinkled her nose as she recalled it but Horton noticed her hand was still steady. 'I told Jonathan that I had tried to comfort Owen over Arina's death only he mistook my intentions and tried to rape me. I said I'd shot him in self-defence, but this could never come out. I'm a public figure and the media would destroy my reputation and career. Jonathan didn't believe me, because he'd overheard Arina talking to Owen in the garden. So I promised to pay off all his debts and give him more money if he helped me. He jumped at the chance. I must say it took some stomach to haul Owen into the boat.'

And if she could do that then Horton didn't think she'd have any compunction about killing him.

'We put one of Jonathan's collapsible wheelbarrows in the boat and early Wednesday morning, when it was still dark, we went into Bembridge on the high tide. At this time of year, as you know, there isn't a soul about. Both Jonathan and I know the harbour like the back of our hands. We put Owen in the wheelbarrow and placed him in the bunker on the Duver.'

'Why?' Horton asked, baffled. 'Surely it would have been easier to have thrown his body over the side of the boat and leave him to be washed up later, if at all.' Like she was planning for him.

She scowled as if annoyed at the memory. 'It would but there was Thea. Owen might have confided in her. She might make a nuisance of herself and besides I had to have someone to take the blame for Jonathan's death.'

Horton stiffened. Dr Clayton's words flashed through his mind. A clever killing by a clever killer. Also a ruthless one by an evil woman.

Laura was saying, 'Jonathan telephoned Thea and left an anonymous message telling her where to look for her brother's body.'

So Thea wasn't psychic. Why had she lied? If only she'd told him about the call at the beginning he might have saved her life, and caught Owen's killer sooner.

He said, 'Then Anmore kept watch from a safe distance, saw me arrive and wondered who the devil I was when I seemed so friendly with the police.'

'Yes.'

She shifted slightly as though her arm was beginning to ache. The tide was going out. And he'd be going with it if he didn't do something — and soon. Quickly he scanned the horizon for any sign of a human being or a weapon but no sane person was out in this weather, and it was an isolated spot. There was only the abbey to his left and he didn't think the monks would be walking along the shore in the wind, rain and dark.

She said, 'Jonathan watched you go to your boat, and then searched it after you left. He didn't discover you were a policeman though, and I didn't know that either until you showed up with Steve.'

'Which of you knocked Thea out and then tried to set light to us?'

'Jonathan, of course. I had to make sure that Owen hadn't left anything incriminating behind, which could point to me.'

He tensed with fury. 'And you thought he'd kill Thea too.' The time was almost here. Soon he would have to make his move or it would be too late.

She frowned, annoyed. 'I didn't know Thea had been released. Jonathan let himself in with Owen's key, and knocked Thea out before she had a chance to see him. Then you showed up so he decided to destroy any evidence and hope it would look as though Thea, unbalanced, had attacked you and then set light to the house. It's time to go, Andy.'

The gun came up. The sea was crashing onto the shore beneath him. There was no way out. He held his breath. He wouldn't hear the trigger being pulled above the sound of the wind and waves. It would be quick and relatively painless. He steeled himself. His heightened senses screamed at him. He had microseconds of life left. There was only one thing he could do. And he did it.

CHAPTER TWENTY-SEVEN

A sharp hot pain smashed into his arm before the freezing cold water sucked the breath from his body. It wasn't deep, but there was enough water to pull him under. He was still alive. For how much longer though was another matter. When he resurfaced, as he must, she would be there, standing on the jetty waiting for him. Suddenly, the water close by hissed and spat. She was firing at him.

He half swam and half waded in his sodden heavy clothes until he was under the jetty, grabbing at one of the wooden posts; his clothes weighing him down, the freezing water numbing his body, and the heavy waves threatening to drag him back. He tried to calculate how many rounds she had fired, and how many she had left. Had she exhausted her supply? He hoped so because he couldn't stay here for much longer.

Using the jetty stilts to guide him, he slowly hauled himself up the shore until there was soft shingle and sand beneath his feet. He felt as though he'd been in the water a lifetime, though he knew it was only a few minutes, if that. Then he was free of it, but there was a sharp climb up the beach to the summer house and Laura would surely see him in the electric light that still blazed from the cabin.

Crouching low he looked down the jetty towards the sea. Yes, there she was, leaning over and peering into the dark water. Then he blinked, hardly able to believe his eyes as incredibly another figure came up behind her. Who the hell was it? He couldn't see. By its stature it was a woman. Bella Westbury? No, it was far too slender for her. Who then? Julie, the hired help? His heart sank. His escape would be more difficult now. How did he know she too didn't have a gun or had fetched more ammunition for Laura? There might even be bullets left in Laura's gun. He had to get to a phone.

Laura turned and froze. Then suddenly the two figures were wrestling, and seemed in danger of falling into the water. His heart somersaulted. Jesus! It wasn't Julie, but Thea. She was alive. But not for much longer if Laura had her way.

He sprang up, cursing through his chattering teeth, and propelled himself onto the jetty, his speed and agility hampered by his sea-soaked clothes and his shivering body. He cried out as he grasped the jetty with his wounded arm, the pain ripping through his body. Then he was running towards them. Were there any bullets left in that gun? He hoped to God not. Would Thea get hurt? At last, he was there, grabbing Laura, pinning her arm behind her.

'She attacked me,' Laura cried. 'She's mad. She killed her brother and Jonathan, and she tried to kill me.'

Horton stared at Thea's thin, drawn face and saw anxiety and fear. He turned to Laura. 'Good try and it might have worked if you had stuck to your original story and hadn't already confessed to me.'

'Prove it,' she shouted defiantly.

'I think this is proof enough.' He indicated his arm which was throbbing like mad.

'She grabbed the gun from me and shot you.'

Horton followed Laura's gaze and saw that Thea was holding the gun. Suddenly, realizing it was in her hand, Thea looked as though she was about to throw it in the sea when Horton quickly said, 'I'll take that.' He held out his hand but

Thea seemed reluctant to pass it over. Quietly he said, 'It's OK, Thea. I know what happened.'

She handed it over. Keeping his strong right hand on Laura, and trying not to think of the pain in his left arm, he managed to disable the gun, seeing with relief that the magazine was empty anyway.

'You've got no evidence to show I was involved in any of these murders,' Laura cried. 'She's the killer. She's unbalanced. Owen told me.'

'It won't work,' Horton said, dragging her towards the summer house with a feeling that maybe it would. She would deny everything she had told him. They had found no evidence that Laura had been in Anmore's barn, and even if they did, she'd claim she had met Anmore in his barn on other occasions. And her car had not been seen anywhere near it. She must have parked it some distance away and walked to the barn, killed Anmore and then walked back to her car using a torch to guide her. There would be no evidence on her boat either, because they'd have washed it down, and the sea would have destroyed the rest. But they might get something from the summer house, though Jonathan had probably hosed it out and scrubbed it down; a tiny shard of glass meant nothing. Even then they couldn't actually prove Laura had shot Owen. And no one could prove she had killed Arina, unless a witness came forward, which was unlikely, or the silent Julie would help them, but somehow, he doubted that. All he could get her on was the Whitefields land fraud, but even then, she'd claim that she had been young, and completely infatuated with Jack. And she knew it.

Was there something he had missed? Something that would prove she was the killer. She stared boldly and defiantly at him in the bright light of the summer house. Thea looked worried. Horton could imagine what was going through her mind. They would still believe she had killed her brother, and now her prints were on Laura's gun. But they had no real evidence to prove that Thea had killed Owen or Anmore, and she hadn't even been in the country when Arina was killed. She was safe . . . but even then his gut told him a clever barrister would make mincemeat of him, and tear Thea to shreds, and unfortunately, Laura Rosewood could afford the best there was.

As if reading his mind she repeated with conviction, 'There is no evidence linking me to any of this.'

With disgust, Horton thrust her on to the sofa. He was chilled to the bone and Thea was also soaked to the skin, but he couldn't use a blanket or any type of covering in here and risk contaminating any fragment of evidence that might still conceivably exist from Owen's murder. He didn't want to think about the maggots and how Jonathan must have cleaned this place out.

He said, 'They'll believe the word of a police officer rather than you.'

'Not one who was recently suspended for raping a girl,' she declared smugly. Thea eyed him warily. 'Especially when you stormed into my house, assaulted me and forced me to lie. I was running away from you when you attacked me. I had to shoot you in self-defence. Or perhaps I'll claim that Thea showed up to kill me because she knew that Owen had confided his concerns about his sister's health to me. She wrestled with me, took my gun and shot you. I am a very persuasive woman, Andy, and a highly respected one with very good contacts in the police and the European Commission.'

He believed her. She was clever all right, but maybe not quite clever enough. It was time to tell her something which, he hoped, might provoke her into a fit of remorse, though he wasn't counting on it.

With as much confidence as he could muster, he said, 'It's all been for nothing, Laura.'

She looked dazed. 'What do you mean?'

'All these deaths. You needn't have done them.'

'You're talking rubbish,' she snapped.

Now for it. 'The scandal at Whitefields that Christopher Sutton told his daughter about had nothing to do with your land deal. It was Sir Christopher's role there fifty years ago.'

'What are you talking about?' She eyed him with irritation.

'Sir Christopher was transferred from the British Military Hospital in Tripoli during his National Service in late 1958 because he was caught in bed with a female member of staff. He was sent to Whitefields where he agreed to help out on secret drug experiments with the mentally ill patients. He didn't much mind because it was his field of specialism, pioneering new mind drugs and therapies.' Horton didn't know this for a fact but he could hazard an educated guess that this was the scandal that Arina had alluded to, and why Bella Westbury had been his housekeeper.

He said, 'The year in question, 1959, was the height of the Cold War. And that was the secret Sutton confessed on his deathbed, which you overheard Arina telling Owen. And one which would cause an international political scandal if it ever came out. It had nothing to do with your sordid, money-grabbing crime.'

Laura was eyeing him as if he was mad, but he thought he detected a glimmer of uncertainty in her keen blue eyes — though that could be wishful thinking on his part.

He continued. 'When Arina died so suddenly, Owen began to wonder if it was true and if the security services had silenced Arina. So he attempted to find out. He called on Dr Nelson, Sutton's colleague at Tripoli, who told him about the nurse and Sutton being sent away. When you hinted to Owen that you might know something about Whitefields he thought you might have discovered this secret through your political contacts, or that perhaps Sir Christopher had hinted to you what he had been doing there. Owen understood and was more than willing to go along with your demands for caution and secrecy because he knew how dangerous it was. You killed him for the wrong reasons, Laura. Owen had no idea about your fraud or the fact that you'd been involved in the murder of his parents.'

'Rubbish!'

But he could see her trying to grasp this new knowledge. Horton threw Thea a look. She seemed in control of her emotions, but he guessed the turmoil inside her. 'You could have got away with it, Laura. You could have carried on quite happily. It's all been for nothing.'

The truth was beginning to sink in. There wasn't so much confidence about her eyes. But still with a trace of defiance, she said, 'You still can't prove I've killed anyone.'

'I think Inspector Horton can,' Thea said quietly.

'What do you know about it?' Laura hissed at her.

Thea dashed a glance at Horton. She said, 'I had the last postcard my mother sent me lodged in a book called *The Lost Ghosts of the Isle of Wight*. It was a photograph of Whitefields, but I didn't know where it was, and what it meant, until I visited Gordon Elms and saw the painting on his wall. I asked Owen about it and then he told me what Arina had said about Whitefields. He was scared the house was bugged so we talked in Owen's wild garden.'

Which, Horton recalled, was where Evelyn Mackie had seen them talking on the Friday before Owen's disappearance.

'That proves nothing,' Laura declared contemptuously.

'There's a witness.'

Horton stared at Thea, shocked.

She gave him an apologetic glance. 'I only discovered it this afternoon, which is why I came here. I didn't know whether she would be here and what I would do when I got here if she was, but I needed to be where Owen had died.' She shivered and hugged her arms around her slender chest as her sad eyes scoured the summer house. Horton wanted to go to her, but he couldn't afford to take his eye off Laura Rosewood.

Pulling herself together, Thea continued. 'I've been staying at Northwood Abbey in the guest house. I needed to be somewhere safe. I didn't know who I could trust. Jonathan Anmore called me at the hospital and told me that he knew who had killed my brother. He asked me to meet him by the marina in Yarmouth.'

And Horton knew that Laura had asked Anmore to call Thea to incriminate her further in her brother's death and to frame her for Anmore's murder.

Thea said, 'I got a lift from Mr Elms but as soon as I was at Yarmouth I felt a premonition of danger.'

'Why didn't you call me?' Horton cried, half annoyed and half in anguish.

'How could I? Who would believe me?'

Horton recalled his own disbelief of Thea's psychic powers on the Duver the morning he'd found her and felt a stab of guilt as she continued.

'DCI Birch made it quite clear to me from the beginning that he thought I was mad. I have a record of mental illness. It would only be a matter of time before everyone believed I had killed Owen. They'd have said I had an accomplice to help me get Owen's body to the Duver. They'd have thought of something to prove I did it.'

Sadly, he knew that was true.

She was saying, 'I was going to cross to the mainland, then I realized that running away would make me look guilty. I didn't know where to go until I saw a poster advertising Northwood Abbey and I thought the monks would take me in. I managed to hitch a lift to Fishbourne with a woman who was catching the ferry to Portsmouth. She was returning to London after being on the island for a week. From there I walked to the Abbey.

'There's a rule of silence at the Abbey. No one can speak to me except the monk designated to take care of me. Tonight, he could see how upset I was so I told him what had happened. Then amazingly he said he'd seen my brother. The resemblance between us is striking. He'd seen Owen walking along the beach early on Saturday afternoon, and spoke to him, but Owen didn't answer. Brother Joseph said Owen seemed upset and deeply troubled. He watched him head towards the pontoon with a woman whom he described to me. It was her.' She pointed at Laura. 'Brother Joseph heard a gunshot shortly afterwards, but he thought it was the farmer shooting rabbits. He didn't connect it with Owen, why should he? The Abbey doesn't have a television, radio and limited contact with the outside world, so he had no idea what had happened.'

Laura leapt up. 'I'm not going to prison,' she cried, and before Horton could stop her, she was out of the door and running towards the jetty. Cursing, he raced after her, but he didn't have the speed with his wet clothes and his freezing body, not to mention his arm feeling as though it was on fire. She was heading for the RIB. He knew he wouldn't get there in time to stop her.

Then she stalled, and quickly he saw that the RIB had broken its mooring and was tossing on the tumultuous waves about three yards out to sea.

She dashed a glance at him. 'I'm not going to prison,' she repeated.

'Laura, it's over.'

'No.' She turned back to the sea and in that instant Horton knew what she was about to do.

'Laura. No.' But already he was too late. She was in the sea.

Frantically he peered around but there was no lifebelt or line to throw her. He peered into the pitch-black evening. Where the hell was she? Then his eyes picked out what he thought was a figure. Incredibly she was trying to swim towards the RIB. She'd never make it. He made to dive in after her when Thea grabbed his arm.

'Leave her,' she said urgently.

He strained his eyes out to sea, every instinct within him aching to go after her, but he knew that Thea was right. He was exhausted and he would be pretty useless with his wounded arm. Already the darkness had swallowed her up. She might make it. He should have tried.

'We have to call the coastguard and the lifeboat.' He turned and began running towards the house, knowing his mobile was useless after the soaking it had taken. His footsteps were heavy. He was too slow. If only they could reach her in time . . .

He crashed through the door, rushed for the phone and called the station. He told them to alert the lifeboat and coastguards. Then he called Cantelli.

'Are you still on the island?'

'We're just heading for the car ferry, though I don't much fancy the crossing in this weather.'

'Postpone it.' Horton gave him instructions on how to find *Tideways* and rang off. Cantelli would take him to A & E.

He replaced the phone knowing they wouldn't find Laura Rosewood alive. He felt drained and exhausted, but turning to Thea standing behind him, he knew that she was feeling worse than him. Swiftly he crossed to her and put his arms around her, feeling her thin, shivering body lean into his chest. Resting his chin on the top of her head, he closed his eyes and tried not to see the body of Laura Rosewood washed up on a beach, or the bloody, maggot-infested body of Owen Carlsson in the sand. Maybe Thea was thinking the same. He felt her pain, borne silently. She shed no tears. Maybe they would come later, maybe never.

After a moment she pulled away from him.

'Are you OK?' he asked. He always seemed to be asking her stupid questions, but she nodded.

'I didn't think she'd run away like that. I thought she'd try and bluff it out. She could have said Brother Joseph was mistaken, or that Owen had come here and left, or that I'd gone after him and I'd killed him.'

'There was too much building up against her. But being wrong annoyed her more than anything. She was angry at herself, for being trapped. She wasn't thinking straight. I should have stopped her.' He moved away from Thea.

'There was nothing you could do. You're bleeding, and freezing. What chance would you have of surviving? To die trying to save a killer would be a waste of your life.'

Horton knew she was right, but he didn't like it. 'I'll fetch us some blankets.'

'No. I'll go.'

He flicked the kettle on, then pulled off his sodden jacket and peered at his blood-stained T-shirt. His arm was throbbing and burning but he could see that the bullet had only taken a chunk of flesh out of his upper arm and hadn't penetrated the muscle.

Thea returned within minutes with a blanket draped around her shoulders and another for him. She was also carrying a first-aid box.

She began to clean his wound. He watched her for a moment, feeling a deep tenderness towards her that, given time, he knew could become more. After a while he said, 'Why didn't you answer the phone after Owen went missing?'

'For the same reason I didn't talk to Mrs Mackie, and why Owen and I talked in the garden. We didn't know who we could trust.'

'You trusted me the first time we met — why?'

She gave a small, tired smile. 'Let's just say it was a matter of instinct.'

He returned the smile, deciding not to press her further on that one. He felt his affection deepening with each passing moment before the bitter voice of past betrayals echoed in his head. Well, that could sod off for once.

Thea said, 'Both Bengal and I would be dead if it hadn't been for you. How is he?'

'Wormed his way into Evelyn Mackie's affections, I'd say.' Like you have into mine.

'Good. I'd like him to find a comfortable home.'

She wouldn't be taking him back to Luxembourg with her then. Would she even be returning there? He guessed so and felt a pang of disappointment. He hoped it wouldn't be too soon. But those were questions for another day. Now he asked the question that had been bothering him.

'Did Jonathan Anmore tell you where to find Owen?' Laura Rosewood had said he'd called Thea, but Thea hadn't answered Terry Knowles' calls so why should she have answered Anmore's call?

She sat down beside him, her pale blue eyes sad and hollow with fatigue. Her hands were shaking slightly. Her chin came up and she held his gaze. 'No, he didn't.'

He knew it was the truth. He took her hands in his. They seemed so small and so thin. She made no effort to withdraw them.

'I couldn't tell you where I was, Andy, though I wanted to.'

He liked hearing her say his name.

The silence hung between them for several seconds. Horton felt reluctant to disturb it but there was still a question he needed to ask. 'Who was the girl, Thea? The one you asked Peter Bohman about?'

She took a breath. 'I kept seeing this girl in my mind just before Arina was killed. She was in a stark white room, wearing a white gown, and she was warning me of evil and danger. She warned my mother too, only she either chose to ignore it or couldn't avoid it. I think the latter, which was why she sent me that postcard of Whitefields. It feels like an evil place, and a sad one. I think the girl was from there and my mother had seen her just before she came across Laura and those men. Oh, this girl isn't real, not now anyway. She lived once. Sorry if this sort of talk bothers you.'

'I never said . . . Did this girl tell you how it would end?'

'In the sea, but I didn't know whether that was my fate or someone else's. It's all right, you don't have to believe.' She gave a timid smile.

Maybe he did. Suddenly he was back on the old golf course at the Duver but this time as a child. A woman was ahead of him. She turned and called his name, then laughed.

'She loved you.'

Horton started. 'Who did?' he asked sharply, his stomach churning. She held his gaze and he saw this was no act.

'The woman you're searching for,' Thea said quietly.

Horton felt sick, then a flicker of hope, then bewilderment.

'You're very angry with her for hurting you.'

He made to withdraw his hands but she clung on to them.

'Listen.' She leant forward with a new urgency in her voice, as the sound of a car pulled up outside. 'You don't have to believe me, that's up to you, but I just want you to know that I felt her presence on that first day we met. When you touched me, she was there so powerfully that for a moment I forgot about Owen and that was incredible. I felt your anger, and her pain. I could hardly breathe.'

Car doors slammed. Footsteps on the gravel drive. His heart was pounding. The blood pulsating in his ears. He had about twenty seconds before Cantelli rang the doorbell. He so desperately wanted to believe her, but could he? Dare he? Ten seconds. Voices outside. Was she telling him the truth? He took a breath.

'Thea, should I look for her?'

She held his gaze. 'That's for you to decide, Andy.'

'Does she want me to?'

The bell clanged through the house.

'What do you think?'

There was only one possible answer.

THE END

ALSO BY PAULINE ROWSON

THE SOLENT MURDER MYSTERIES
Book 1: THE PORTSMOUTH MURDERS
Book 2: THE LANGSTONE HARBOUR MURDERS
Book 3: THE HORSEA MARINA MURDERS
Book 4: THE ROYAL HOTEL MURDERS
Book 5: THE ISLE OF WIGHT MURDERS

Thank you for reading this book.

If you enjoyed it please leave feedback on Amazon or Goodreads, and if there is anything we missed or you have a question about, then please get in touch. We appreciate you choosing our book.

Founded in 2014 in Shoreditch, London, we at Joffe Books pride ourselves on our history of innovative publishing. We were thrilled to be shortlisted for Independent Publisher of the Year at the British Book Awards.

www.joffebooks.com

We're very grateful to eagle-eyed readers who take the time to contact us. Please send any errors you find to corrections@joffebooks.com. We'll get them fixed ASAP.

Printed in Great Britain
by Amazon

50689056R00158